THE DEVIL'S BRIDGE AFFAIR

THE DEVIL'S BRIDGE AFFAIR

ROB GITTINS

HOBECK

This edition produced in Great Britain in 2022

by Hobeck Books Limited, Unit 14, Sugnall Business Centre, Sugnall, Stafford, Staffordshire, ST21 6NF

www.hobeck.net

This book is entirely a work of fiction. The names, characters and incidents portrayed in this novel are the work of the author's imagination. Any resemblance to actual persons (living or dead), events or localities is entirely coincidental.

A CIP catalogue for this book is available from the British Library.

ISBN 978-1-913-793-91-3 (pbk)

ISBN 978-1-913-793-90-6 (ebook)

Cover design by Jayne Mapp Design

Printed and bound in Great Britain

PRAISE FOR THE DEVIL'S BRIDGE AFFAIR

'A thoroughly enjoyable, entertaining read.'
Sarah Leck

'Intriguing, compelling and darkly enjoyable… I've not read many books in two sittings this year!' Alex Jones

'A pacy thriller that will challenge many of your preconceptions.'
Angela Paull

For Jill Foster and Alison Finch

PART ONE

He seized the devil and bound him for a thousand years.
But after that, he must be set free.
Revelation 20:2

DEVIL'S BRIDGE

LIGHTNING SPLITS THE SKY, night somersaulting into day.

And in that moment a life is lost.

The storm's been raging for the last hour, gales blowing in from the sea, the ocean taking revenge on the land, a long-standing penance for an ancient misdeed.

Trees and bushes prostrate themselves under the assault. If this was a fight the referee would have stopped the unequal contest many rounds ago. No one should even think about being out on a night like this, let alone goading the elements to deliver down on their heads their most savage retribution. But these teens have been partying hard.

They started hours ago, shots, then more shots, some Ket, then MDMA, before the long-suffering landlords of the pubs down in the town, some of which were in imminent danger of being totally wrecked by those end of term revellers, drove them out into a wind that was already howling round the small streets, smashing into signs, upending bins, ripping tiles from roofs and hurling them down onto otherwise deserted streets; a night, in short, that was already beginning to threaten Armageddon.

Which was when the teens struck out for the bridge. It was where all parties always ended. Sometimes crazed souls hung from the parapet, but the cumulative effect of those shots and more shots and the Ket and MDMA meant that most congregated at the foot of the ancient structure, staring out, unseeing, towards a sea in the near distance they'd stared at almost every day of their lives, as they spilled from houses and headed for schools, playgrounds or the one town park; but one soul on the bridge tonight will stare out over the sea no longer.

The night's dislocating enough without the human pigs. The young girl's dress, torn from the climb up to the gully beneath the bridge and the whipped branches smashing into her with almost every step, almost gives way the moment one floats in front of her, which is exactly what the over-sized hulk from the year above wants, of course.

Instead, she bites back the panicked scream that's all she can hear inside and yells at him, sensing, if not seeing, the huge grin behind the latex mask as he moves on to hopefully more gullible, or rather more wasted, prey. He's heard that girls are always far more up for it after a shock, and in a triumph of hope over experience is already trying the same ploy with a small gaggle of fifteen-year-olds, one of whom now seems to have now all but totally collapsed.

Another of his companions is attempting a more traditional approach. His hand has been inching ever closer to the knickers of her friend for what seems to him like a lifetime, but, can only be a few moments. As the next lightning bolt strikes, and encouraged on by it, he slips an excited finger under the thin elastic, beginning to knead the soft skin inside.

The girl tenses, but it's nothing to do with the attentions of her excited companion and his even more excited finger, or the gargoyle in the Scream-type mask that now floats past on the outer edge of her vision.

Illuminated in the forked white light she sees a figure on the very edge of the bridge above, struggling with a second figure. And then she hears a distant scream, mistaken for the wind by most of the partygoers tonight, but this is more high-pitched, intense, before it's snatched away by a darkness that descends as quickly as it vanished a moment before.

The young girl starts to tremble, an atavistic reaction to an evil she can now sense all around, perhaps, and the boy mistakes it for arousal. Encouraged, another of his fingers joins the first. Then the boy freezes as the girl starts to scream too, and this isn't mistaken for the wind by anyone, because all those teens hear now is pure and simple terror.

The owner of the Scream mask doubles back immediately. Lots can and will happen in and around that gully and under the bridge tonight; lots of things are and always have been tolerated, but sexual assault is definitely not.

'Bastard.'

The boy's fingers slip from inside her knickers as the first blow lands, smashing him to the ground. One of the girls moves to her friend's side, taking her now-shaking body in her arms, trying to proffer words of soothing comfort, but another friend is also staring up at the now-unseen bridge, has also just witnessed that same macabre tableau, those same two figures caught in the lightning and what had to be a fateful struggle; how could it not be when they were that high up in the air? The still-shaking girl, who can't help herself, screams again.

Her rescuer, now divested of his latex mask, stares, puzzled. What the fuck did that boy do to her? The boy himself is moaning on the ground, his head still ringing from the sudden blow, and the rescuer gives him a kick for good measure.

Then another crack of lightning splits the sky, throwing the bridge into clear relief once more.

And those same two girls, still staring up at it from hundreds of feet below, can see that while there were quite clearly two struggling figures up there just a few moments before, there's now just one.

BEX – THE WANNABE

I CAN'T REMEMBER the headline and the report was only a few lines long. The reporter probably wouldn't have even bothered writing the story at all if it hadn't been for the name of the town. But it's always had that ring to it. Something that makes people pause and look at you for a moment when you tell them where you're from. That echo of something drenched in other-worldly menace that probably made that reporter pick up the story in the first place and run with it that day.

Because something bad always has to happen in a town called Devil's Bridge, right?

When we were young it was one of the first things every child was taught. The local legend. The tale of how the town got its name,

The story was that centuries ago, the devil himself visited. He'd never been to the area before, but he'd heard that the scenery was stunning. He walked in over a mountain path, stared down into the valley, then walked on into the small settlement below. Mountains towered behind him on three sides, the sea forming a fourth wall in front.

The first person he came across was a beautiful young

woman sitting at the bottom of a steep gorge by a river that flowed down from the mountains and out to the sea, her faithful small dog at her side. The young woman was upset, distraught even, and the devil paused to speak to her.

'What's the matter?' he asked.

'I'm in such a terrible muddle,' she told him. 'I just don't know what to do.'

The young woman nodded across the water, flowing fast at her side.

'My cow has wandered across the river, and I can't get her back.'

The devil looked across the water to the cow staring mournfully at them, then he turned back to the young woman, whose beauty, now he was closer, was dazzling.

'What you need…' the devil said to her, '…is a bridge.'

Then he smiled at her, a smile that seemed warm and reassuring, but which chilled the young woman for reasons she didn't quite understand.

'I'll build you one.'

The young woman's small dog began to move away, growling softly as he did so, but the devil maintained his same warm, reassuring tone and smile.

'Why don't you go home, and in the morning, there'll be a bridge waiting for you.'

The devil paused, looked across the river at her stranded cow, then back at her, and his eyes almost seemed to drink her in.

'All I ask is to keep the first living thing that crosses it.'

Almost before she realised what she was doing, the young woman nodded.

'All right,' she said. 'I'll see you in the morning.'

Then she went home, buoyed by the idea of being reunited with her cow but still feeling chilled.

The next day she woke and called for her small dog. Together they went down to the river, and she couldn't believe her eyes.

Because in front of her, dim, almost ghostly in the early morning mist, was a brand-new bridge, the first her hometown had ever seen, spanning a river that seemed to be flowing even faster that morning.

Suddenly, out of nowhere, her visitor from the previous day appeared on the other side of the new bridge. At the same time the early morning mist began to clear, and she saw her cow standing by his side, as if waiting for permission to cross.

'I told you I would build you a bridge.'

The devil smiled at her, a smile that was still like no other smile she'd ever seen before.

'Now it's your turn to keep your promise'.

The beautiful young woman, still seemingly totally entranced by the near-miraculous sight before her, walked towards the new bridge with the devil watching her every step of the way. But then, just as she put her foot on it, she stopped and took out a biscuit from her apron pocket. Then she hurled it across the bridge, and as quick as a flash and before the devil could do anything to stop him, her small dog chased after it, snatching up the biscuit in his mouth as it landed on the other side before racing back again.

'You stupid girl,' the devil yelled across at her, his eyes flashing with what looked like firebolts, spittle flecking his lips and cheek as he stared at the human prize that had eluded him.

'Your useless farm dog's no good to me'.

He turned away, and, for a moment, the beautiful young woman thought he was going to vanish as quickly as he'd appeared, perhaps embarrassed at being outwitted by a simple country girl. But then he turned back and looked at her. And now, suddenly, he was calm, and for reasons she again didn't understand, that was even more chilling than all his previous fury.

Then the devil told her that he would have taken just her once she'd crossed his bridge. But now, and thanks to her trickery, he would re-visit and he would come in different guises and at different times. Each time the most terrible things would happen on or around his bridge, and in the end the town would come to curse the blessing he'd bestowed. And then, suddenly again, he was gone.

People came from far and wide to marvel at the new apparition suspended high in the air above that plunging gorge. Shepherds drove their flocks across, and the town prospered like never before. And as time passed, the young woman dismissed all the stranger had said to her that morning.

Soon after, she married and had a child. Her first born, a boy, was strong and healthy, and as soon as he could he began to play outside with all the other children in the town.

Then, one day, he went missing. The young woman searched high and low and then a terrible premonition gripped her. She dashed up to the bridge, where a shocked traveller told her he'd just seen a child talking to a stranger, and then the child had fallen to his death. The distraught young woman scrabbled down to the gully below where she found the body of her son.

Following his burial, the young woman went mad. She left her home and went to live in a cave near the bridge to warn all who passed by not to go near it. But no one listened to her tales of the devil and his doom-laden predictions because they knew it was just a story and the devil wasn't real. And so it seemed, because the devil, so we were told, was never seen near the town again.

But that wasn't true because the devil has visited again. The accident I was reading about right now, if it was an accident, was testament to that. The problem being the guise he'd assumed this time.

Was it Ethan James, the boy, now a man, whose name's before me, who I haven't seen for years but have probably thought about every day since?

Or was it a young woman called Tanya Adams, someone else I've also never managed to forget?

It was a question that obsessed my home town back then and must now be tormenting it again.

I look out through the window onto a street that leads down to the local station.

Then I stand, newspaper in hand, and go to catch a train.

NIA – THE MUM

ETHAN'S OUT ON A RUN. I'm getting ready. I've been getting ready for the last hour and I'm no nearer managing it than I was an hour ago.

Ethan's little dog, Sami, a Shih-Tzu, is in here somewhere, buried in the small mountain of clothes that covers every inch of our front room. Dresses, tops, jeans, more dresses, more tops, more jeans. Don't get me wrong – I'm no upmarket clothes horse, just a hoarder. But today everything's out and everything's being tried on, different combinations, different looks, a hundred decisions made and then unmade, one step forward and then, as I wheel in front of an old mirror I've manhandled in from the hall, ten steps back again.

Ethan's key sounds in the lock and Sami suddenly appears from under an old blouse I'd forgotten I even had and wish I'd never bought, bounding to the door as he always does when he hears his master's tread out in the hall. For a moment Ethan endures his usual death by a thousand ecstatic licks. Then he walks into a front room that looks like the proverbial bomb's hit it and his face says it all.

He knows what I'm doing. He knows why I'm doing it. And I

know he knows, which is why I nod across at the clock and launch straight away into Grumbling Mum mode.

'It starts in twenty minutes.'

Ethan keeps looking round the clothes-strewn room as I nod at his T-shirt and jogging shorts.

'Go and get a shower – you stink of teenager.'

But Ethan's eyes are still taking in the tops, the shirts, the jeans, the dresses. Then he looks back at me and his tone's mild and gentle, but I'm not fooled. There's steel in there too.

'It's only a parents' evening.'

'Don't say "only", it's important.'

Sami's back under yet another pile of clothes, sniffing, checking for moths.

'Most people'll probably turn up in tracky bottoms and trainers.'

'So, I don't want to let you down – take me out and shoot me.'

'Mrs Adams isn't going to be bothered how you look. It's my grades she's going to be talking about.'

Then Ethan pauses, the expression on his face saying it all.

Worse luck.

I pause too. It hasn't been the best of times for him this term. It hasn't been the best of times for any of us. I keep hesitating, struggling for a moment.

'Your dad's coming.'

Ethan just looks at me.

'He called. This morning, after you left for school. Like he said, this is a big one, your exams coming up next year and that.'

Ethan's eyes don't leave mine.

'He's not bringing…?'

I cut across, shutting that one down straight away. It was the very first question I asked, too.

'Just your dad.'

Ethan's eyes turn back to the obstacle course that's our new-look front room.

'So, he's the reason for all this, yeah?'

'No.'

Which is a yes and Ethan knows it because he's that kind of boy, wise beyond his years, as my little sis, Ella, always says. But maybe, and these last few months in particular, he's had to be.

I struggle again.

'I just don't want him looking at me and thinking, thank God I'm not with her anymore.'

Ethan keeps looking at me.

'Do you want him to be with you?'

Which is when it comes back as quick as a flash, because this really is God's honest truth.

'No.'

I think.

'Do you want to be with him?'

I bat it back again as if we're playing word tennis.

'No.'

I hesitate for another moment, then turn away, start hunting among more discarded dresses than you'd find in your average Oxfam shop.

'What are you doing?'

'Looking for my tracky bottoms and trainers.'

I smile across at him and Ethan smiles back, a shared, warm comfortable sort of smile. Then I nod across at the clock again.

'Fifteen minutes.'

Ethan, still smiling, turns and heads for the stairs.

Then I find them.

My trainers.

Caked in mud.

And, suddenly, it's this morning again and I'm waking up, feeling something blurring my vision, reaching my hand up to my left eye before bringing it back streaked in blood, then sitting bolt-upright in bed to see the bruise on my thigh already turning yellow-brown and the weals and scratches on my ankles.

And for a few more moments I just stay there, frozen.

AL – THE DAD

I SEE them as I'm parking the car.

Well, trying to park the car – space is at a bit of a premium right now. There's a school fete on this weekend, stalls and rides and stuff. It's a fund-raising event – they do a lot of them these days – raise cash, help out the beleaguered school budget.

Joel, my boss, is providing a bouncy castle. PR, he calls it, all very community-spirited and good-hearted and nothing at all to do with the great big banner that's going to be splashed across the front: 'Sponsored by Joel Adams Construction'.

All of which means that the yard where people normally park is closed off, so I've had to go round a couple of times looking for a spot on the surrounding streets. That's when I see them, a hundred or so metres away, pulling up in Nia's old car.

I haven't actually seen Nia for a couple of months. Her choice, not mine. I can't blame her – the break-up hasn't exactly been easy. What break-up is? Ethan very quickly became the go-between, ferrying messages between the two of us. At the same time as trying to deal with it all himself, of course.

I keep wanting to ask how he is, how he and his mum are coping, even though I know it's a stupid question. What's he supposed to say? How's life in what's suddenly become a single parent household? How's living with a mum who couldn't get to the end of a single sentence when it first happened without dissolving into floods of tears? The answer's always going to be pretty obvious.

Then, across the street, Nia sees me, and the moment she does she turns and heads on into the school. She was short enough on the phone this morning, and it looks like I'm going to be in for more of the cold shoulder treatment now. That just leaves Ethan, hovering by the school door looking as if this is the last place he wants to be, or maybe that's down to the company he's about to be keeping. I take a quick, deep, breath, lock the car and make my way over to him.

I read a story once about the last walk of the men and women who were about to be hanged under the courtroom of the Old Bailey. Apparently, the roof of the passage on that final journey grew lower and lower the closer they came to the gallows. It was meant to destroy their spirit before their body was dispatched too. No prizes for guessing why that particular not-so-useful nugget of not-very-illuminating information has popped into my head on the walk over to my waiting, wary son.

I nod at Ethan, who nods back at me. For a moment neither of us speak. But then I do finally come out with it. Maybe it's like an itch you just can't stop scratching.

'So how are things?'

Ethan nods towards a big sign on the door that reads, 'Parents' Evening'.

'That's what we're going to find out, isn't it?'

I should just play along, and maybe I would if I hadn't just seen Nia heading into the school like that. But suddenly I've had enough of it, of the half-sentences and pregnant pauses, the air so heavy with what isn't being said it feels like it's crushing us.

Or maybe it's something else. Something that's happened in just the last few days, something I've no idea how to raise and even less idea whether I should.

'I know we haven't had much chance to talk since—'

I stop. What do you call it? The split? The bust-up? The desertion? I stumble on as Ethan just looks at me, and I already know that this is such a bad idea.

'And I know this is difficult—'

It's getting more and more excruciating by the moment, but I plough on, regardless.

'But sometimes—'

I stop again, struggling even more now.

'People move on—'

Ethan cuts across.

'Our front room looks like a dress shop.'

I stare at him.

'Mum's done her make-up at least three times that I know about.'

He looks at me steadily.

'You might have moved on – well, you've moved out, so I suppose you must have.'

Ethan nods at me again.

'Not too sure she has.'

Then he turns, opens the door, and follows Nia inside.

I stand there for a moment. Then I reach my hand into my pockets and bring out the note.

It's the sixth one we've had. I intercepted the first three, but Kate saw the fourth and then the fifth. I don't think she's seen this one, but I can't be sure. A conspiracy of silence seems to have descended in the last week or so, neither of us dignifying them by speculating where all this hate mail might have come from or who might have written it. But we're just fooling ourselves – we think about it all the time.

And I always thought Kate was the calmer of the two of us, but these last few weeks I've seen a different side to her. Making me worry what might happen if we ever do find out where they've come from and who's written it all.

NIA – THE MUM

I'M BOTTLING IT, and I'm not.

No, I really do not want to see Al right now, not straight after Ethan stumbling in on ClothesGate. I know I'm going to have to some time this evening, of course – that's why we're here, to discuss our son. But at the moment none of that matters as much as my really wanting to see Ethan's form teacher, Tanya.

I catch up with her outside the time-honoured confessional known as the Ladies. She's with a woman who has her back to me, but as she turns, I see it's Megan, the headteacher. They're in a concentrated little huddle and no wonder – it's a big night tonight, and there are probably a hundred and one things they have to talk about, a hundred and one kids whose welfare is about to be discussed, maybe even decided this evening too.

Because fifteen's that kind of age, isn't it? It was for me, and it probably will be for every one of the milling pupils I can see up and down that corridor right now. One single piece of bad advice, one unfortunate comment from the wrong person at the wrong time and a whole future can go one way or the other. Meaning Tanya really doesn't have time for yet another over-anxious mum.

'I just—'

I stop as quickly as I started. A gang of kids, boys and girls led by Jimmy Shand, one of Ethan's old pals from way back in primary school, pauses as they pass, some collective antennae picking up potential gossip as they see me in what looks like a wracked mini conference with two of Ethan's teachers. I see Bex Hughes there too, another of Ethan's old friends from that same church primary that now seems to belong to a different life and a dozen lifetimes ago. And now, with those teen eyes joining the two adult pairs of eyes also still looking at me, I'm at even more of a loss how to begin to explain why I'm standing here looking every inch like a tongue-twisted teen myself.

With anyone else I might have expected a suggestion that we talk later, or that we move to one of the nearby classrooms if Tanya decides she can actually spare just a moment or two right now. But then she reaches out a hand and I suddenly find myself propelled into the nearby toilet, where Tanya flicks the bolt on the door, cutting off the now-openly inquisitive stares of that gang of kids on the other side.

Then she leans back against one of the sinks, and Megan, who's followed us in, leans back against another.

'Lezzers!'

From outside, I hear Jimmy's muffled yell followed by an explosion of delighted laughter from the rest of the acolytes. If I'd been fifteen, I'd probably have joined in myself.

As it is, I just lean back against one of the cubicle doors.

'You've both heard what's happened. Me and Al.'

I stop again. Of course they've heard; this is only a small town and the school's not that big either.

Besides, and now I hesitate, nod at Tanya.

'He works for your other half. You must have.'

She smiles back, sympathy dimples flecking her cheeks.

'Joel mentioned there'd been some trouble—'

She hurries on.

'He wasn't talking out of turn, it's just…'

I take a deep breath as Tanya tails off. Maybe this is something we really should be talking about in the actual Parents' Evening itself but bringing it up in front of Al, with Ethan listening in and looking on, is just defeating me right now.

'Ethan's been struggling ever since, then we got his latest report, the one you sent through last Friday.'

I pause.

'Seems his grades are struggling too, yeah?'

Tanya nods back as a rattling sounds on the door, some girl trying to come in perhaps, or maybe it's Jimmy wanting to feast his eyes on the orgy.

Megan intervenes cautiously.

'It's nothing we can't put right, I'm sure.'

Tanya nods in firm agreement. Maybe they were already discussing him as I approached.

'But it is one of the things I wanted to talk to you all about.'

Which is good to hear. But it's not the real reason we're in this toilet tonight.

'The only thing is, Al's coming too.'

I glance involuntarily towards the door, almost as if I'm expecting him to suddenly materialise or something.

'Well, actually he's already here.'

I tail off once more, not sure now how to say what I want to say, so Tanya says it for me.

'And you don't want me or anyone else putting their big fat foot in it.'

I think of saying, no. But I don't. Because I've had a bellyful lately of all the wrong sort of comments made by all the wrong sort of people when the two of us are out in the town, and I really don't want Ethan to suffer any more of them this evening.

Tanya just smiles again as I hesitate, those sympathy dimples deepening.

'Let's just concentrate on getting Ethan back on track, shall we?'

Then she puts her hand on my arm, a simple, instinctive, gesture of support, and I smile back.

BEX – THE WANNABE

I REMEMBER THAT EVENING WELL. It was a big number, mocks just finished, the real exams less than a year away – all of a sudden, the atmosphere inside the school had changed, teachers coming down harder on us all the time, essays and assignments being marked harder and harder too. Even the high-flyers were feeling the heat, and as I'd never been a high-flyer, as my dad had always reminded me, I was never going to stand a chance.

'I've just been slaughtered.'

I stop Ethan as he's walking in. I really need some air right now. Behind me, the hall's packed with tables, teachers on one side, parents and pupils opposite. Five minutes ago I was one of those pupils flanked by both my parents and it was excruciating.

Pete, our Language Tutor, was chatting to Mairead Hunt and her mum and dad. They were the appointment before us. Mairead was already marked for greatness, which in Devil's Bridge meant if not Oxbridge, then Bristol or maybe one of the London colleges. Heady days, for some anyway. The formal part of the meeting was over and Pete – he always insisted on first names – was making small talk with all three of them as the session wrapped up.

Which was when I stole a sideways glance at my waiting dad, and my heart sank. Already his lips were compressing into that thin white line I know only too well as his eyes fixed on the chatting, oblivious Pete. I glance sideways at Mum, but she isn't looking at me, only at him.

Mum didn't actually need to be here or listen to what Pete or any of the other teachers have to say about me; her verdict on her only daughter was set in stone years ago and nothing is ever going to change it. I heard her talking to a couple of our neighbours once, uncaring whether I could hear them or not, telling them that I just didn't have it, the one quality she obviously prized above all others – sticking power, that all-important and clearly-missing grit. And from that moment on it was all I saw in her eyes; it didn't matter what I did or how hard I tried.

She slipped her hand around Dad's arm, a silent warning not to make any sort of scene, a warning we both knew was never going to be heeded, and it wasn't. As Mairead and her mum and dad finally moved away, Pete beamed across at us from behind the table.

'Sorry to keep you waiting.'

He gestured at us to take our places in the still-warm seats, but Dad remained standing, staring down at him, lips still compressed in that thin white line.

'Five past.'

Pete's smile faded as Dad nodded across at a large clock on the hall wall.

'That's the time we were given. It's gone ten past now.'

Pete's smile was fast becoming a ghost of its former self.

'These things never quite run to time, I'm afraid.'

Dad, still standing, nodded down at him again.

'And they never will, not if you lot waste time chatting about the ins and outs of a duck's arse.'

At the next desk another of the teachers looked across. A couple of passing classmates paused. Pete smiled again, but his smile was now ice.

'Well. Let's start now, shall we?'

It would never have made any difference. Pete's too good a teacher to let something like that influence what he now had to say. I was always going to get roasted. I can already hear my mum delivering her verdict later on my academic efforts or lack of them, and I can see Dad nodding back, those thin lips compressing in disapproval once again, but not disappointment, because to be disappointed meant he had expectations, and the truth was they both came here tonight with none.

Ethan doesn't reply, just smiles back, and there's more than an element of the sacrificial lamb in his smile too. He is next up, not with Pete, but with Mrs Adams, our English teacher, first name Tanya, although, and unlike with Pete, none of us has ever used it, at least not to her face. Where Pete always tries to make out he's a friend as well as a teacher, she's always kept more of a distance.

I shake my head, eyeing Pete, who is now laughing and joking with the next set of parents, who are laughing and joking with him in turn, and hiss at Ethan again.

'Reckon I could have him for libel.'

Ethan looks round the room, spotting his own mum and dad waiting now, too, another set of parents getting to their feet in front of them, their session with Mrs Adams coming to an end.

'Slander.'

I look at him as Ethan's mum signals across to him.

'What?'

'Libel's when you write it down; slander's when you say it.'

'Oh, great. So now my mates are calling me thick too.'

Ethan's smile widened.

'You're not thick.'

Then out it came. Quick as a flash. Almost before I realised what I was actually going to say.

'We're still mates though, yeah?'

Ethan looks back at me and I shuffle uneasily, affecting

nonchalance, but not coming within a million miles of bringing it off.

'Just haven't seen too much of you this last month or so.'

Now my cheeks are beginning to turn red. I might as well have hung a sign around my neck. Bex Hughes fancies Ethan James. The weird thing is I don't think I actually realised it till then. The moment my tongue ran away with itself and ambushed me.

I pray Ethan hasn't noticed, at the same time hoping he has, but he just looks behind me. The group with Mrs Adams is now moving onto the next teacher on their list, Ethan's own parents approaching the vacated chairs.

'My turn.'

Ethan draws a single finger across his throat, execution-style, and flashes me a wry smile as he heads over to take his seat. My eyes follow him all the way.

Then Mum gestures across at me impatiently. The next appointment, which is mercifully running to schedule this time, is about to be endured. Dad is standing a few metres away on a raised lectern where another small row of tables has been assembled for the evening and is looking down at me, waiting too.

And suddenly a picture flashes before my eyes.

I'm small, really small. We're out on a walk and Dad wants us to cross the devil's bridge. But I'm holding back, shaking my head; I won't do it and he's getting more and more irate. What's wrong with her, he's asking Mum. We'll hold her hand, make sure she's OK – tell her!

But I'm still shaking my head. Maybe that's when she first decided I lack the only quality that truly matters. We finally turned back without crossing over and Dad didn't speak to me for a week. Anyone who disobeys him always receives the same silent treatment. He believes I was scared by the massive drop below and didn't trust him enough to guide me across without mishap. He takes it as a lack of trust, a failure of faith in him, somehow.

But I wasn't scared, I was spooked. Because all I could see, as I stood there waiting to cross, was his body falling from the very centre of the bridge, my mum screaming in horror as she saw my small hands pushing him over the edge.

NIA – THE MUM

'IT'S NOT that the last few essays were bad. OK, yes, the marks were lower than usual, but that wasn't the real problem.'

Tanya nods across at Ethan.

'It's more what was there before, that little extra you always seemed to put in, just hasn't been there in the essays and coursework you've been producing lately.'

I see Al steal a quick, sideways glance at me. He doesn't say anything, but he doesn't need to.

'So, I want you to try a couple of exercises. Just so you can get a handle on what the examiners will be looking for next year.'

She picks up a book from the pile in front of her.

'Let's take the set play for this year, Macbeth.'

Ethan nods, not saying anything, but all this is clearly going in.

'Write three or four pages on it but do it from Macduff's point of view. Imagine he's writing a diary, the story of the play if you like, but it's as he sees it, so if he's not present in a scene you can't write about it. It's a way of accessing perspective and it'll really help if there's a question on him in the exam.'

But then she hesitates, as if she knows that she's now starting to skate on thin ice, but also knowing she has no choice.

'When I was fifteen, we did Lear.'

Tanya nods across at another book on a pile on the desk, an old angry man on the front staring up at the heavens.

'We got taken down to see it in the New Theatre. I'd hated Shakespeare up to then – all those weird-sounding speeches, I just couldn't see the point. But seeing it on stage like that, all of a sudden, the whole thing just came alive.'

She glances, quickly, first at Al, then at me.

'I know you missed our own trip.'

I see Al's cheeks begin to mottle. That trip took place just a day or so after Al moved out. Shakespeare and stage plays hadn't exactly been high on any of our agendas back then.

'But, fortunately, there are a few decent film versions you can watch. I've got a couple – you can borrow one if you like.'

Then Tanya looks at me. She doesn't look at Al. Given what she's about to ask, there's not a lot of point.

'Are you going to be in later?'

I stare back.

'I could drop it round.'

I keep staring, flustered. 'I don't want to put you out.'

'I'm passing. Joel's taking us to pick up some stuff for Danny's party – two already, I can't believe it.'

Tanya smiles. I smile back, some sort of parental reflex action at work maybe.

Then suddenly a scream sounds behind as a giraffe falls in through one of the open windows.

AL – THE DAD

FIVE MINUTES later and order's been restored.

Joel, who's Tanya's husband as well as my boss, has manhandled the outsize toy back out onto the yard with the help of a few of the dads, including yours truly. All the time he's giving Jonno, another of the blokes from the firm, the mother and father of all rows for letting it slip off the wagon and crash through the school window like that. Now it's squatting next to an equally outsize bouncy castle, which is practically blotting out the last of the evening sun, a few other lads from the firm already mucking about on it as it inflates.

By the door, Tanya's staring up at it. Joel, his spirits and habitual good humour restored after administering that bollocking, is grinning back at her.

'Great, isn't it?'

Tanya keeps staring as Joel clambers up and bounces up and down on it himself, a couple of the boys who are up there with him losing their footing as he does so.

'That thing, forget it.'

Joel nods across at the wayward giraffe, now being shuffled across to the far side of the yard, before nodding at the bouncy castle again.

'But once the school's finished with it, I thought we could put this up for Danny's party.'

We all stare at turrets that seem to stretch up to the sky, the same thought in all our minds, Tanya giving voice to it.

'He's two.'

Joel grins wider.

'He'll love it.'

'How's he even going to get up on it?'

And suddenly, and out of nowhere, returns a memory so real and vivid it's as if I'm actually living it again. But, before I can say anything, Nia cuts across.

'We got Ethan one for his fifth.'

I look over at Nia, who's clearly lost in that exact same memory.

Tanya gestures at it.

'Five, maybe. *Two*?'

I nod across at Ethan, grinning now.

'He didn't get a look in. Couldn't get the parents off it.'

Then I turn back to Nia.

'His mum was the worst of all.'

Nia splutters back.

'Closely followed by this muppet.'

I grin, more memories returning all the while.

'Just don't drink and dive like she did – half an hour up there and we couldn't get her out of the khazi for the next hour.'

Quick as a flash, she hits back.

'At least I made it to the khazi.'

Then, just as suddenly, she stops, and an uneasy silence descends. And Nia tries her best, she really does, but everyone can see the tears that now fill her eyes.

Ethan steps forward, his voice soft and reassuring as if he's the adult and she's the teenager.

'Come on.'

He nods over towards the car.

'Let's get home.'

Then suddenly everyone pauses again, as from behind it begins. What sounds like a low, agonised, keening. Joel looks towards the bouncy castle where Terry, another of the blokes from the firm, is holding onto one of the inflated supports, shaking his head, refusing all attempts to shepherd him down.

For a moment no one knows what to do. Then Joel moves across, puts an arm around Terry and leans close, talking to him all the while, promising him he'll have all the time he wants up there after the fete.

Terry's been a fixture at the firm for as long as I can remember. Not that he actually does very much. Given how he is, it's not as if he can. But it makes no difference. Terry's always there, each and every day. Some people in the town say the enormous pains Joel always seems to take with him are a testament to his big heart.

But I've heard rumours. Little things that Nia's let slip over the years. But I've never investigated too deeply and probably never will. Too many skeletons in my own closet for that.

NIA – THE MUM

An hour or so later I'm sipping from a large mug of cocoa and Ethan's swigging from a can of coke.

We didn't speak all the way back in the car. We didn't speak when we let ourselves back into the house to endure another death by a thousand sloppy licks from Sami. Not that things are awkward; they never are. There's lots to talk about: the parents' evening, him seeing his dad again, me letting myself down a bit, well, more than a bit, out in the schoolyard in the shadow of that bouncy castle, being watched over all the while by that outsize giraffe. But none of that's even mentioned. Ethan just strokes Sami's soft white fur and tells me a joke that really doesn't sound like much of a joke at first.

'It doesn't make any sense.'

'Think about it – it's a good one.'

Ethan nods down at the adoring Sami as I chew away at the tagline.

'What's a Shih-Tzu?'

Ethan nods. I give up.

'It's a dog.'

Ethan shakes his head, grinning wider all the while.

'Zoo with no animals.'

For the next minute at least, I don't do anything apart from giggle, helplessly, because Ethan's right – it is a good one.

That isn't why he told me it though, and I know that, because all of a sudden, tears well in my eyes again, and as I don't want him to see them, I head out into the kitchen to pour some more hot water in my cocoa, but then I stop as I see the half-open bottle of wine by the fridge.

It's a trick of the light obviously. But for a moment, as the last of the sun sets outside, it's as if there's a red streak on the neck that almost looks like blood. And just for a moment I'm back there again; it's this morning and I'm waking up, looking at that blood and those bruises, and thinking, why the fuck has all this started again?

Then I hear the ring on the bell outside.

For a moment I just stand there, disorientated, then suddenly I remember.

Tanya.

She's standing outside as I open the door, a DVD in hand. Joel's in the car, the engine idling. I can just make out the booster seat in the back and the dim shape of their little boy, Danny, sleeping.

'There was honestly no need.'

Tanya just smiles back. She smiles a lot; I've noticed that about her. Some sour souls in our small town say she's got a lot to smile about: good job, married to the very fanciable and very successful Joel and a lovely little boy in Danny. But some people would begrudge anyone just about anything.

'I was passing. I told you.'

Then she hesitates, that warm smile wobbling slightly, as if she doesn't know if she should say what she's about to say next.

'And you're OK, yes?'

I know what she means. It's that scene with Al out in the

schoolyard, the scene that never really became a scene thanks to Ethan.

I nod back.

'Yeah – and sorry.'

Behind, the exhaust fumes from Joel's idling engine are rising into the night. And out it comes again in some great big rush. Which is crazy – I really don't know her that well, certainly not well enough to be trading confidences on the doorstep. Maybe it's that warm smile again. Or maybe she's like Ethan. The kind of person you just feel easy with.

'It was just listening to you and Joel sorting out Danny's party.'

I struggle.

'It was like stepping back in time, I suppose. All of a sudden, I was remembering me and Al doing the same for Ethan.'

I stop suddenly, feeling foolish, but Tanya doesn't seem to find anything foolish about it.

She just nods at me again, that same warm, easy smile on her face and presses the DVD into my hand, then she turns, and she's gone.

JOEL – THE HUSBAND

TANYA COMES BACK to the car, checking on Danny the moment she gets back as she always does. It doesn't matter if she's only been away a few moments, it's always the same routine – deft hands smoothing the blankets around and underneath him, making sure he's still securely tucked in. Then she nods at me, and I put the car in gear, glancing at Danny still sleeping in his booster seat in the back as I do so, which is when I pause.

Tanya doesn't notice; she's choosing some song on the entertainment menu, but through the rear-view mirror I see it. A curtain in one of the upstairs windows in Nia's house moving slightly, as if someone's behind it, looking out.

I only notice it because I've got my foot on the brake and the red lights are illuminating the front of the house. I take my foot off the brake as I keep looking through the mirror and the curtain stops moving straight away, as if whoever's up there knows I've caught them watching.

Then the music sounds, soft and low through the speakers, and I set off towards home.

I used to have this toy when I was a kid. I still have it actually. I kept it back after we had a big clear-out when my parents died.

I told Tanya I wanted to pass it on to any kids we might have, but the truth is I still bring it out sometimes when no one's around.

It's a simple kaleidoscope. You look through a hole in the top, twist the bottom, and everything changes shape, all the colours merging each into the other. Twist it again and it happens again. A million different patterns every time you turn the cylinder so every time you look at it you see something different.

What I saw earlier this evening out on the school yard with Ethan was simple. The way he stepped up when no one else did, the way he took his mum's arm, how he spoke to her before steering her towards her car. There was nothing showy about it; he was just a caring kid who took over when she needed him, and I was impressed. To be honest I'm not sure I'd have been able to do that at his age. I'd probably have just looked at the floor and shuffled my feet, waiting for someone else to do something, preferably quickly so I could get back to my mates. But Ethan didn't and I respected him for it. He seemed like a decent kid.

Meaning that the cylinder still hadn't turned. The different shape that was there all the time hadn't revealed itself. The true colours, his true colours, still hadn't revealed themselves.

Not that I knew any of that then, of course, but I still must have sensed something, because, for a moment, I feel a sudden rage boil up inside me. I've been so much better at controlling it lately. Since meeting Tanya, these sudden flashes of anger have only really flared up once or twice, and that's been at work when there's been some problem or other, so it's never really mattered too much.

It mattered once, of course. It mattered a lot, but I really don't want to think about that, so why all of a sudden am I? Maybe it's being here outside Nia's house. Maybe that's why I'm tasting again that hot dryness in my throat and why my head's starting to pound. Maybe it's nothing to do with an unseen figure who may or may not have been spying on us from behind a bedroom curtain.

Maybe it's something else.

BEX – THE WANNABE

THE PROBLEM'S OBVIOUS, isn't it? It's the same problem for all of us.

Every little moment, each and every single little thing any of us saw or even didn't see, maybe just imagined we'd seen, every word and every look, they all became magnified somehow. Everything Ethan and Tanya did was suddenly being put under this big collective microscope, and everyone started remembering things they didn't realise were there before, and I know that because I did it myself.

I'd see her out and about in the town as well as in school; we all did. Tanya was a fitness freak as well as our English teacher. She wasn't obsessive – she just went out for a run once a day, in the evenings usually after school finished, so now and again all of us at some point or another would catch a glimpse of her as she ran past.

This one night, it was soon after that parents' evening, I saw her again. There was nothing so unusual in that, but this time I saw Ethan walking down the same street. Nothing actually happened. I can't even be sure she saw him, to be honest, even though I could see he'd spotted her. Not that he did anything either; he just paused for a moment to watch as she jogged by, and then, after a moment, maybe even less, moved on himself.

So why did that one single, stray encounter stick in my mind? And why do I keep replaying it? Was there something weird in him standing there watching our English teacher as she took her usual jog along that street? Or has that memory become filtered somehow because of all that's happened since? Was it just a totally innocent look he gave her? Or was it something more than that, some sort of portent, a harbinger, if I'd had the eyes to see it at the time, of the shitstorm to come? Why did I even notice Ethan and her out on the same street, apart from the fact, as it's obviously going to be hard for me to deny, that I did have more than a mild case of the hots for him?

Which is that old problem again, the question all of us have had to wrestle with ever since. What's fact and what's fiction? What's real and what's not?

The geography of the town didn't help, the way every house was hemmed in by the mountains on three sides and the sea on the other. And most of those houses were also built in such a way that they looked out on other houses too, which all added to the sense of a pressure cooker just waiting to explode.

And of course, there was our town's name and that age-old curse. The ancient story about the devil returning for all those mortgaged souls. Maybe every generation since has wondered if they'd be the ones to pay that long-standing debt, meaning that whenever bad things happened, and they must have happened to other generations as well as ours, it was always there.

That sense of the past finally catching up.

DEVIL'S BRIDGE

'DID YOU SEE THAT?'

The girl who first screamed doesn't answer but she doesn't need to. The same human pigs still mill around, oblivious, protected by their latex horror masks from the real horror that's just unfolded a few hundred feet above their heads. Other party-goers in different masks swoop among the pigs, similarly unaware of all that's just happened. But those two girls are only too aware.

They can't see anyone up on the bridge now, but that's only because the moon's retreated behind a cloud. When it reappears, they'll have a clear sight once again, and all the two girls now want is for that cloud to remain in place for ever.

One of the girls looks at her companion.

'What the fuck happened?'

But the question's redundant. They both know what happened. They both saw those struggling figures and they both heard the scream. And they both saw the immediate aftermath as well, that sole figure high up on the bridge, the devil's bridge, where before there were two.

The boy who dealt the blow is still staring at them, still unsure what's going on here, and the boy he felled is still moaning on the ground. He's hurt, but not badly hurt. He'll have a sore head in the morning, but he'd have had that anyway. Then the moon begins to peek from behind the shifting cloud, the night's party-going casualties becoming illuminated as the flickering fingers of light pick out more and more drunken bodies.

But the two girls just keep staring at the high bridge above them.

Where is it? That's all they're thinking. Where's the second of the figures that was up there those few moments ago, but isn't now?

Then the moonlight begins to lick at the bridge itself. And as it does so it picks out the same figure still just standing there; impossible to tell if it's male or female, young or old. Or even, to the two young girls in their heightened state right now, human or not. The figure up on the bridge, perhaps sensing something, half-turns. The two girls both scream again, and, for a moment, the figure on the bridge freezes.

Then, with its face still in shadow, it looks down towards the two watchers below on the ground.

AL – THE DAD

JOEL SEES HIM FIRST.

I'm finishing levelling one of the slabs for a small estate we're building on the far side of town. The slab's one of the most important parts of any building job. Get that right and you've got a home that could last for decades, maybe a lot longer. Get it wrong and we'll be back every year for the rest of our working lives fixing the problems.

Joel doesn't like problems, as he's made clear to us time and time again, so Ethan could have walked past fifty times today and I still wouldn't have seen him. Later, Joel tells me it was something about the set of his shoulders. As if he was carrying the weight of the world on them. I've never really had Joel down as the observant type, but I suppose he must be, because my usually brisk and business-like boss approaches me.

I'm checking the levels for the umpteenth time. It's another of those lessons drummed into us – check, check and check again, so it's even more of a surprise that he interrupts. He's usually the kind of employer who insists on total concentration on his sites. No blaring music from a tinny old radio, no chat apart from necessary communication. For Joel, plain and simple work's always been the even simpler name of the game.

'Terry's running a couple of errands for me.'

I look up at him, slightly puzzled as ever by the fact that Joel's trusting him to run any sort of errand at all.

'We could do with an extra pair of hands for the next hour or so.'

Joel glances across the road and now I see Ethan as well. And suddenly, almost as if I'm having some sort of out-of-body experience, it's like I'm looking at myself. We both look as if we have that weight on our shoulders right now. Then again, with all that's happened in the last few months I don't suppose that's any sort of surprise.

'He'll just tell me to take a running jump.'

'It'll be cash in hand.'

'Nothing to do with the money.'

Ethan's stopped to talk to a couple of his mates, or maybe they've stopped to talk to him. Either way he doesn't look too interested, which is another thing he and his old man have in common right now. Don't get me wrong – I turn up on time and I do my work. There's no choice anyway, not where Joel's concerned. But the fact of the matter is that I'm not all that interested these days either.

'You know what they say – if you don't try…'

I smile back quickly, a smile that's no smile at all.

'Do you think I haven't?'

'That mean you can't try again?'

I look across at Ethan once more. And keep looking.

For the first few minutes it's the same old story. Ethan's mates wander off the minute I approach and now he's looking at anything and anyone but me. Cars passing behind, people passing too, Joel across the road supervising a wagon that's just pulled up to dump a load of concrete, making sure its wheels stay on the tarpaulin we've laid down so there's no mess trailing back down the surrounding streets – Joel being his usual stickler, in other words.

'It'll be an hour, max.'

Ethan doesn't reply.

'Joel says he'll front you twenty quid.' I smile again or try to. 'Wish he was paying me twenty quid an hour.'

For a long moment I don't think Ethan's actually going to say anything at all, that he's just going to keep on looking at anyone or anything but me. But then, suddenly, he makes eye contact for the first time.

'So, why me?'

I pause, momentarily thrown, and not just by the eye contact.

'I told you. We need an extra pair of hands.'

'So, it could have been anyone?'

'I didn't mean it like that.'

'So, what did you mean?'

And suddenly, I've had enough again. Of walking round on eggshells, holding my breath every time I open my mouth, trying to work out what I should say before I even know what I'm going to say.

'OK, it's a made-up job. We can probably manage anyway.'

Ethan just keeps looking at me.

'And it wasn't my idea either, it was Joel's.'

Behind us the tanker driver's just put one wheel onto the tarmac next to the tarpaulin and Joel's reading him the riot act.

'He saw you.'

I pause, struggling.

'And he was there at the school, and he saw all that with your mum as well. He probably thought it'd be a chance for the two of us to talk.'

I look towards Joel and the tanker. Maybe I could still do some good today, stop a delivery driver losing a vital part of his anatomy.

Then Ethan cuts across.

'Think I'd worked that out for myself.'

I look back at him.

'I was just waiting for you to be honest and say so.'

I keep looking at him as Ethan holds my look.

Ten minutes later it's going better than I could have hoped.

Joel's with us, Terry's back from his errand, and that's a tale in itself. Ethan's grinning for the first time in what seems like a lifetime, and, for a few moments, I allow myself to feel some sort of cautious hope.

Until suddenly I see it.

We all do.

The ghost-like gargoyle approaching from the road.

KATE – THE NEWBIE

SOME DAYS you just can't win, can you? Sometimes, no matter what you do, it always turns out wrong.

We've had a run of that lately, things going pear-shaped. So far as honeymoon periods are concerned, that's ended pretty quickly for me and Al. In darker moments I have wondered why we couldn't have just kept all this the big secret it was at the start, but I know the answer of course. And I probably wouldn't have it any other way, or love him, if he hadn't done what he did and dragged it all out into the open like that. Despite everything people in this town might think, and definitely despite everything Nia will always think, neither of us were ever going to be happy creeping round behind people's backs.

So, I should have known. When I came out of work that afternoon, dived into the newsagents for some milk and bread and saw that display stashed by the till, I should have just paid for what I needed and left. But all of a sudden I thought, let's do something spontaneous for a change, something fun, which, let's face it, has been in pretty short supply lately.

We finished early at the garage. I work there as a receptionist. So, I thought I'd go and pick him up, let Al ride home in our car for a change instead of being thrown about in the back of one of Joel's vans by one of his lunatic drivers.

It's a lovely summer's afternoon. Through the open window as I pull up, I can hear Joel with Al and one of the other lads. Joel's got a spirit level in his hand and is giving it large, in his usual way. Joel's a big man, physically, and a big personality too, but despite all his bark and bluster I've always seen him as a bit of a softy deep down. Their voices float across the site to me as I kill the engine, which in the case of our old car is very definitely putting it out of its misery.

'I said, level.'

Al's voice floats back to me.

'It is.'

Joel snorts in derision.

'Can I borrow your brain, Al, I want to build myself an idiot.'

Another voice, a voice I don't recognise and can't place for now, chips in.

'We've checked.'

Joel has his large back to me, and for now that is all I can see.

'Were you two born lopsided or have you just grown that way?'

I rummage around in my bag for a moment, check my look in the mirror, then open the car door as I hear a long-suffering Al again.

'Check it again; we'll never hear the last of it if we don't.'

'Never hear the last of it from the poor sod who moves in, more like.'

Then I pause. Terry's now walking past, holding something in one of his hands. I don't know why, but he's always made me uneasy. Maybe it's just the way he is. Ahead, Joel keeps talking as I hover just out of sight, waiting for my moment.

'Every time they put a plate on the table, their dinner'll slide onto the floor.'

Then Joel stops as he sees Terry.

'Got it.' Terry holds out a child's skipping rope. Joel stares at him and, as they're distracted, I approach. I can already see Al now grinning broadly. For his part, Joel keeps staring at the skipping rope and he isn't grinning at all.

'What's that?'

Terry stares back at him.

'You told me to get a rope.'

Joel looks at the rope, then back at him, something approaching stunned wonder in his eyes. As I'm about to find out, this is a good one even for Terry

'For the Open Day, at the school.'

Terry just looks blank, and Al steps in.

'The tug of war.'

Joel takes the small skipping rope from him, stretches it out to its fullest in his giant hands, then looks back at Terry, and even he's beginning to get the point by now.

'It's teachers against parents and pupils, not Snow White against the Seven Dwarves.'

By now Al's in fits. I'm grinning too as I come up to them, although no one's going to see that. Joel doesn't register my approach; he's still just staring at Terry, who doesn't see me either, as he's shuffling his feet.

But then Al sees me, and his mouth hits the floor.

Gotcha.

Joel turns and almost drops the child's rope, and even though they can't see it, I've got the biggest, widest grin on my face right now.

Loads of kids are wearing these masks out and about in the town. It's getting towards the end of term, party season, a reminder to Al and to myself that in amongst all the angst and the soul-searching and the constant debates about Ethan and Nia and money, which is all we seem to talk about these days, we can actually let our guard down now and again and act like big kids too.

But Al isn't smiling as I take it off.

'Thought I'd give you a lift home.'

Then Terry moves to one side, and I see the other builder with Al, or at least who I assumed was the other builder. But now I see Ethan staring back at me.

I just catch Joel shoot a quick sideways look of fellow-feeling, sympathy, his way, but Al doesn't even see it. He's looking at Ethan instead, who's already turning away.

'Ethan—'

Al calls after him, but he just keeps on walking. Then Al looks back at me as Joel diplomatically melts away too, shepherding Terry with him.

I hiss at him. 'You could have told me.'

'I didn't know.'

'All you had to say was that Ethan was working with you today and I wouldn't have come within a mile of the place.'

'He wasn't supposed to be working at all; it was just a spur of the moment thing.'

Al pauses, frustrated, hurt and angry all at the same time.

'Joel's idea, not mine.'

I flare at him again.

'You still could have called me.'

He flares back at me.

'I didn't know you were going to turn up.'

Then, at the edge of my vision I just catch a glimpse of Ethan as he looks back at me from the bottom of the street.

Al doesn't see him; he's still facing me. For that moment it's just me and Ethan as we lock eyes.

What is it that I'm seeing?

I go over it time and again in the days that follow.

What is it I see in his eyes that I'm catching in that unguarded moment?

NIA – THE MUM

I FEEL like a guilty school kid. Which is ridiculous, double ridiculous in fact, because I'm not actually doing anything wrong, but I still feel as if I've just been caught out.

'Nia?'

I bolt up from the letterbox, turning at the same time, which is when I twist my knee. As I feel it give way, I grab onto Tanya, who's standing behind me, knocking her off-balance and crashing the pair of us down onto the small path that leads from the road to her front door.

I just lie there for a moment, gasping and panting on the ground, Tanya lying beside me.

'Oh, God.'

Struggling, I prop myself up on one arm and look down at her.

'Are you OK?'

For a moment I think she might be having some sort of fit. Her face is blood red and she doesn't seem able to speak. I hunch closer, increasingly convinced I've just done her a serious injury.

'Tanya?'

For a moment longer there's this awful silence. Then out it comes. One of the biggest, loudest, barks of laughter I've ever heard as Tanya stares back up at me, barely able to get the words out she's spluttering so much.

'What—?'

Tanya stops, can't continue for a moment.

'What the—?'

Then she stops again. One of her neighbours has been cutting his front lawn and he's now looking, cautiously, over a small dividing hedge at us, which only sends Tanya off into more fits and splutters.

I struggle to my feet, trying to help her up at the same time as stammering out some sort of explanation, but Tanya shakes her head, finally managing something approaching one coherent sentence at least.

'Tell you what.'

She nods, still gasping, towards the front door.

'Why don't you tell me inside?'

Ten minutes later, we're sitting in Tanya's kitchen, coffees in front of us, the birthday present I've brought for Danny, which I'd been trying to stuff through the letterbox, on the table.

It was meant to be a simple thank you for all she was doing for Ethan until it turned into something more resembling an assault. Tanya hasn't stopped giggling about it all the time she's been filling the upmarket percolator. It could have been horrible, embarrassing, yet it's anything but.

Maybe that's why within just a few more moments of giggles and cooing over Danny's present, talking about Ethan, that DVD, his school play, I find us talking about the parents' evening and me and Al.

'It was weird, you know.'

I look at her, sipping my coffee.

Which is perfect, by the way.

Of course.

'The two of you. Out on that yard.' She smiles. 'If I hadn't known, I'd never have imagined there was anything wrong.'

I struggle back a sort of smile.

'Yeah, well, it came as a bit of a shock to me too.'

Tanya looks at me and now there's something in her eyes, something I haven't seen before. She always comes across as so calm, so confident, but now she looks different. Vulnerable, almost. She struggles for a moment as I keep looking at her, then puts her mug down on the table.

'It's my worst nightmare if you want the truth.' She takes a quick, deep breath. 'OK. Joel's no George Clooney—'

'Joel's hot.'

Out it comes; I can't help myself. It's always been my problem – if something's in my head it's out there.

I stop, flushing suddenly. Does she know? Not that there's all that much to know, but there was a time, long before Tanya, way back when we were all in school together, when there was something between me and him. Not that it led anywhere and not that it probably ever would. But for those few days that summer, there was that moment in time.

But Tanya just smiles, wryly.

'A lot of women think so, and not just women, for God's sake – girls too. I've seen the looks he gets when we're out sometimes.'

She hesitates, indicating her running gear and trainers stacked by the back door, the reason she came home in the first place.

'And I'm not getting any younger.'

I keep looking at her, all those runs she's always going on now coming across in a different light.

'It wasn't just that with me and Al. The latest model.' I pause. 'Well, it was, but—'

Now it's my turn to put down my coffee.

'You must know some of this anyway, about Al's old business. Joel must have told you.'

Tanya nods back, cautious.

'I know he tried starting up on his own.'

'I really thought he could make a go of it. OK, not on Joel's scale, but he's a good builder, I kept telling him, too good to be working for someone else for the rest of his life.'

I stop suddenly again.

'No offence.'

But Tanya just smiles that easy smile of hers again.

'Actually, Joel's always said much the same.'

I take a quick, deep breath, all this still raw. Maybe it always will be.

'It started OK, but then he ran into trouble. People not paying bills as quickly as they promised, at the same time as he had bills of his own to pay. And the people he owed money to always seemed able to shout louder than he could shout at the people who owed him.'

I break off for a moment, shaking my head. 'That sort of stuff's probably meat and drink to Joel, but it really got to Al.'

I pick up the coffee, which is getting cold by now, but I drink it anyway.

'The worst thing was he didn't tell me. Maybe he thought I'd think less of him or something. So, then he started staying out later and later – working, he told me.'

I pause again. 'Seems most of the time he was sitting in the pub or his car trying not to think about his problems.'

Tanya tenses slightly. She knows what's about to come next; it's all too obvious. Maybe it always was. To everyone except me.

'It wasn't too long before he found someone to talk to, though.'

I look back up at her steadily. I've gone over this a thousand times and it's clear now, or at least I think it is.

'Al seeing someone else; that wasn't my fault. The business though. Maybe that was.'

Tanya breaks in, quizzical.

'Your fault for believing in your husband, for wanting the best for him and your family?'

'Didn't quite work out like that, did it? Thank God Joel took him back, that's all I can say, or we'd have been in real trouble.'

Tanya breaks in again, more hesitant this time.

'And there's no chance you and he…?'

I close that one down straight away.

'No.'

She looks at me, quizzical again.

'One strike and he's out?' She hurries on. 'I don't mean to sound judgemental – if I'm honest, it would be with me. I don't think I'd ever be able to get past it. And so far as Joel's concerned, if he thought someone was coming onto me—'

She stops suddenly, gives a small shudder. 'I definitely wouldn't like to poke that bear.'

'It's not just that. I've got Ethan to think of.'

'You've got a life to live too.'

'The last thing he needs right now is any more upset. He's been brilliant, don't get me wrong – well, he's had to be – but…'

I struggle again.

'He's only fifteen.'

BEX – THE WANNABE

I SEE her again this evening.

Nothing unusual about that, only this time I'm in Jimmy's van, well, Jimmy's brother's van, just me in there along with three testosterone-fuelled teenage boys.

'Where is he?'

I've told them to wait for Ethan, that he's coming with us – OK, maybe that's more hope on my part than any sort of promise on his. I just hope I'm sounding suitably casual about it all.

'He's got two minutes.'

'OK.'

'Then we go.'

'I said.'

But then Jimmy breaks off as he looks through the window. I follow the look just that little bit too eagerly. Is it Ethan?

Then a couple of the other boys lean forward as they also follow Jimmy's stare, and I see for myself what's driven all thoughts of Ethan out of his mind and out of the mind of every other testosterone-fuelled teenager in that van right now as Tanya jogs past.

It's weird. It's not that she's any sort of goddess. And she always dresses down too, in school and out of it; even her jogging gear's really loose-fitting. But she still has something, even I can see it. And it's only too obvious in the way the pairs of eyes next to me in that van are drinking her in right now.

'Sad.'

Jimmy shoots me a half-pitying glance.

'Jealous?'

'She's older than my gran.'

Which isn't even remotely true, but it doesn't make any difference. Jimmy just stares at Tanya again as she heads on into the school, feasting on the sight for another few precious seconds.

'Well, I would.'

I look at the other boys and their faces are saying it all.

So would they.

'Playing in a sand pit. At your age.'

It's earlier that day. Ethan stops as I stare at him. He's filthy. Boots caked in all sorts, jeans just the same. OK, he hasn't been in a sand pit and I know it, but he still looks as if he's been rolling around in something like a five-year-old. I found out later he'd been working with his dad, which was maybe why he also didn't seem to be in the mood for conversation, so I had to be quick.

'A few of us are going up to the Rec.'

Ethan looks back at me.

'We may even go up to the bridge later; they say there's going to be a party.'

I've started now, no point in not finishing.

'Jimmy's brother's picking us all up from outside the school at six.'

I reach into my pocket, hand him a spliff.

'Be plenty more where that came from.'

Ethan looks down at the spliff, hesitating.

I grin at him. 'You smoke it.'

He grins back.

'I know.'

'Just checking.'

Ethan's grin grows wider.

'Shut up.'

'Hate to lead you astray.'

Which, given what I have in mind for the evening, isn't strictly true. I nod at him again, briskly.

'If you're there, see you then.'

I don't wait for a reply. But as I walk away, I can't help a small glow starting inside.

Ethan hasn't said yes.

But he hasn't said no either.

And now, sitting in Jimmy's brother's van, I'm doubly glad he hasn't, although I'd never admit it to anyone. I've known this lot for most of my life; most of us started in school together, and that's primary, not the high school we're in now. I know them as well as I know anyone.

But the fact remains I'm the only girl in the van right now. Some more girls should join us later, particularly if we do head up to the bridge. If the rumours about that big party that's going to kick off turn out to be true, no one's going to want to miss out on it.

But I can't help wondering what might happen if I remain the only girl tonight with all these boys. For some reason I'd just feel easier if Ethan was here too, which doesn't make much sense, I know, because it wouldn't exactly even up the boy/girl split, would it?

Maybe it's that place. The bridge. It still gives me the creeps for some reason, and it's nothing to do with that weird image I still have of pushing my own dad over the edge. It's not the story behind it either or the name.

It's just something about it. Something that's always made me wonder what might happen up there if things got really out of hand.

NIA – THE MUM

I'VE BEEN RUNNING LATE all week; we've an inspection coming up. It's not Ofsted like they have in Ethan's school from time to time, which seems to terrify everyone from the headteacher to the caretaker. Life in a hospital records department isn't that interesting. It's not much more than a licensing check by the local Health Board in truth, but everything still has to be right.

Ethan's books are all over the kitchen table, along with the DVD Tanya dropped off for him. Ethan himself is upstairs. I can hear the shower running. As I put the kettle on a few moments later, I still hear it running, and as I finish my mug of tea more than ten minutes after that the water's still pounding down.

And this is pushing it a bit. OK, we're not on any sort of meter, but the steam in that bathroom must be approaching Turkish bath proportions by now. I'm just about to head up there when the shower, mercifully for our condensation count, cuts out.

A few minutes later, Ethan appears, booted and suited and towelling his hair. And, yes, that is pushing it a bit too. He isn't wearing a suit and he's wearing trainers; he doesn't actually own a pair of boots. But he's definitely taken pains with how he's looking. Not that I let him know I've noticed, at least not straight away. I just nod at the books and the DVD instead.

'Been getting down to it then?'

Ethan hesitates, then nods back, cautiously.

'So, how's it going?'

And there it is again, that fractional hesitation before he nods again.

'Good.'

'It's helping, then?'

'What?'

'The DVD that Mrs Adams dropped off.'

I still find it peculiar, I must admit. Schools are definitely more informal these days, but it feels strange to me to use Tanya's Christian name in front of Ethan, even though I use it myself to her face every time we meet.

Now he's looking at a spot just behind my left ear, always a sure sign something's going on with that son of mine.

'Only thing is, I need a couple more books.'

I look at his freshly towelled hair.

'Thought I'd nip down the library.'

I try, not altogether successfully, to suppress a smile.

'What, now?'

Ethan nods again, his eyes still fixed on that same spot.

'It's open till late.'

I'm still trying my hardest not to break out in giggles.

'Good idea.'

Ethan turns for the door, and I watch him every step of the way. Then, just before he lets himself out, I can't help myself.

'Does it kill flies too?'

He looks at me, puzzled.

'That aftershave you've just had a bath in?'

Caught out and knowing it, Ethan hesitates again. Then he sees the smile spreading across my face and I nod at him.

'Go on. Enjoy yourself. You deserve a bit of time off.'

And, with a parting grin, he's gone.

I stand there for a moment longer, and I'm still grinning as I rinse my mug and put away his schoolbooks and the DVD. Because it's kids, isn't it? Just normal, teenage stuff, the kind of stuff everyone does, the kind of stuff I used to do back in the day, and I don't begrudge him a single, solitary moment of it.

Which is when, suddenly and out of nowhere, a memory returns. Or maybe it isn't out of nowhere; maybe it was being up there, in Joel's house, with all those pictures of him and his family all over the walls.

I was around the same age as Ethan is right now, maybe a little older, and we'd just been out on the first of our dates, although date is definitely putting it a bit strongly. It was evening and we'd headed up to the gorge beneath the bridge, where I'd had what I'm pretty sure was one of my first proper snogs – tongues, the lot, although strictly nothing else. Even then I knew I was punching above my weight. It wasn't just the fact Joel was a year or so older than me – I just knew he was always going to set his sights a bit higher than plain old simple Nia from the local council estate, and so it proved. But, briefly, during that sixteen-year-old summer, I was one local girl who very definitely dared to dream. Until what happened, anyway. Neither of us was much in the mood for any more moonlit trysts after that.

Suddenly, I jump as a loud crash sounds. I stand there, frozen for a moment, then dash next door to find a small table lying on its side. I stare round because it's Sami, it has to be – he's tipped it over as he sniffed behind it or something, and I can't see him right now, but he always does that; goes to ground when he thinks he's done something wrong.

I right the small table, move back into the kitchen and take a deep breath, trying to dismiss both my sudden panic and that apparition from years before that just floated in front of my eyes.

But for some reason, and for the rest of the evening, I can't dismiss either.

JOEL – THE HUSBAND

I DO it all the time, that's what people forget – day in, day out, every day of the week. In my game you have to work people out. It's an instinct. You either have it or you don't, and you may as well pack up and go home if you don't, because you're not going to last five minutes.

I work with brickies, plasterers, roofers and chippies who'll pull the wool over your eyes as quick as look at you. The building game's full of chancers and you quickly learn to sort out the wheat from the chaff, particularly when you run your own business. I've run mine for years now and I pride myself on being able to spot a dodgy story at a hundred paces.

So, I know that when Tanya told me what happened that night, every single thing she was saying was the absolute truth.

She'd gone into the school after her evening run. It was a regular ritual and anyone keeping watch on her would have known that. A run after school, a shower in the changing room, some prep in the staffroom for the next day and then home.

Going into the changing room, she sensed something. She didn't know what exactly, but there was no one out on the school yard a moment or so before, and the only person she saw as she was walking down the corridor was the caretaker, who'd just finished his usual checks for the night and was letting himself out of the side door back onto the street. So, whatever it was she sensed, or thought she sensed, she just put it to the back of her mind.

Tanya had her shower in the empty changing room as usual. She didn't have that same feeling while she was in there, but as she came out of the shower, and as she was standing in front of one of the mirrors, towelling her hair, she had it again.

This time it was more specific. This time she felt as if someone was in there with her.

Tanya looked round, but she still couldn't see anyone. The changing room is open plan, but there are some cubicles at the far end, and Tanya called out, just in case. But there was just silence. She turned back to the mirror, which was when she thought she saw an image behind her, but it was fleeting, unfocused. The mirror was still steamed up from the shower and she didn't really get a clear sight. Tanya wheeled round again, getting spooked now, but there was still no one there.

So, this time she went up to the cubicles at the far end of the changing room, opened the doors and looked in each and every one just to make sure, but they were all empty.

Then Tanya did what she always does. She sorted out her prep in the staffroom for her classes the following day, then she came home. Just like she's done dozens and dozens of days before.

But this day's going to be like none of those other days.

From this day on nothing's ever going to be the same.

MEGAN – THE HEADTEACHER

It was a normal, busy, school day, but most of us were really concentrating on the fete that was taking place later on. Who's manning which stall? Are all the relevant health and safety protocols in place? How can we coax every last little bit of cash from the protesting pockets of occasionally reluctant attendees? What we weren't meant to be focusing on was a life-size toy giraffe.

Most of the teachers have been in since first thing, setting up before they began their teaching. The caretaker was in even earlier to open up for Joel to check on his bouncy castle. It still feels more than a little alien, in truth. I went into teaching all those years ago to teach, but the higher I've risen through the ranks to what some see as my current exalted position of head-teacher, which I'm increasingly coming to see more as a poisoned chalice, the more I seem to resemble an accountant trying to balance the books and usually failing.

But these days all schools have to do what they can, hence the bouncy castle.

And the giraffe.

Don pulls up alongside. I've known him years – we were at school together ourselves. But he's not here today as an old mate.

Don's the newly installed head of governors and it's his first school fete. Well, his first anything actually, seeing as he's only been a governor for three months. His daughter, Keira, started in the school a year ago. I don't think he knows yet what a school governor actually does, but as no one else in the school seems to either, including its headteacher, it doesn't matter too much. But his new post does come with its own parking space in the school yard with a sign that reads, 'Reserved: Head of Governors', which is giving him a grandstand view of the new arrival right now.

Don wasn't there at the parents' evening so he's staring at a long neck and the head that's sticking out from the sunroof of my car for the first time. And as the giraffe measures fully twenty feet from top to bottom it's sticking out of that sunroof of mine a long way, too.

For a moment Don just keeps staring while I look back at him. I had a lot of those sorts of stares, along with honks of horns and yelled comments, as I drove through the town up the series of steep hills and bends to the school. I had the same sort of stares, and the honks of horns and yelled comments, as I drove home with it after the parents' evening too.

He turns to me, but I cut across.

'Don't ask.'

Behind, the caretaker's just opened the gates and parents and pupils are beginning to swarm inside. The bouncy castle, predictably, is already proving to be the biggest attraction. Partly to distract attention from my unwanted companion, in fact totally to distract attention from my unwanted companion, I nod across at the large – very large – banner on the front of the inflated castle.

'That sign.'

Don, reluctantly, tears his eyes away from the over-sized stuffed toy and looks across at it.

'You don't think it could be just a tiny bit bigger?'

It seems to dominate the whole of the yard. 'Sponsored By

Joel Adams Construction.' And with people now starting to jump up and down on the inflatable castle, the sign's bouncing up and down as well, making it look even bigger.

Don hesitates. 'It is a freebie.'

Then he checks an entry on his phone. He's got the accounts for the day ticking up on a spreadsheet. Another advantage of having an actual accountant as a governor.

'And Joel's donated five hundred quid to school funds.'

I spread my arms wide.

Why hadn't he said so sooner?

'Make it as big as he likes.'

That matter dispensed with, a now grinning Don looks at the giraffe again and I grow defensive once more.

'It's a donation from the toy shop in town – what was I supposed to say? Can't look a gift horse in the mouth.'

'It's a giraffe.'

'Whatever.'

'You can't even see its mouth.'

'Shut up.'

Then we both stop as Tanya approaches, leaving a small gaggle of teachers behind her.

'OK, we've been having a chat.'

Tanya nods up at the rogue donation too. What to do with it was one of the first tasks I set my staff today.

'First, we thought, guess the height. But then we thought, too obvious. So, then we thought, best name.'

I look up at the giraffe, dubious already, and, as if she can read my mind, Tanya nods.

'But that'd be a real hostage to fortune. Some of the ones the staff came up with were filthy enough.'

Above us the giraffe's neck moves slightly in the wind, almost as if it's listening.

'Then we thought, who are we trying to kid? No one's going to want it anyway. So then we thought, make it the booby prize.'

Tanya nods across the yard to a loose group forming around a large, knotted rope.

'Whoever loses the tug of war has to work out what to do with it.'

I don't hesitate for a second.

'Brilliant.'

Which is when a scream cuts across the yard.

It's just an accident, that's all. The kind of thing that happens ten times a day in any school. An excited kid chasing across a yard; a group of older kids heading in the opposite direction. Irresistible force meets immoveable object – result: the kind of accident we have to deal with all the time.

Except...

One of the other teachers heard it. Not everything; she only caught snatches of the exchange, but from what she told us later Bex Hughes seemed upset that Ethan James hadn't shown up for some date or other the previous evening. It wasn't a row exactly, but it wasn't far off.

Bex stood there for a moment as Ethan walked away. Then Bex turned away too. A moment later, we all heard the scream.

No one can actually know if the small girl was deliberately smashed into the side of that stall. Bex bumped into her as she walked away, but the yard and the playing field were packed – it could have just been one of those things. In any event the staff were rather more concerned with treating the nasty-looking head wound the girl suffered as a result, which, as it turned out, necessitated a trip to the local casualty department and four stitches.

But I've been around hundreds of kids in my time. And every now and again you get a feeling about one of them. And I'm getting that feeling now as I look at Bex, keeping her distance as concerned teachers huddle around the injured girl.

The feeling that this one's trouble.

NIA – THE MUM

I HEAR the music as I turn the corner at the bottom of the street, although I've no idea what's playing. Ella always said my musical taste stalled at George Michael and never got going again. Some might take offence at that, but to me it's a badge of pride. Sometimes I think if I never heard anything again apart from the warbling of Gorgeous George I'd die happy.

I'm meeting Ella at the house, collecting Ethan, then we're all heading off to the school. Normally she wouldn't go near the place after she finishes work. She's not a teacher – education's something that also stalled more than a little bit for her, as she'd be the first to admit. Not that I was that far behind in the stalling stakes. I stayed the course so far as school was concerned, but that was much more down to luck than good judgement.

But Ella left at sixteen, then drifted. She dabbled with a bit of hairdressing and did some office work, but then she did a catering course and ended up as an Education Centre Nourishment Consultant. In my day, they were plain old dinner ladies, but that's what the bright spark who hired her called them. And it wasn't just Ella who found her new job rechristened like that; another old classmate of mine became a hotel receptionist only to find herself rebranded as a Guest Services Agent. Another friend who'd worked the perfume counter at Boots ever since she'd left school walked into work one day to find she'd become a Beauty Ambassador.

But none of that's on my mind right now. All I'm thinking about as I approach the house is that music pounding from inside.

Ella nods out across to the sea behind us.

'You can hear that over in Wexford.'

I glance up towards Ethan's front bedroom window. That may not be strictly true, but it isn't far off.

'What do you know about music?'

'Says the girl who had 'Careless Whisper' on repeat cycle for a whole year.'

See what I mean about my musical taste? And the way my sister never, ever, lets me forget it?

'It's a good song, still is.'

'And who cried herself to sleep for the whole of the next year after she found out he was gay.'

I look up at the bedroom window again, keeping quiet at that one.

Guilty as charged.

'It is a bit loud, isn't it?'

'A bit?'

I call up towards the window.

'Ethan.'

Nothing. Apart from the music. Which if anything now seems to be sounding even louder.

'Ethan!'

Still nothing.

'What's he doing up there?'

Ella shrugs.

'Teenage boy. On his own. In a bedroom.'

I look back at her, sour.

'That's supposed to make you blind isn't it, not deaf?'

Ella, grinning, follows me inside, making for our small kitchen to make herself some coffee as I head up the stairs.

I haven't actually seen Ethan this morning. Or last night. He came in late, but I wasn't too bothered. How many Saturday nights had I done it? Headed out with my mates, sneaked back in at least half an hour after I was supposed to, trod up the stairs, praying the steps wouldn't creak and wake Mum and Dad, who were probably wide awake anyway, smiling to themselves in the darkness as they remembered their own teenage rites of passage.

But that music is definitely still too loud. And the fete's starting in half an hour.

I tap on the door.

'Ethan?'

Still nothing from inside, and suddenly I freeze. He hasn't had one for years, not since he was a small boy, but he did have the odd asthma attack back then. I push open the door quickly, move inside even more quickly, then stop dead.

It's weird, it really is, but for a moment it's like looking at a stranger. Ethan still hasn't heard me – the music's deafening now I'm inside, but that isn't the reason he doesn't even register I'm there. He's just standing in the middle of the room, mobile in hand, and it's as if there's nothing and no one else in the world right now.

Just him and that mobile.

I move forward, tap him on the shoulder.

'Ethan.'

Suddenly, he wheels round. I just catch a flash of something on the screen, but all I then see is Ethan's face filling my eyes as he yells at me, as in really, really, yells.

'Don't do that!'

I just stare back at him for a moment. Then he yells again, even louder this time, his eyes even wilder.

'Don't creep up on me!'

Then, still gripping his phone tight in his hand, he moves past and heads downstairs.

I stand there for a moment, rooted. He has never in his life done that before. He has never pushed his face into mine and yelled at me like that, and, for a moment, I have no idea what to do.

Then what I actually do is pick up a shirt of his that's lying on the bed, then I pick up a pair of jeans discarded on a chair to wash them too. Moving as if on automatic pilot, doing anything and everything apart from think about what's just happened, in other words.

Which is when something falls out of one of the pockets of his jeans.

And all of a sudden, I've something else to think about.

KATE – THE NEWBIE

We get there about half an hour after it started and the bouncy castle's already doing a roaring trade. It's a pound for three minutes, with all the money going to school funds. Judging by the queue they'll be able to build a brand-new school by the time the day's through.

Al's nervous, his eyes darting everywhere from the minute we park the car, and there's no prizes for guessing why. We've come across each other in the town, run into each other out on the street or in the shops. In our sort of town, you really can't help running into people. Nia's not been too hostile up to now, but that's no guarantee she won't suddenly make some sort of scene. So right now, Al isn't the only one who's feeling more than a little nervous, but as it happens it's not his ex we see first, but his boss.

'Al, you're on my team.'

Joel nods across at a sign next to the bouncy castle advertising a tug of war.

'And we can't lose, OK?'

Then Joel nods over at Tanya, who's helping out on one of the stalls, parents and kids in front of her taking pictures of themselves with different coloured wigs and costumes – policemen, nurses, firemen.

'Blame my wife.'

But Al's eyes are still darting everywhere. I don't think he's even heard Joel. I step in, and not for the first time lately where a distracted Al's concerned.

'The part's in, by the way.'

Joel looks back at me, puzzled, his mind clearly only on tugs of war and bouncy castles.

'That problem you've got with your sat-nav?'

Al breaks in, finally trying to engage.

'First world problems, eh? Remember them old bangers we used to drive around in? So old we had to insure them against fire, theft and Vikings.'

He always does it – whenever he's nervous, out they come, the really bad jokes, but suddenly I'm not listening. It's ironic, but for all his darting eyes I've seen them before he has: Nia, Ethan, and Nia's sister Ella now walking onto the yard.

Joel obviously sees them at about the same time too, and Al now follows his look. As he does so I see Joel shoot him a quick glance you could have walked to the end of and still not quite deciphered. But then, and equally suddenly, he melts away just like he did before on that site.

I don't speak. For a moment, Al doesn't either.

'I'll just go and say hello.'

I look back at him, wary.

'Break the ice. Then we'll go and check out some of the stalls, yeah?'

I struggle for a moment, but how can I say what I actually want to say without coming across as some kind of whiney kid? But maybe I am a whiney kid, because I say it anyway. And I smile, I try to soften what I'm saying, but things like this, days like today, they lay down a marker. Get a day like today wrong and you get things wrong for good.

'We talked about this.'

Al's eyes are darting behind me again.

'I haven't come here to be pushed into the background.'

'You won't be.'

'Al—'

'Just give me a minute, that's all.'

I watch him as he crosses the yard, making for Nia, Ella, and Ethan, who've now stopped by another of the stalls manned by a member of staff who must have spent the whole of the previous night up to her elbows in cupcakes, given the number on display. He doesn't look back once, and if he feels my eyes on him, he gives no sign.

So, I just stand there, on my own, a woman apart, which is my fault, I know – I'd have said it myself about anyone else in my position. I knew he was married when this whole thing started. Situations like this, no matter what we've agreed about putting on a united front, just go with the territory.

And I know I have to give him space to ask about the notes too, because he made it crystal clear before we came out that he was going to. Initially, he tried treating them as some kind of joke until that latest one, detailing exactly what was going to be done to us in general, and me in particular. That was far from any kind of laughing matter. Al even talked about taking it to the police.

As he said last night, he doesn't think it's Nia. He just doesn't think it's her style – she's always favoured the direct approach if she wants to say something. As he said too, it could just be some overly moralistic local maniac we don't know, which isn't as crazy as it sounds, because this town has always housed all sorts of weirdos just waiting to crawl out of the woodwork. But he is going to try, subtly, to ask.

Then I stop as across the yard I see Al now move close to Nia and take her in his arms.

NIA – THE MUM

'Girl trouble.'

I look back at Ella. Ethan's wandered off somewhere. He moved away the minute Al began his solo trek across the yard towards us.

'Bound to be.'

I hesitate.

'He did go out last night.'

Ella nods at me in that point-made sort of way that always used to wind me up big time when we were growing up. Usually because she was right, but not this time though. This time she's way off the mark.

'Did he say where? Who with?'

Ella shakes her head sagely, not even waiting for a reply.

'Keeping it secret, that's a sure sign too. He sneaks off on some date, then him and Little Miss Gym Slip have a tiff.'

I cut across at that, spluttering, can't help myself.

'Who?'

'Well I don't know who she is, do I? Neither do you. But he goes out – something happens.'

She grins.

'Or doesn't.'

I eye her, pictures in my head I very much do not want to see.

'He comes home, broods on it all night and then takes it out on his mum.'

She nods at me, point-made-style again.

'Think you did the same when you found out about George Michael. None of us could talk to you for months.'

Then suddenly I catch sight of him, away on his own, the rest of the kids all in little huddles out on the field or by the stalls in groups. It hasn't struck me before, but for the last few weeks I haven't seen Ethan with anyone. Whenever I've seen him, coming home from school or out in the town, he's always been on his own.

I turn back towards Ella.

'Have you talked to him lately?'

'He's fifteen. They don't talk, they grunt.'

'But he's been OK? When you've seen him in school?'

'I only ever see him in the dinner queue these days.'

Now Ella pauses. 'He's not been eating much; I have noticed that.'

Then she grins again.'Don't say it. Food I dish up – you're not surprised.'

But then her smile fades as I keep looking across at the solitary Ethan, now passing one of the stalls on the far side of the yard.

'He's fine, Nia. Relax.'

But he isn't and I know it.

And I know why.

I just don't know how serious it is yet.

AL – THE DAD

I FEEL Kate's eyes on me all the way over. I can't blame her, I suppose. But what are we supposed to do, walk over there together hand in hand?

Nia looks tense – I notice that straight away – and worried, but I don't think too much of it at first. She usually does right now and that's down to me, I know. Yet another reason not to do anything stupid. Then I hear her talking about our son, and suddenly everything else is wiped.

'Is Ethan OK?'

Nia looks up at me and I can see that everything else is wiped for her now too. For that moment it's as if all that happened between us hasn't happened at all – we're just two parents again with only one concern, and that's our child.

Ella, diplomatically, moves away. She did a lot of that in the weeks and months before I moved out, leaving us to a whole series of humdinger slanging matches. But today it's another slanging match that's much more on Nia's mind as she tells me all about walking in on Ethan.

I stare at her, can't quite believe what I'm hearing. Nia and Ethan have always had a special sort of bond. He's not a mummy's boy, not how that sounds anyway, he's just always gone to her, been able to talk to her, tell her things, and from way back when he was really small. So what she's telling me now is really not right.

'It's not just the way he yelled at me or the way he looked at me. There's something else.'

Then Nia stops, really struggling now. And suddenly I can't help it – I just reach out. I can't even remember if I actually hug her or just take her arm. All I do know is that for the first time in months there's some sort of actual contact.

It's just unfortunate to say the least that Kate chooses that moment to make her approach.

'Hi.'

Nia looks behind me as I wheel round. And for that moment I don't speak. I can't – it's like being wrenched from one reality to another, from a world in which there's only one focus and that's Ethan. But before I can say anything anyway, Nia steps in. She always was a lot quicker at recovering her wits.

'Caught us, eh Al?'

I stare at her, as bewildered as Kate.

'Bang to rights.'

Nia nods at her.

'We've got a thing going on. No point hiding it though, is there? Not from an expert like you – you'd spot the signs straight away.'

Then Nia turns away. For a moment neither myself or Kate speak. I don't think either of us even look at each other. It didn't seem like a rehearsed speech on Nia's part, something she'd been planning to say. I think it just came out, spur of the moment. Which doesn't alter the fact that it doesn't exactly help. Or that it makes this difficult situation even more fucking impossible.

But then I look across at Nia in a huddle with Ella again.

What did she mean, there's something else?

NIA – THE MUM

'Look.'

I join Ella by one of the craft stalls. Al and Kate are where I left them a moment ago, but I'm looking across at Ethan again, who's still just wandering round the yard, not talking to anyone, still no one talking to him.

Ella looks down at my hand, or, more accurately, the spliff I'm holding in my hand.

Then she looks back up at me.

'I found it in the pocket of Ethan's jeans just before we came out. The ones he went out in last night.'

Ella keeps looking at me.

'Just calm down.'

'Calm down? My son is on drugs.'

'It's a spliff. That doesn't mean he's on drugs.'

'So, what else is he on?'

'You don't know he's on anything else.'

'I didn't know he was on this till I found it.'

Ella shakes her head.

'Ethan is not on drugs.'

I gesture down at the spliff again.

'So, what's this, Scotch Mist?'

'Remember the school disco when you were in Year 11, you sneaking off for a crafty fag, Mum catching you?'

I cut across, impatient.

'A crafty cig's one thing.'

But she cuts across in turn.

'Kids experiment, that's all I'm saying. And I'm not saying it's right, but don't go over the top before you actually know what you're dealing with here.'

I nod across at Ethan, now looking at his phone again.

'And how am I going to do that?'

'What?'

'Find out what we're dealing with?'

I roll on before Ella can respond as I keep looking at him, the answer literally before my eyes.

'That'd tell me, I suppose.'

'What would?'

'His phone.'

Ella stares at me again.

'He was looking at it when I walked in on him in his bedroom.'

'Course he was. They live on them these days. You should see them in school – their mobiles are practically welded to their fingers.'

'They live their life on them, yeah?'

I nod back at her, my own point-made moment, before continuing.

'So, if anything is going on, anything his mum really should know about, it'll be on that.'

Ella stares at me as pennies start to drop.

'You can't.'

I just look back at her.

'Apart from the fact he'd never forgive you if you do start prying like that, and that's as in never, do not pass Go and do not collect two hundred pounds.'

I cut across again.

'It wouldn't be prying – it'd be me trying to find out if there's anything I should know about.'

I gesture down at the spliff again.

'Whether this is going to open a window on something more serious, which is maybe why he went off on one like that.'

But Ella just shakes her head in turn.

'You can't, as in how would you even do it? Get into his phone? They're all password protected, you know that, and most of the kids change their passwords every five minutes too.'

I pause, struggling with that one.

'As for him going off on one, what were you like at fifteen? Mum couldn't even look at you sometimes.'

Ella pauses, then squeezes my hand, gentler now.

'He's a teenager.'

'So just ignore it?'

For a moment I hover on the edge of a nightmare I really don't want to revisit.

'Hope it'll all go away?'

'I didn't say that.'

'Like I did with his dad?'

I nod back across the yard towards Al, back with Kate, the two of them now with Joel, everyone getting ready for the tug of war.

'All the warning signs were there then too, weren't they, the late nights, his phone switched off whenever I tried to call?'

Ella just keeps looking at me.

'And what did I do? Told myself it was nothing, turned a blind eye, ignored each and every warning sign time and again.'

Ella reaches out her hand, massages my arm again, gentle, helpless.

'Nia—'

But all of a sudden, I'm not listening. Because now I'm looking beyond Al and behind Kate and Joel, and then I start looking around the yard.

'Where's Ethan?'

MEGAN – THE HEADTEACHER

I've been over and over it, again and again. Every single moment of that afternoon: the fete, Tanya – searching for some kind of clue, I suppose. Something I must have missed at the time that should have warned me something was seriously wrong.

All the major players were there. Tanya, Ethan, Joel, as well as Ethan's parents, Nia and Al. On that small schoolyard were assembled all the major protagonists in all that was to unfold, but the only thing on my mind was still that fucking giraffe.

All right, that's not strictly fair. There were other things too, a million and one other things in fact, but that's par for the course. Ask any headteacher in any school up and down the country – this isn't one job, it's dozens. But that's precisely why any decent headteacher should always keep their wits about them, keep their eyes peeled every moment of every day, especially when they're in the school itself tuning into all those different vibes. Picking up on the very first hint of trouble.

I truly believed that if anything was happening in or around my school then I'd know, maybe not straight away but soon enough. But on this occasion, I didn't even come close.

It doesn't matter that it was already too late by then. It doesn't matter that the totally unthinkable had, apparently, already happened. That wasn't the point. The point was that storm clouds were gathering and even a half-decent head should have known that. And that's not because we're blessed with the gift of second sight; it's just something in the way the atoms arrange themselves in the air sometimes. A feeling, deep in the pit of your stomach, that at least one of the souls whose well-being is in your hands for those few hours of the day has a problem. It's an instinct that develops naturally over the years or should do. But it's an instinct that let me down badly that day.

Looking back there is just one moment that does give me pause for thought, though. I'm passing by the tug of war, which is just about to start, and Joel's talking to Ethan, or trying to talk to Ethan, which is what makes me pause like that.

'Ethan, you can help out too.'

Then Joel stops, his words hanging in the air as Ethan just keeps on walking. He's heard him, I know he has, and Joel knows he has too. A quick, sideways flicker of Ethan's eyes betray him as he moves on.

I see Joel about to head after him. He runs a tight ship with his business, everyone knows that – doesn't take any nonsense. And Ethan's just a boy. Joel wouldn't put up with that kind of treatment from anyone, let alone a pimply youth not long out of short trousers.

Then Joel looks across the yard, sees Nia and her sister in a tense-looking huddle by one of the stalls. A few feet away Al is standing with Kate, the pair of them in a tense little huddle too. Then he looks back at Ethan, who's still walking away, and obviously decides to cut him some slack. With all that's going on right now, he's probably thinking it's no wonder Ethan acts a bit strange from to time.

NIA – THE MUM

I TURN the corner at the bottom of the street and begin to make my way up the hill towards home.

'Deep breaths.'

Ella's keeping pace with me every step of the way. I nod at her, barely listening and she knows it.

'Talk to him, listen to him.'

Then she stands in front of me, physically blocking the path to my own front door.

'Do not, as in not, go off on one.'

Then the door opens and Ethan himself appears, ready to go out again, and I hold out the spliff, waving it in front of his staring eyes as Ella closes hers.

'What the hell's this?'

Five minutes later, we're in the kitchen.

Ella's left us alone. She's had her say, tried her best, and much good it's done too, as the daggers stare she shot my way as she left made all too clear. Ethan's sitting at the table, the spliff in front of him, his body language telling me he's not exactly my number one fan right now either.

'Just get off my back, will you?'

'What does that mean?'

I stare back at him as I struggle to impersonate a truculent fifteen-year-old. 'Everyone does it? Chill out?' I shake my head. 'Well, my son doesn't.'

Ethan cuts across.

'It was in my pocket, right?'

'What?'

'That's where you found it?'

'So?'

'So doesn't that tell you something?'

He keeps looking at me as if I've got special needs.

'If it was in my pocket, I haven't smoked it.'

'Yet.'

'And I wasn't going to.'

'So where did you get it?'

And now Ethan hesitates. 'What?'

'Who's your dealer?'

He splutters as if that's the most ridiculous thing he's ever heard in his life.

'I don't have a dealer.'

'Fairies delivered it in the night, did they?'

Ethan stands.

'I told you. Just leave it.'

I stand in front of him, in no mood to leave anything, but he just shakes his head.

'I'm not telling you where I got it or who I got it from. But I promise it wasn't from a dealer. I don't even know any dealers, OK?'

Then he moves past me and heads up the stairs. A moment later I hear the music click on again. I look towards the stairs, the music sounding louder now. Then I head for the stairs myself.

It's like a re-run of those few hours before. A moment later I push open his bedroom door to see Ethan staring at his phone again. But this time I don't give him time to look round – I just snake out a hand instead and yank it from his grasp.

'Texting him now, are you?'

Ethan just stares at me, stilled and stunned, as I look down at his phone, stilling too as I now see what's on the screen.

For a moment I don't move, and I don't speak, perhaps because, like Ethan right now, I can't.

Because this is the moment.

The moment I know that Ethan is in trouble, as in real trouble.

That all of us are.

DEVIL'S BRIDGE

The figure on the bridge hasn't moved.

Of the other figure, the one who was there and isn't any more, there's still no sign. Where that second figure is, they don't know.

What the remaining figure is doing just standing there up on the bridge, they don't know either.

The human pigs have stopped circling and the rest of the partygoers are removing their different masks too, adding them to a growing pile on the ground.

One of the girls breaks in.

'I want to go home.'

But the girl who first screamed doesn't move.

'How?'

Her companions all turn, stare at her.

'There's only one way out of here.'

The rest of her friends follow her stare up towards the one steep path that leads out of the gorge, the path that leads towards the bridge where the figure, still cast in shadow, is immobile. It's impossible even to tell which way he, she – it – is facing right now. Down towards them, up towards the ink-black sky, or are those eyes fixed on something or someone else instead?

Then the boy who dealt the blow takes charge, gestures round.

'OK, this is simple. There's loads of us, look.'

But no one does look. As one, all eyes seem to be irresistibly drawn to that figure up on the bridge.

'We just go up there together.'

The girl, the one who first screamed, starts to shake. To even contemplate moving a single inch closer to that creature is simply ambushing her. An image suddenly flashes through the young girl's head of herself and nine companions stepping across the bridge side by side, marching in step just as countless generations before them have done, thrilling to the way the structure seems to rumble beneath them – as if they're testing it to the limit, perhaps even beyond.

Only that danger's never been real. Deep down they all knew the bridge would hold, but this is different. All the old certainties seem to have vanished, borne away on a night now so dark it seems impossible to conceive of light ever penetrating again.

And the girl starts to shake some more, not hearing what the boy who dealt the blow is saying, let alone beginning to take it in.

All she can think is, someone's dead.

Someone's dead, and she watched it happen.

PART TWO

Be alert, for the devil prowls like a roaring lion, looking to devour
Peter 5:8

AL – THE DAD

Kate doesn't like it; I don't expect her to. But she understands, and that's why, despite everything, I just know that what we have is going to work.

All that with Nia at the school fete has unsettled me big-time. We still do the tug of war, and we win as well, thank God, because Joel would have been poison in the morning. Something about a giraffe, but I wasn't actually listening. All that's on my mind right now is Ethan.

'Just go.'

I hesitate, can see what it's costing her to say this, but she knows what it'd cost me not to go, too.

'I won't be long.'

'I don't care how long you are.'

And now I'm trying, as ever, to make everything right.

'I'll pick up a takeaway on the way back.'

Kate smiles, and there's more than a touch of sadness in that smile now too.

'You don't need to bribe me.'

'I don't mean it like that.'

But I do, and she keeps smiling, in that soft, slightly sad way that always makes my heart lurch.

'Ethan's your son – it's natural. Something's wrong and you want to find out what. And you couldn't do it before, so go and do it now.'

I nod back, stupidly grateful. Kate's right – it is natural and it's right. But so little has been natural and right these last few months that I find myself apologising in advance for simple things like popping in and checking on a son when I'm more than usually worried about him. I swoop down, kiss her briefly, then turn to the door.

'Extra poppadom'd be nice though.'

Which is when she flashes me that other smile, the one more redolent of promise than sadness, the one that lights up the sky, and all the way over there I'm smiling back at her even though she isn't there.

I know what people think – the people who don't know her, anyway. The First Wives Club has its tentacles everywhere, not just in Hollywood films – it's here in our small town too. But Kate's not like that. She's warm and she's understanding and she's kind. And driving over to see Nia and Ethan, I love her more than ever.

I don't even notice the storm that's beginning to whip up or the rain that's beginning to hammer down on my windscreen.

I just keep smiling all the way.

NIA – THE MUM

ELLA COULD BE RIGHT – it could all be down to a girl. Maybe Bex, the girl we'd seen hanging around him at the parents' evening, trying not to make it look too painfully obvious that she was interested in him, but failing totally of course. In other words, what was behind that totally uncharacteristic outburst up in his bedroom could just have been normal teen angst, if we're lucky.

It could have been sparked by something else if we're not, like bullying, which happens even at his age, although it might take different forms from my day. Online, anonymous, something nastier than just girl trouble, in other words – the sort of thing that could really cast a shadow.

It could have been everything I first feared, as in drugs, that single spliff the gateway to something much more worrying. Small towns can be the worst for that sort of thing. It may seem idyllic, but this is no rural haven, even if it might look like one to tourists on their two-week summer break.

What I've been looking for is the usual tick-list, in other words. The kind of thing I can talk about to Ethan, to Ella, maybe even to Al – the kind of thing we could sort out and put behind us.

But what I'm looking at right now isn't on any sort of tick-list I've ever thought about before.

Ethan's just staying silent. But he doesn't duck his eyes when I look at him like he's always done before when I've caught him out, so this is different too. Even the simple way he's just standing there is something I haven't seen before. And the look on his face is strange too, and I can't work it out at first, but it's almost relief. As if some part of him is actually glad this is out there.

But what's out there? I don't know, much as I don't know how long I've been standing there staring at that phone, trying to take in what I'm seeing and totally failing.

What I'm looking at is clear enough. The picture's only too clear, in fact. It's Tanya, Ethan's form teacher. The woman who brought round that DVD; the woman who made me coffee when I dropped her little boy's birthday present over by way of thanks.

What isn't clear at all, and what I can't even begin to get my head round, is why there's a naked picture of her on my son's phone.

'Ethan.'

But then I stop, floundering even more. All the time Ethan just stares at me. And it's getting stronger now, that feeling he's almost glad all this is happening, is actually pleased in some way that I walked in and snatched the phone from his hand like that.

'How did…?'

I stop again, then take the deepest of deep breaths, trying desperately to order my thoughts, get my brain, my thought processes, or what passes for it and them right now, back under some sort of control.

And once again there it is. That same, silent, almost level, stare. As if he's waiting for me to catch up.

'Look, whatever's happened, just tell me, OK – whatever it is.'

I don't know how long all this might have gone on for. I don't know if he might have stayed like that all evening, taking refuge in that strange, almost eerie silence, with me babbling away more and more incoherently in front of him, or whether the floodgates would have suddenly burst, and it all would have come spilling out.

I never get the chance to find out because now there's a ring on the bell.

AL – THE DAD

I SAID I wouldn't be long, and as an act of good faith I decide to stop and pick up the takeaway first. Almost as a guarantee that I probably won't go in, even if I'm invited, which is a fond hope anyway. I'll just stand on the doorstep, do what I said I was going to do – check Ethan's OK, that there's been no more upset of the kind there was before, whatever that was actually all about, and then go.

The smell of Kate's korma percolates through the car. It seems stronger than my more incendiary tikka masala for some reason, and my stomach's rumbling within sixty seconds of setting off from the best takeaway in town, just a street or so away from the school.

Briefly, I wonder about giving Nia a quick call on my mobile instead of actually calling in person, but as I'm only a few streets away by then I press on, vowing to myself that it's going to be straight back home and into the korma, masala, rice and chips, not forgetting that extra poppadom for Kate.

Nia opens the door. Only she doesn't because she doesn't look like Nia, which makes no sense, I know. She also has a phone in her hand. It's not her phone, which is very definitely getting on a bit now. This is a state-of-the-art brand-new smart phone, which means it has to be Ethan's.

But I start in straight away on my well-rehearsed spiel, tell her I'm just passing on my home from the takeaway, subtly, or at least hopefully subtly, planting the reason why I can't stop even if she wants me to, but as she can't get away from me quick enough these days, why I even bother I don't know.

I also mention Joel – I remembered that on the way over too. Before we left the fete, he had a quick word with me, telling me about this really strange exchange he'd had with Ethan, who totally ignored him, which only made me worry about him even more.

Still Nia doesn't speak. Then she holds out Ethan's phone. I take it from her and look down at the screen. Then I forget all about chicken korma, masala and rice, and even the extra poppadom. All the hunger pangs in my stomach vanish as well.

All of a sudden there's nothing else in the world. I don't even register the storm, which is really gathering pace now.

All there is in the world right now is just me and Nia and that phone.

NIA – THE MUM

AL'S SITTING NEXT to me; Ethan's facing us both.

He still hasn't said anything. Maybe he thinks he doesn't need to – maybe he thinks that photo on his phone says it all. But he's wrong, because I for one have a hell of a lot of questions and no answers, and by the look on his face so does his dad.

'This is some sort of joke, yeah?'

I stare sideways at Al, hardly believing my ears.

'A joke?'

Al hurries on, qualifying that immediately.

'A prank.' He nods across at the still-silent Ethan. 'Something you or you and your mates have knocked up or something?'

I look back at Ethan. I hadn't thought of that. Then again, I haven't actually thought anything – everything's just been a fog.

'A mock-up, you mean?'

Al nods.

'The kind of things kids can do with photos these days. They could take one of me and turn me into Brad Pitt.'

Slowly, somewhere deep down inside, hope's stirring. Because if that's what this is really all about, then maybe this isn't too bad after all.

I keep looking at him. 'Is that right? Is that what you've done?'

That small kernel of hope keeps growing as Ethan casts his eyes down to the floor.

I hunch forward.

'Ethan, if this had got out, if anyone else had seen this...'

Then I stop, a horrible suspicion suddenly gripping me.

'It hasn't, has it? Please tell me you haven't sent this to any of your friends?'

Still keeping his head down, Ethan shakes his head.

'You haven't shared it online with anyone?'

Ethan shakes his head again.I look across at Al, who looks back at me, a silent exchange of relieved eyes.

Then Al leans forward, trying to take charge.

'All right, so if it's only you, well, so long as you get rid of it, and that's as in right now…' He hesitates. 'No harm done, I suppose.'

I stare at him again. Did I just hear that? Al hurries on.

'You know what I mean.'

'Al, if I hadn't come back, if I hadn't seen that…'

I gesture down at Ethan's phone, the screen saver now, mercifully, cutting in.

'But you did come back. You did see it. And no one else has. Ethan's just told us.'

Ethan hasn't actually said anything, but I don't labour the point. But that really should tell me, shouldn't it? All the warning sirens should be sounding loud and clear, and maybe they are. Maybe I just don't want to listen.

Al turns back to Ethan.

'Even so, it could have landed you in the biggest trouble you have ever been in, in your life.'

For a moment Al struggles as that nightmare scenario opens up, as if he can see it unfolding step by step in front of his eyes.

'For God's sake, if Mrs Adams had seen this – or the head-teacher.'

Operating almost on automatic pilot, I supply the name.

'Mrs Williams.'

Al looks at Ethan again, almost wonderingly.

'You'd have been suspended. Maybe even worse.'

I look at him too.

Why is Ethan still not saying anything?

Why is he just sitting there like that?

Al hunches closer. 'You haven't got any more?'

Al hunches ever closer, beginning to panic all over again as images of that parents' evening we all attended flash through both our minds. There wasn't just Tanya there, there were loads of other female teachers as well.

I stand up, not even waiting for an answer. 'Right. That's it. I want your laptop.'

Then I nod at his phone, still on the table.

'And I'm taking this too. I'm going through every photo you've ever taken on here, just to be sure. I want to see every file, every folder.'

Ethan cuts across.

'I haven't.'

'You haven't what?'

'I haven't taken any more pictures.'

I stare at him. And I keep staring as those few words echo over and over inside.

Then I pick up his phone, the screen firing once again into life, and I nod down at the naked picture of Tanya.

'Does that mean you did take this?'

Ethan just keeps staring back at me.

AL – THE DAD

I DON'T UNDERSTAND what Nia's saying at first.

Ethan gets it straight away, but he's got a head start, hasn't he? I'm just floundering as I look at him, then back at Nia. For her part, she just keeps staring at him.

'This hasn't been mocked-up on some computer?'

She keeps looking at him.

'This is an actual photo?'

For a moment I don't think Ethan's going to say anything. And just for that moment, the takeaway that's still sitting on the front seat of my car floats into my mind. I've no idea why I suddenly think of it. Maybe because I don't want to think of the new possibility Nia's just forced us to confront. The question that Ethan, at first anyway, doesn't seem to want to answer.

But then out it comes. Not an answer as such, just a nod. But a simple, definite, nod.

I take a deep breath. OK, this is bad. It's worse, much worse, than we've imagined so far, but I'm still thinking that with a fair wind and a large slice of luck we can rescue it, meaning I'm not thinking properly at all, am I?

'OK. How? Where?'

I pick up the phone, trying to ignore the naked woman who

now appears in the centre of the screen – my boss's wife, for Christ's sake! I try to concentrate on the other details I can pick out behind her.

'Those are showers, yeah? The ones in school?'

I've never been in the female shower block at Ethan's school, obviously, but we've worked on similar shower blocks in a couple of other schools, and they all have that same institutional look to them.

'So, you sneaked in there and took it.'

Ethan suddenly cuts across, insistent.

'I didn't sneak anywhere.'

I stare at him again. What's the point of him denying this now?

'So, you just walked into the shower block, bold as brass, said, "Hello, Mrs Adams, just stand there for a minute while I take this snap of you?"'

A different atmosphere's beginning to creep into the room. And if I thought things had been tense before, this is something else. It's almost as if neither of us want Nia to say what she says next. As if we'd both prefer to just delete that photo and let Ethan go up to his room while I go off with my takeaway. As if part of her and a big part of me too, in truth, really would prefer just not to know.

'You're not trying to tell us she knew about this?'

And now I cut across, trying desperately to cling onto an option that seemed a lot worse than anything we'd feared a moment before, but is now beginning to look like a lifeline.

'Ethan, stop messing about, will you? OK, you've done something wrong, something really stupid—'

I stop as he interrupts once more.

'We haven't.'

I stare at him again.

'You haven't what?'

'Done anything wrong.'

Suddenly, I'm aware I can't hear anything going on outside

the house. For these few moments all sound in the world seems to have stopped. I don't break the charged silence and I don't think Nia's going to speak either. But then she repeats the one word that's now reverberating inside her head and my head above all the others.

'We?'

NIA – THE MUM

It's like I'm pushing against a door I don't want to open, knowing that behind it there's something I really don't want to see. That it's going to open onto a future that should never be allowed to exist. But it's not going to make any difference whether I push it open or not, because what's waiting on the other side is there anyway and there's nothing we can do about it.

'You're saying...?'

I stop. Al's fallen silent by now, but his eyes, like mine, are fixed on our son.

I try again.

'You and Mrs Adams?'

Then I stop again. Even now I can't do it, can't take that last final step, can't make this real by putting it into actual words.

Al cuts in.

'Ethan, if this is some sort of joke then stop it now, because we are getting seriously worried here.'

'Why should you be worried?'

I stare at him.

'No one forced me. Or Tanya.'

All I can hear now is that name.

Tanya.

Not the more formal name he should be using, the name any kid should be using when they're talking about their form teacher.

Just Tanya.

And it sounds so horribly familiar.

So intimate.

So wrong.

'We wanted to.'

Silence hangs heavy between us for a moment, before Al cuts in once more.

'Ethan, this is ridiculous.'

Then Al stops, and I stop too as all of a sudden it's like the floodgates opening as Ethan hunches forward.

'We've been talking for ages – more than talking – she's been saying things. I wanted to know if she was saying what I thought she was saying – I watched her as she went into that changing room, then I followed her inside.'

We just keep staring at him as Ethan pauses for a moment. And I can see why in his eyes. It's almost out of a desire not to betray the memory, to not let any of this down in his mind by missing out a single detail.

'She meant it. She meant it all. So we went to this room, at the back of the classrooms. Afterwards she took some pictures of me.'

Ethan nods back at his phone.

'Then I took that picture of her.'

Ethan pauses again, his chest rising and falling, the thrill of the confessional coursing through him.

We're like statues. We just stare at him again while all around us, our world, the world we knew, the world we thought we'd always know, comes crashing down.

MEGAN – THE HEADTEACHER

I REMEMBER every word of our exchange that evening. Particularly the last words I spoke to Nia and Al before everything imploded.

All the stalls had closed, the parents and pupils gone. I'd just finished liaising with the caretaker about what we could leave out overnight and what had to be put away before I turned back to Don, who was working his calculator, the expression on his face giving me cautious hope at least.

'So? What's the total?'

I shoot a quick glance round the yard. Everyone really has put a hell of a lot of effort into all this. I'm just hoping against hope it's been worth it.

'Haven't really been keeping track.'

I eye him, amused. He hasn't been doing anything else.

'But roughly?'

The answer comes back, promptly.

'Four thousand, two hundred and six pounds.'

Don peers at the figures on the display.

'And sixty-seven pence.'

'And that's to the nearest sixty-seven?'

'Exactly.'

I nod across the yard, relaxing now. As global figures go, compared to a post-Covid National Debt for example, it's not a lot. It's not even going to do that much to help run a medium-sized school such as ours, but it will definitely pay for a few extras. And it's also going to be useful ammunition the next time I try to persuade hard-pressed staff to give up some precious free time to man some stalls.

Don cuts in, puncturing my sudden reverie.

'Just one fly in the ointment.'

He nods across the yard. I follow his nod, stopping dead as I see the giraffe, still there, still alone and looking destined to stay that way.

I stare back at him.

'I thought that had all been sorted out. The losing team in the tug of war?'

Don doesn't reply, just sweeps an explanatory hand around the yard, empty now not only of parents and pupils but, and all too obviously, the losing team themselves, who have clearly scurried away without their unwanted memento.

Then I hear a voice from behind.

'We need to see you.'

The newly arrived Nia is standing there, her ex, Al, by her side.

I nod back, a practised smile on my face. It's a smile I've used a lot today. It's a smile I use a lot out in the town too. Almost every parent I come across always seems to regard any encounter with me as fair game. No matter how fleeting, no matter where it might be taking place, in their eyes anyway it's always a precious chance to talk about their even more precious offspring.

'Can it wait, Mrs James?'

I nod around the yard. 'We're just finishing up.'

By Nia's side, Al cuts across.

'It's about Ethan.'

Surprise, surprise. Not that I say that; I just keep the same practised smile on my face.

'If you've any concerns, you really should see his form teacher, Mrs Adams.'

At this point that practised smile of mine does begin to wobble a little. Because now they're both just staring at me. Not saying a single word. Just staring.

Don looks across, also picking up on the charged atmosphere that seems to have suddenly crash-landed like an Exocet.

'Let's all just keep calm, shall we?'

It's a few moments later. We're back in my office and Nia's fixing me with the sort of thousand-yard stare I've tried to perfect in the past when faced with truculent kids or a recalcitrant member of staff.

And right now, she's managing it much better than I ever have, and no wonder. Even to my ears, all I'm saying sounds unutterably feeble. But what am I supposed to say? Let's all just sit here and totally panic.

By my side, Don, who's definitely panicking but is trying his best not to show it, picks up the baton.

'I think what Mrs Williams is trying to say is that there could be any number of explanations for this.'

'And we've been through them. Each and every one.'

Al gestures at Ethan's mobile, which is now on the desk in front of us.

'This is a mock-up. We tried that one. Ethan snuck in and took it without her knowing. We tried that one too.'

Nia cuts to the chase.

'She slept with him.'

We all turn towards her.

'She's his teacher and she slept with him.'

I look across at Don, a silent appeal for help he can't give. Then I look back at Nia and Al, feeling more lost than I've ever felt in my professional life. Yes, there have been all sorts of minor and occasionally major misdemeanours to deal with over the years, from truancy to vandalism to drug abuse. This is the twenty-first century, for Christ's sake – every school has to deal with a hundred and one things on that sort of scale almost daily. But this?

I look back at the photo again; can't seem to help myself, can't seem to drag my eyes away from it. Then I clear my throat.

'We'll get Mrs Adams in. Talk to her.'

And there it is. The second most unutterably feeble thing I've said in about as many minutes.

Nia and Al just stare at me again.

'We do have to get her side of the story.'

Don, bless him, steps in once more. At first, I think maybe he's dredging up some half-forgotten nugget from some dimly remembered crib sheet he may have scanned when he first took up his post as governor. Then I realise he's scrolling through his phone, trying desperately to establish the correct procedure here, and thank goodness for that, because right now I haven't got a clue.

'We'll also log this with the Education Authority. And, of course, HR.'

Taking my cue from him I lean forward in turn, trying to strike some sort of conciliatory note at the same time as desperately trying to sound as if I also know what I'm talking about.

'If a pupil makes an allegation, any sort of allegation, then there are protocols we have to follow, and we will follow them to the letter, I promise you.'

Then I break off, smarting under another of those thousand-yard stares.

'Mrs James, what else do you want me to do?'

'Nothing.'

I stare at her again. By my side, Don stares too, her reply side-swiping the pair of us. Whatever response we might have expected right now, it wasn't that. Nia stands, her face setting, determined, picking up Ethan's phone at the same time.

'I'll do it.'

And then she's gone. With Ethan's phone her in hand, and with all of us still staring after her, she opens the door and makes her way back down the corridor and out towards the yard. Al stands too, about to follow. Like the rest of us, he doesn't know exactly what his ex is going to do right now, but he probably has a shrewd suspicion she isn't about to go home, make herself a cup of cocoa and write the whole thing off to growing pains.

But then he turns back to us.

'You think he's lying, don't you?'

All I can do is look at him as he repeats his question.

'You think Ethan's making all this up?'

'No one's saying that.'

But Al just turns, and then he's gone too.

Don and I exchange looks. Outside, we can hear the sound of an engine firing into life. For a moment neither of us speaks. Then Don says exactly what we're both thinking right now.

'Hope to God he is, though.'

I look skywards in silent imprecation.

JOEL – THE HUSBAND

'YOU'VE PAID GWEN?'

Tanya's just dashed downstairs, Danny in her arms.

I nod back.

'And a tenner on top.'

Danny's squirming, trying desperately to get to Gwen herself, who's equally desperately trying to avoid any sort of contact right now.

'For the cornflakes.'

I've been trying to clear them up for the last ten minutes. Gwen's been trying to do the same for the last half hour. I've got a feeling we'll be finding traces dotted around the room and under the sofa and the chairs for the next few years.

She looks shattered, and no wonder. A couple of hours with a two-year-old must have sounded like a doddle yesterday evening when her mum, one of Tanya's friends from school, offered her the gig. Easy money. The strained smile on her face when we walked back in a few moments ago told a very different story.

It's chaos, in other words, and that's not just down to Danny. We're in the middle of preps for his birthday party. That's where we've been for the past couple of hours since the fete finished, getting balloons, streamers, then more balloons and more streamers, as well as picking up a cake that another of Tanya's mates has made for him. I tried floating the idea that maybe it was all just a little bit, ever so slightly, over the top, only for Tanya to cross to the kitchen window and look out at the now-deflated bouncy castle in pride of place on our rear lawn. Which you'd probably have to say was a fair point well made.

Then the doorbell sounds from outside.

I call across to Gwen, asking her to answer it as I take the still-squirming, still-babysitter-obsessed Danny from Tanya, so I'm looking away from the door right now. Visitors aren't exactly unusual. They're usually work-related, one of the builders updating me on a site problem or another of Tanya's teacher friends from school popping in with some fresh titbit of gossip. But then Gwen calls across to me, and something in her voice tells me straight away this isn't a builder or a teacher.

A man's standing in the doorway, a man I don't know, with a police warrant card in his hand. By his side stands a uniformed police officer, a woman I do know. I was at school with her brother. I wrack my brains for a moment, trying to remember her name, which, in retrospect, always strikes me as more than a little odd. When two police officers suddenly appear on your doorstep, you'd think the first thing that would go through your mind would be what are they doing here, not what are their names?

Then, suddenly, out of nowhere, I place her. She's a few years younger than her brother, the boy I was at school with, and she's called Georgie, always shortened to Gee.

The senior officer, the plainclothes officer, introduces himself as Detective Inspector Donovan McCarthy, just in case we haven't taken in his name from the warrant card, then looks at Tanya.

And asks if he can have a word.

DI MCCARTHY – THE COP

FIRST IMPRESSIONS.

They say it's the most valuable time in any investigation, and it's true. Those first few minutes of any interview or exchange, be it formal or informal, taking place in controlled conditions in some nick somewhere, in an interview under caution in a private house like this one, or courtesy of just a few snatched words out on some street. Because it's the time people actually say things. Things they shouldn't, things they might regret, the kind of things that might come back later and bite them, hard. The moment you catch them off guard.

After that, they get used to what's happening, adjust to the idea that they're under the kind of scrutiny they've probably never experienced before, and then they adapt and, quicker than you'd ever believe possible, become more guarded, close down. So, in those all-important first few moments you really do have to hit with everything you've got.

'Do you know an Ethan James, Mrs Adams?'

Tanya, sitting opposite in her large and expensively appointed front room, nods immediately.

'Of course; he's in my class.'

I study her for a moment, letting the silence stretch. Another old trick. Let the mark fill in the blanks and make sure there are no distractions too, which is why it's just the two of us in her front room. Her husband has been kept out of all this.

Tanya hesitates as the silence lengthens.

'Has something happened?'

She's looked bewildered up to this point. Now she's beginning to look totally lost.

'For now?'

Her forehead deepens into an even more puzzled frown.

'What is all this?'

I reach down, open a folder and take out the report we've just received.

'Ethan's made an allegation.'

Actually, technically speaking, it was Ethan's mum who made the allegation, but this really isn't the time to split hairs. She still keeps staring at me and I don't say anything either, just let that silence lengthen once again. See if I can tease out any of those unguarded responses.

But she just keeps looking at me, so I hand over the report.

She looks down at it straight away.

And keeps on looking.

JOEL – THE HUSBAND

No one's telling me anything – what they're doing here or why that other officer wants to talk to Tanya. Gee's just sitting with me, looking as if it's last place in the world she wants to be right now.

'It's just school stuff. That's all I was told.'

I stare at her. I've been pacing the kitchen like a caged animal for the last few moments. Danny's finally fallen asleep in his buggy; Gwen's been collected by her taxi and is on her way home. I can hear nothing from the other side of the closed door. What Tanya and that other officer are talking about is a total mystery, but Gee knows, and she's squirming like a fish on a hook right now as I try and find out.

'Two coppers call round in the middle of the night.'

'It's not exactly the middle of the night.'

I cut across.

'Gee, I don't know your mate from Adam.'

Then I stop in turn as she deflects.

'He's no mate of mine. They've drafted him in from somewhere – he only arrived last week.'

'But I know your dad. I was at school with your brother.'

I move closer, lowering my voice.

'For God's sake, Gee.'

She struggles for a moment longer, then glances towards the closed door to the sitting room. Then she leans towards me, lowering her voice in turn.

'It's something about a kid in her class.'

I stare at her, now even more puzzled.

'I don't know all the ins and outs, and that's God's honest truth, but he was on his mobile talking to someone in HQ on the way over.'

'A kid in her class?'

Gee nods.

'So why are the police involved? What's Tanya supposed to have done, hit him or something?'

Now she's really struggling.

'Not hit him, no.'

I keep staring at her, growing more bewildered by the second.

'What then?'

Gee looks towards the still-closed door, increasingly nervous, then lowers her voice even further. I almost don't catch what she says. Then when I do, I wished I hadn't.

'Something else.'

'What?'

'That's what he's saying anyway. The kid, whoever he is. I don't know his name – they haven't told me.'

Gee glances towards the closed door again, fearful, then she looks back at me.

'He's saying that something happened.'

She pauses for a moment.

'Him and her.'

DI MCCARTHY – THE COP

THAT REPORT, the statement we took down in the nick that I've just handed to her, that's the softening-up process. The appetiser. Cleanse the palate, if you like, for the main event.

Next, I slide across the table a photo, and it's large, an A4-sized print. You can pick out every detail.

'And this was found on Ethan's phone.'

For a moment she just stares at it, and now I'm watching her even more intently. Because if it is going to happen, now's the time. The time something might crack.

'Ethan alleges that you and he have been having a relationship.'

Her eyes grow wider. Her breathing deepens. But her eyes as she looks back up at me are steady and they don't leave mine at all. Not for one single moment.

So, what is that first impression? What am I thinking, sitting here, in Tanya Adams's front room, in these first few moments after she heard the allegation that is going to change her life and the lives of so many others as well? I can see shock; I can see bewilderment and I can see confusion. But that's all I can see. I certainly can't see what I've been looking for more than anything else right now, and that's guilt.

She remains frozen – there's no other word for it. She hardly even seems to be breathing right now.

'Did you know this photo was on your pupil's phone?'

For a moment longer she remains silent. I'm wondering if she might not even have heard me, and I'm about to repeat the question.

Then she shakes her head.

'Of course I didn't.'

'Do you know how it came to be there?'

Tanya glances back down at it again, but then looks away as if all of a sudden she can't bear the sight of it.

'I've no idea.'

'Ethan also says you took pictures of him, on your phone.'

Tanya just keeps staring at me.

'That he took naked photos of you and that you did the same.'

'Photos of Ethan?'

She hunts in her pocket, bringing out her mobile a second later, handing it to me.

'Where? Look.'

I take it. I'd have asked for it anyway. But then I nod down at the photo again, something about this really not making sense.

'Mrs Adams.'

I struggle. Partly because this is always going to be seriously strange. I'm looking at a naked photo of a woman I've never met before with the real-life woman herself no more than a metre or so away.

'OK, you're not looking straight at the camera, I can see that, but Ethan can't have been far away from you when he took this.'

Her eyes, reluctantly, return to the photo.

'How could he have taken it without you even realising?'

Her response comes back straight away. Once again there seems no attempt to dissemble or evade.

'I don't know.'

She keeps staring down at it.

'I know where it was taken, though.'

I nod back at her. So do we, but I want to hear it from her own mouth. I want to keep her talking, then talking some more. No one has ever tripped themselves up in any police interview, formal or informal, by staying silent.

'That's the changing rooms at school. The girls' changing room. I use it in the evenings after I've been out for my run.'

Then Tanya looks back up at me, and something starts creeping across her face now, a slow realisation seeming to begin to dawn.

'Last night.'

She stops, looks back down at the photo, then up at me again.

'That's when he took this.'

She holds my stare, steady and level again.

'He was in there last night.'

NIA – THE MUM

THE POLICE OFFICER turns up about nine in the evening.

There's no phone call beforehand, no warning – he just appears on our doorstep. I think he's alone at first, but then I see a younger uniformed, female officer with him. I've seen her out and about in the town, but I haven't seen him before.

He introduces himself as Detective Inspector McCarthy, showing us his warrant card at the same time. The younger officer does the same. It's the procedure you see time and again on the tele, and it seems so familiar and so alien, all at the same time.

The older officer, the Detective Inspector, asks to see Ethan, and I say yes straight way. Why wouldn't I? After all those sham promises of action and professions of concern down in the school, I'm just glad someone seems to be taking this seriously.

I show him into the sitting room. Al comes through from the kitchen. He's texted her a couple of times, but now he's just come off the phone to Kate. I heard snatches of the conversation as I went to the door. Something about a takeaway.

Ethan hasn't spoken for the last hour or so. It's as if he's said what he had to say and now he seems to be away somewhere in a world of his own. Maybe he is, because we certainly can't reach him. But Detective Inspector McCarthy brings Ethan back down to earth quickly enough.

'Mrs Adams believes that you must have got into the girls' changing room without her realising.'

There's no preamble, no small talk, no questions. Just the first in a series of statements he's reading from notes in front of him.

'She can only imagine you'd hidden yourself in there somehow.'

Ethan stares at him, his eyes growing wider all the time.

'She alleges that you took that picture of her without her knowledge.'

Ethan cuts across, finally speaking, nodding at Al and me.

'No, I already told you I took pictures of her, and she took pictures of me.'

But the police officer just rolls on.

'She categorically denies any relationship exists between the two of you aside from that of teacher and pupil.'

Ethan stares back at him again.

'Mrs Adams, in short, alleges that you are a fantasist, Ethan.'

Still holding that same steady stare, he nods at Ethan.

'A fantasist and a peeping tom.'

Ethan doesn't say anything. He just stares at the police officer for a moment longer, before looking back at me and Al. Then, suddenly, he stands, pushing past us all and banging out into the hall before heading up the stairs, his footsteps echoing through the house, the bedroom door slamming shut behind him a moment later.

I stare after him, then stand myself.

AL – THE DAD

For a moment I've no idea where she's going. Where Ethan's gone is obvious enough. You could have heard his feet running up those stairs out in the street. And you could have heard that bedroom door slam behind him up in space.

In the immediate aftermath we all just sit there for a moment. Nia, the plain-clothes copper who showed us his warrant card when he came in and whose name I've already forgotten, and his young female sidekick, all of us enduring the dead weight of a silence that seems like concrete.

Then Nia stands and walks out too.

I look after her, expecting to hear the same, if lighter, tread heading up those same stairs, followed by the first of a series of urgent taps on Ethan's bedroom door, followed, hopefully, by a low, hushed exchange as she does what she's always been good at, reaching out to and calming our son. But I don't hear any of that. All I hear is the sound of the front door opening instead.

And that's it. It just opens. Nia doesn't even bother closing it behind her – she just walks out into the night.

I sit there for a moment longer along with my two unexpected and unwanted companions, because everything's too much right now. I'm still trying to take in all that's just happened, not just in the last few minutes since the coppers arrived, but before that too, and I'm not even remotely managing it.

I'm not even thinking where Nia might have gone or what she's doing. I'm probably just assuming she's stepped out for some much-needed air. Then something, some instinct, tells me just where she's going and exactly what she's about to do.

I stand quickly, muttering a low curse at myself for being so thick, panic rising inside all the time. I don't even look at the coppers, who are now staring at me, and just head blindly for the door. On the way out onto the street I fumble for my phone, hitting the speed dial button for Ella.

I see Nia ahead as I come out of the house, already turning the corner at the end of the street. Ella answers on the second ring and I tell her to get over to the house, as in now, that one of us will explain everything, but just get over there please, and don't talk to Ethan. Don't even try, just sit there and wait till one of us gets back.

I'm passing my car now, which is parked where I've left it, that long-forgotten takeaway still on the passenger seat, destined for one place and one place only now and that's the nearest bin.

Then I put my phone away and hurry after Nia.

JOEL – THE HUSBAND

TANYA HASN'T STOPPED pacing since the coppers left. Round and round – first the kitchen, then the sitting room. Danny's been crying for the last half hour too. Maybe he's picking up on the vibe. He doesn't need feeding or changing, I've checked, so now I'm trying to soothe him at the same time as trying to calm Tanya, two totally hopeless tasks right now. I've never felt more useless or powerless in my life.

Then Tanya springs for the phone.

'Lucy.'

'Who?'

I stare at her as she begins to punch in numbers. She's already tried calling Megan, her head, both at the school in case she's still there and on her home number. She hasn't had a reply from either, just a standard answerphone greeting in both cases asking her to leave a message. Tanya did, although it was more of an anguished, garbled rant. So far Megan hasn't called her back.

Tanya's also called a couple of the other teachers to see if they can shed any light on this, but from the cheery way they greeted her it was obvious they were completely clueless as to all that was happening, and she cut both calls without even telling them what it was about. Right now, she wants answers, and she needs someone who can provide them. She also desperately needs help, and there doesn't seem to be a single soul in the world who can give her any.

Tanya, the phone still in her hand, nods at me.

'From the union.'

Dimly, a face swims before my eyes, a woman I've met a few times, a girl Tanya was in college with.

Then Tanya stops as her call is answered. She doesn't even wait for Lucy to say anything, just plunges straight in, another wracked rant at first but becoming a bit more coherent as I hear Lucy on the other end of the line trying to calm her. In my arms, Danny's crying louder now.

'Can you get here? Tonight? Or tomorrow first thing, please, Lucy. I can't get through to anyone at the school – Megan's not responding. I've left two messages already but she's not taking my calls.'

Then Tanya stops as Danny's crying suddenly ratchets up a few more notches.

Because from outside comes a loud banging on the front door.

AL – THE DAD

I TRY TALKING to her all the way over, but Nia just keeps striding on, eyes forward, legs pumping. From her house, our old house, to Tanya and Joel's can't be much more than a quarter of a mile, but it feels like one of the longest journeys of my life, with every step along the way sounding like the chimes of doom.

All the time I'm bombarding her with questions. Where's she going? What does she think she's doing? I've no idea and I don't think she does either. But I know what's propelling her on like this. It's the same sight that's haunting me now too – Ethan staring back at that copper with that stunned, totally disbelieving look on his face. All my ex-wife's most basic instincts have kicked in, and it's turning her into what she always has been and always will be so far as our son is concerned, a lioness.

And yes, even in the middle of all this, I'm probably aware that it's all been given an extra edge by what's happened in the last few months. She hasn't been able to protect her son from any of that. He's seen her at some massively low points lately, meaning that she's inflicted, by proxy at least, some massively low points on him in turn. She hasn't been able to do the one thing she must have wanted to do above everything else – return the world to how it was, give him back the life that has been taken from him. But she can do something about this. And the proverbial wild horses aren't going to stop her, which means all I can actually do right now is match her step for impotent step. And hope to God that Joel has taken his wife out for a curry too.

We turn the corner at the entrance to Joel and Tanya's street. For a moment I don't even look towards their house, which is the largest one in a small development at the top of a small hill, looking down on all the others. But I don't need to – I can see from the look on Nia's face that my silent prayer to the Gods hasn't been answered.

I look behind her to see lights blazing from almost every window.

Meaning Joel and Tanya are home.

MEGAN – THE HEADTEACHER

EVEN THOUGH IT'S late in the evening by now, the emails from the local authority are coming in thick and fast. Tanya's phoned as well, but I haven't responded. I can't.

Don's still with me, and as I scan the latest email, he looks over my shoulder at the same time. Even at this early stage every one's putting everything in writing, creating a paper trail. Everyone already seems to know they really have to watch their backs on this one. No one wants any unguarded comments, in any chance phone call, to come back later to haunt them, which is one of the reasons I can't respond to Tanya's phone call right now.

The itemised points in the latest email are brief, succinct, and unequivocal. And they mirror the points made in the previous emails too.

At this stage, we just have to keep a lid on this. Yes, we have to follow procedure, but so far as we can we have to keep all this between the school authorities and the principal parties involved.

I look to the skies, offering up another silent prayer.

And then maybe, maybe, we can get through it all with the minimum amount of damage done to everyone.

JOEL – THE HUSBAND

THAT LOUD BANGING on the door turns into a hammering. On the other end of the phone, I can hear Lucy still trying to calm Tanya, but as the hammering continues outside, Tanya cuts the call, moves towards the door, and tells me to leave this to her.

Neither of us knows for sure who it is, although logically it's going to be one of two people right now, Nia or Al. I've already mentally discounted Al – confrontations aren't really his style. He's no shrinking violet, and if anything ever kicks off on site, builders being combustible characters, he'll weigh in with the best of them. But big public face-offs aren't really his thing, and if that hammering on the door's anything to go by, a big public face-off is exactly what's on the cards right now.

Not that it's fazing Tanya. Unlike Al, she's never been the type to shy away from anything and isn't about to start now. You don't get to be a teacher in a modern secondary school without having steel somewhere. She might have been a mess up to now tonight – and who wouldn't be after seeing that picture of herself on Ethan's phone? – but no way is she going to dissolve into little bits, and why the fuck should she? I can see it in her eyes, and I'm already wishing the rest of the world was here right now to see it too. Because she isn't the one who's done anything wrong.

'What the hell is all this?'

Nia starts in on her the minute she opens the door, but Tanya hits back, straight away.

'Mrs James, just go home.'

Right from the start Tanya's keeping it formal. No first names, even though I know it's been first names between them up to now. But tonight, she's trying at least to keep all this professional. Not that Nia even seems to notice.

'Ethan's fifteen years old. He's a kid, for Christ's sake.'

Now I'm moving towards the door myself. Danny's mercifully quietening, sleep finally beginning to claim him. Tanya's voice floats out onto the night air as I join her on the front step – firm, steady, not overly confrontational, trying to sound reasonable even, but not giving a single inch at the same time.

'And nothing, I promise, nothing has happened between me and your son.'

I can see Al now, standing by Nia's side, providing the same sort of support to her that I am to Tanya, I suppose. He doesn't even look at me, which is typical Al again. He isn't about to turn tail and run, but it's all too obvious he isn't exactly relishing this either.

Nia's just staring at Tanya. 'I've seen that picture.'

'So have I, and I have no idea how he managed to take it.'

'You know how he took it. He's told me what's been going on.'

'Nothing has been going on.'

Tanya's still trying to stay reasonable, making no huge accusations or indulging in wild denials. She's just making a simple statement of fact, which is exactly the way something like this should be played, presumably, making it even more of a shame that no one's actually told me. Because I'm feeling far from reasonable.

'Ethan is not a liar.'

Which was when I snap. Our lives, our whole world, have just been turned upside down in the last hour or so by the lies that copper flung at Tanya, and maybe we have to take it from him, maybe he was only doing his job, but why should I listen to more of the same from some stupid kid's mum on my own fucking doorstep?

And yes, my voice is probably louder now than it should be, and I probably am actually yelling, but to be fair, who wouldn't?

'He's not just a liar, he's a perve and a creep.'

Al cuts in, doing his best as ever to calm things down. Talk about horses and stable doors.

'Joel, this isn't helping.'

'And this is?'

I gesture at Nia, who doesn't even seem to hear me. Her eyes are still fixed on Tanya.

'How else do you think he took that picture of my wife?'

Which is when the first of the doors begin to open on our small street.

NIA – THE MUM

I don't suppose any of us are exactly thinking straight.

Each of us is just doing what comes naturally right now, acting on instinct. One of your own is under threat – what would anyone do? You fight back. Defend to the death.

In a different world and time and if I'd been a different person, maybe I would have let things take their course, maybe I wouldn't have marched round there like that. But right now, I just want to look in her eyes, the eyes of the woman who looked into mine across that kitchen table, who pushed that mug of coffee across to me, who asked about Al, who talked about Joel – the woman I felt I'd connected with in some way, the woman I felt might actually become a friend. I want to look in her eyes and I want see the very different woman I now know her to be.

Because this is simple so far as I'm concerned. I know my son. I know that Ethan is telling me the truth. Not because I have any actual proof, that single photo aside, but because in some instinctive and elemental way, I just know. The way any mother would.

So now I want to see some admission of all she's done, and maybe if it had been just me and her, I might have done. We might have made some sort of sense out of what the hell has been happening here.

It doesn't help that it's all now getting very public. I'm already sensing, if not actually seeing, more and more lights coming on all around, sensing at the same time people beginning to come outside, as they hear the raised voices echoing around the house at the very top of the small hill.

And suddenly out it comes. Because Joel's cutting words have lacerated me and I'm not having it.

'There's only one perve round here, you predatory bitch.'

Which everyone behind me now hears, and they all hear the next bit too. Loud and clear.

'What else would you call a sicko who sleeps with a fifteen-year-old kid?'

All I can see is a single pair of eyes staring at me, Tanya's eyes.

I search for an explanation, or even just an acknowledgement, albeit a silent one.

But I see nothing there.

Nothing at all.

DEVIL'S BRIDGE

They travel no more than a few metres before that loose, shuffling line of scared teens grinds to a sudden halt, because that's when the next scream sounds.

But there's no mystery about this one. No one stares round wildly, trying to identify where it might have come from. This scream comes unmistakably from within their own ranks.

Like the rest of her friends tonight, the girl's still wearing her party outfit. Sheer tights, high heels and a crop top exposing what's now a washboard stomach but in a few years' time will be anything but. It's little protection against the elements, as her disapproving mum chided just a few hours before, and she's been proved right. The girl's been shivering almost uncontrollably for the last half hour, although that's not entirely due to the cold.

It's also little protection against the blood.

At first, she thought she'd put her foot in one of the small pools of bracken-stained water formed by the storm. But this doesn't feel like water – it's sticky, glutinous, and there's a smell to it, acrid and brittle, almost metallic somehow. It's something she's never really smelt before, but who would smell something like that in that sort of accumulation, apart from maybe in an operating theatre?

The girl reaches down, brushing it away. Then she brings her hand back up in front of her eyes, which is when she lets out that sudden scream. Then the wind begins to pick up again, along with a low whistling sound as the clouds blow away and moonlight steals through once more.

As one the teens look up again towards the bridge, but the whistling sound isn't coming from there.

It's coming from a body wheeling round and round in the gathering wind, impaled on the branch of a nearby tree.

JOEL – THE HUSBAND

TANYA'S already down in the kitchen by the time I come out of the shower. Danny's in his highchair and she's feeding him breakfast. As always, food's everywhere – over the highchair, the kitchen table, the floor, and all over Danny. Some of it's in his mouth, which is about the best we can hope for these days. The TV's on low, behind, some kids' cartoon on screen.

In other words, it's a totally normal day – just like any other day in fact, but it isn't, of course.

I hear the doorbell from upstairs. I'm towelling myself down before heading off to check on one of the sites. We talked about it last night after that doorstep exchange with Nia and we agreed. Tomorrow, we do what we always do. We get up, we sort out Danny, we take him to the childminder, and we go to work. Anything else would feel like some sort of acknowledgement that there's actually some case to answer here, that there's something in those crazed allegations of Ethan's after all. Like I've already said, Tanya's done nothing wrong, and people who've done nothing wrong do not hide away from anyone.

I come downstairs and look at the letter that's just been delivered, which is already smeared with Danny's choice of cereals today as he tries grabbing it from her. He likes lining up all the different packets before pointing to the one he wants, taking a mouthful, then pointing to the next. I'm already counting at least three different samples from at least as many packets. Displacement activity, I once heard it called. Focusing on one thing, trying not to think of something else.

'It's just been couriered over from the school.'

I take Danny's spoon out of Tanya's hand and kneel down in front of our delighted little boy. Another adult to smear with Coco Pops.

'And?'

Tanya's trying, not altogether successfully, to keep the tremor out of her voice.

'I'm not to go into work today.'

I look back at her.

'Or the next few days.'

At the table Danny sets up an extended splutter as he tries to make bubbles out of the milk in his mouth, another party trick he's learnt in the last few days. I try to keep my voice steady too as I concentrate on getting another spoonful inside him.

'Can they do that? Stop you, just like that?'

Tanya just looks down at the letter. The silence grows. Even Danny quietens. Then Tanya picks it up, turns and heads for the garden at the back.

'He's a boy, Joel, a boy, for Christ's sake.'

I follow her out a few moments later, after making sure Danny's OK. Aside from that joint agreement last night that today would be like any other day, Tanya didn't actually say too much. She just held onto me, and I held onto her. We didn't need to say anything. Whatever this is all about, whatever twisted world of his diseased imagining Ethan's inhabiting and is trying to make Tanya inhabit too, we will face it, and we'll do that as we've always done from the very first moment we met, together.

But Tanya's saying plenty now. She paces our rear garden, moving backwards and forwards, the door to the kitchen open behind us, Danny in our eyeline in his highchair, bubbling milk again for all he's worth.

'He's little more than a child.'

Tanya stops, then she goes off again, another circuit of a lawn I've still not managed to edge properly across a path that's still waiting for its final layer of screed before I lay down the paving slabs

'Even if, *if*, I'd done what he's saying, does anyone really think I'd be stupid enough to then tell a fifteen-year-old boy to take a picture?'

Tanya keeps pacing, more fired-up than I've ever seen her before.

'You know what they're like, I've told you – the girls as well as the boys. They never stop, they're always posting things online, anything they can find, and if there's nothing they can put their actual hands on they just mock it up and post it anyway.'

Tanya looks at me, eyes wide in disbelief.

'And I'm supposed…'

Then she stops, almost fighting for breath before she can continue.

'I'm supposed to have not only done that with a fifteen-year-old boy, but to have said to him, why don't you take a picture?'

Tanya keeps staring at me for a moment, then looks down at the letter, still in her hand. And something else shines now in her eyes. The bewilderment and the hurt fades. Then she strides past me into the kitchen, barely pausing as she picks up her coat and car keys before making for the front door.

From the back garden I can see the street at the front of the house through a gap in the hedge. For the first time I see some of our neighbours out there, gathered in small knots outside their houses in a succession of what looks like hushed enclaves. Almost as one they look up as Tanya comes outside and makes for her car, but she doesn't even look at them.

She just gets in the car, starts the engine and drives away.

AL – THE DAD

I HEAD BACK to Nia's before school the next morning.

Not that I imagine for a moment Ethan'll be going into school, and he isn't, of course. He's been up in his room all night, according to his mum. He hasn't spoken to her, hasn't even asked where she went last night. Maybe he didn't even realise she'd gone out. Ella stayed all the time we were away just like I'd asked, and he didn't speak to her either. Nia's right – it's as if he's locked away in some private universe of his own right now, allowing no one in.

I drop Kate off at work and go straight round. I can't exactly go into work myself right now. After last night I don't even know if I'll have any work to go to, but that's for another day, another time. Something Joel and myself will have to try and sort out – it doesn't matter. All that does matter is my son.

I arrive early, but not early enough as it turns out, because a letter's already been delivered. It's way too soon for the post, so this must have been dropped off by a courier. It's short and to the point. It's not confrontational or hostile, but it makes things pretty clear, nevertheless.

In the light of recent events, Ethan is not to attend class for the next forty-eight hours while a series of meetings takes place.

He'll be updated on the outcome of those meetings at the earliest opportunity. In the meantime, if there's any schoolwork he needs then the school will forward it on.

Nia just lets me read the short note. She doesn't say anything, but she doesn't need to.

I head upstairs and tap on Ethan's door. I don't get a reply, so I push it open. Ethan's just sitting on the bed, Sami next to him. He doesn't look up at me as I stand there, and for a moment, I'm not sure what to say let alone what to do, which is when Nia comes up too.

I sit on one side of our son; she sits on the other and I look round for a moment. His bedroom's little more than a box room, really. We always said that one day we'd have to find him something bigger, but over the years the space seemed to wrap itself around him somehow. Posters went up, were torn down, the toys that used to litter the floor were packed away to be replaced by magazines and books and DVDs. His own little retreat reinvented itself time and again over the years, so there seemed less and less reason to find anywhere else for him. He'd got used to it, and so had we. So here he stayed.

I keep looking round. All the big events in his life so far have taken place in this room. His first visit from the tooth fairy, the endless Christmas Eves when we'd will sleep to lull him across to his presents in the morning. All the normal stuff that every kid goes through. I look at Ethan. But what's happening right now is anything but normal. And no kid should go through it either.

'Is it him?'

Ethan looks up at us. It sounds like a sudden thought, something that's just come out of nowhere, but I know him. This is something he'll have been turning over all night.

Nia looks back at him cautiously.

'Who?'

'Joel?'

Neither of us reply. We just keep looking at him, his eyes desperate, pleading.

'Is that why she's saying all this?'

Ethan keeps staring at us, wanting above anything in the world right now for something to make some sort of sense.

'Does she not want to upset him, is that it?'

I look at Nia, who looks back at me, neither of us with the faintest clue what to say to that. Then I try to take some sort of belated charge.

'Never mind what she's saying and never mind Joel either – there's only one person me and your mum are bothered about in all this and that's you.'

And suddenly, back it comes, quick as a flash, something else that sounds like a sudden thought, but something else I'll lay odds he'll have been brooding on all night too.

'Why should you be bothered?'

I blink, stupidly, at that for a moment as Ethan keeps staring at me.

'I told you. No one forced me. No one forced Tanya.'

It's been so simple until now. That's all I can think. All the angst-ridden conversations we've ever had in the past, all those confrontations that seemed so important at the time, they'd all been sorted out so easily. There was one Christmas when Ethan wanted a bike and we told him he had to wait four months for his birthday. It made so much more sense to have a bike at the start of spring rather than in the middle of winter, but he went on about it for days, and the tears you wouldn't believe. But we worked through it in the end, talked him round.

Where the hell do we start with this? I already feel as if I'm in some sort of thick fog, dragging my legs behind me as I plough through what feels like treacle.

By my side, Nia cuts in.

'Ethan, you and Mrs Adams...'

She hesitates, struggling, and then continues.

'That isn't what you think it is.'

Ethan's stare is bold, challenging.

'What are you saying, you don't believe me?'

Nia cuts across firmly.

'No, we believe everything you're saying. We believe that what you say happened did happen. Don't misunderstand, Ethan – this is not me or your dad trying to make out you're a liar.'

I nod at him, the two of us in total accord on this.

'But—'

Ethan's eyes never leave mine as I stop. What can I say? I can tell him, and Nia can tell him, again and again, that we believe every word he's saying, at the same time as knowing that every single thing he's thinking is totally and completely wrong, which sounds like a contradiction, but it isn't.

This is no love story.

Ethan thinks it is, but it's not.

This is something else.

MEGAN – THE HEADTEACHER

I HAVEN'T SLEPT MUCH. For different reasons I don't suppose any of us have, but in a sense that's the point. Not the missing sleep, but the different reasons for it. Somewhere in that is the key to all this.

I write those two letters first thing, the first to Tanya, the second to Ethan. The safeguarding officer at the Local Education Authority told me to do that late last night. She also told me what I had to say, so apart from signing both letters and arranging to have them couriered over, there hasn't actually been that much to do. Except sit and stare at the wall and wonder how a day that could begin with a simple fete in a school could end with at least two lives and probably many more blasted apart like this.

Don, bless him, has been in touch all the time, researching this procedure, checking on that. He's also been in touch with a research group that's done a special study of this kind of abuse, if that's what this is, and he emailed that over to me in turn, just in case there's anything in there that might help.

I scan a random digest of the main points as I try and fail to eat my breakfast.

Many adolescent boys are abused by women – WHAT? – and boys and men are much less likely to report sexual abuse.

Mine's the annotated *WHAT?*, by the way.

Offenders don't sexually abuse for the sex. It's more about power, manipulation, perhaps because there's something they're missing in their own lives.

Head reeling, I keep reading.

Female abusers present themselves differently from men. Women aim to be liked; men aim to be believed.

I make to put it all back on the kitchen table, but not before reluctantly scanning the next entry.

Female teachers often target the quiet, underdeveloped boys rather than the confident ones. They look for vulnerability.

For not the first time in what's occasionally been a trying career, I offer silent thanks to the Gods that things have never quite worked out for me when it came to a lifetime companion and kids. The usual reasons, I suppose – too much work time, too little play time. Occasionally I've seen that as a curse. Right now, I'm seeing it as anything but.

I go to have a shower. For reasons not too difficult to understand I'm feeling more than a little grubby. And, while I don't want to decry what are very obviously Don's best efforts and well-meaning intentions, it really hasn't helped that much.

I get in my car and drive to the school. I've absolutely no idea what to expect from the day ahead. I even half-expect the whole place to have vanished overnight, everything feels so disconnected and disorientating right now.

I turn onto the yard, which is when I see her.

Tanya.

Standing, pale and tense, by the side door to the school.

Waiting for me.

KATE – THE NEWBIE

I DON'T SEE him at first.

One of the other receptionists looks up as the door opens, all ready with the usual practised smile, the obligatory spot of banter. But she doesn't say a word, and whoever's opened that door doesn't speak either. I look up from the electronic appointments ledger I'm checking, on autopilot as I have been ever since Al came home last night. And I don't speak for a moment either as I see Joel standing on the other side of the desk. He doesn't even seem to see the other receptionist. He's just looking at me.

He's just about the last person I expect to see right now, given everything, and he looks as if this is the very last place he expects to be, given everything right now too. Whether it's an impulse visit or something he's been working up to I have no idea, but that doesn't really matter. Here he is and here I am too.

Sue, the other receptionist, clears her throat nervously, as she suddenly remembers something urgent that needs doing somewhere away from the open plan reception area with just these two desks. She leaves, quickly, meaning there's now just one occupied desk, with me behind it.

I struggle to produce a smile. From memory, I think I might have tried to make some lame joke about Joel's sat-nav playing up again. I've no idea what I actually say; I'm just trying to fill the void.

For his part, Joel's staying silent. Then suddenly out it comes.

'I can't talk to Nia. Or Al.'

He hesitates, then continues.

'Tell him, by the way.'

He hesitates again.

'Tell Al this is nothing to do with him, I know.'

I nod back, grateful but hardly reassured. Joel may not be holding Al responsible for the misdeeds or otherwise of his son, but that still doesn't mean Al won't pay some sort of price. Joel's tough, but fair. Everyone says so, but that doesn't make him a saint. If this all ends badly, as in really badly, God knows who else is going to get caught in the fall-out.

Joel struggles again, his voice hissed and low.

'I can't do anything. Just stand back and watch my wife being dragged through the mud.'

He stops and I keep looking at him. What can I say? He stays silent for another moment and I half-expect him to turn and walk back out again. But then out it comes.

'Do you believe him?'

And I still. Because it's like hearing my own voice. My own voice asking myself the very same question.

The girls in the garage have heard all about that exchange on Joel's doorstep by now, of course. Everyone has. But they've skirted round it all morning. No direct challenges and no direct references to it either.

But this isn't one of the girls in the garage. And there's no one else in this reception area, just me and Joel. The two satellite characters in a sense, although he's a lot closer to it all than I am. I'm the new arrival on the scene. How he's feeling I can't imagine, and if truth be told I don't want to.

Joel presses me. 'Do you believe what he's saying?'

I struggle, not meeting his eyes.

'I don't know Ethan, not really – me and Al haven't been together that long.'

But if I imagine for just one second that he's going to let me off the hook that easily, I'm wrong. This is Joel. He hasn't built up his business, hasn't got to where he's got and in such a short space of time by ducking things.

'Would you fancy him?'

I stare at Joel, ambushed by that.

He asks again. 'Ethan? Would you?'

And out it comes, instinctively, with no time for second thoughts, no hesitation, no prevarication, just straight from the heart.

'He's a boy.'

Joel nods at me.

'Tell Al that, will you?'

Then the door opens behind him and another customer walks in, pausing warily as he sees me and Joel. Joel doesn't even seem to see him, just nods at me again.

'Before this gets totally out of hand.'

Then he turns, exits past the arriving customer, who's still half-hesitating in the doorway, clearly wondering if he shouldn't just turn round and come back some other time.

I remain still for a moment as I hear a van door open and then close before Joel starts the engine and drives away. I stay still for a moment longer before I flash a quick smile at the customer and book his car in for the work that needs doing on it today.

And I stay on automatic pilot for the rest of the morning, not even registering the return of Sue, who studiously avoids saying anything about our unexpected visitor, a silence that becomes ever more deafening as the day wears on.

MEGAN – THE HEADTEACHER

I park on a hill, the sea in front of us. Behind is the bridge that gave our town its name, according to that famous, or infamous, legend.

Then I turn to look at Tanya.

Five minutes ago, I was staring at her in disbelief.

'What the hell are you doing?'

This is uncharted territory for all of us and no one really knows what to do. But I know one thing. Tanya isn't supposed to be anywhere near this school right now. For a moment she doesn't reply, but then out it comes. Just a simple one-word plea.

'Please?'

And now I'm really struggling. Tanya's never just been a colleague; she's always been more like a friend. It's the way I run my school, and why not? It makes life easier if you like the people you work with, and I like her, I always have. Everyone says it and it's true – she has that quality about her, easy to get on with, a natural. That same easy, natural quality that's making it really difficult to do what I should do right now, which is go in through that door ahead and close it behind me. At the same time as telling her to get the hell away.

But I don't do any of that. I just keep looking at her, helpless.

'I need to talk to you.'

'Tanya, this is crazy.'

'Just a few minutes?'

She's clearly desperate, distraught even, but there are procedures to follow. So why don't I do what I should do? Is it the thought that maybe, by talking to her, I might short-circuit some of the extended rigmarole we all now know we face? Even gain some inside track on it all? Or is it that uncharted territory all over again? Deep down, do I just not know what to do?

All I do know is that after another moment's hesitation and a quick look round to check that no one seems to be taking too close an interest in this very much forbidden exchange, I nod at my car.

'Get in.'

We don't speak for a moment after I park. Then Tanya brings out the letter, the one I sent this morning.

'So, I'm being suspended?'

I shake my head, firmly. We're still a long way from that.

'No, that's just a notice that you don't come into the school while initial investigations get under way.'

'Oh come on!'

I press on, doggedly.

'It's procedure, that's all. It doesn't mean we're taking any view on the rights and wrongs of all this.'

Tanya shakes her head, more and more vehemently. In her position I'd be doing exactly the same.

'No, this is me being hung out to dry. I get accused of something and the next thing everyone knows I'm sitting at home, barred from my place of work.'

'You're not barred.'

Tanya just rides on.

'And that's the school not taking a view?'

For a moment there's silence again. Then she looks at me.

'So, what about Ethan?'

I still, cautious. It's the first time his name has been mentioned.

'He's not in school today either.'

'And is that his choice or yours?'

I fall silent. What can I say? Yes, Ethan has also been told not to come to the school today, but no formal action can be taken against him in the way more formal action has been taken against Tanya, because there's none that can be taken; that's just the way it is.

Tanya rides on again. 'I've been in touch with the union. Lucy, the rep, she's coming round later.'

Then she breaks off, her whole body now literally shaking.

'Have you seen that picture?'

Out it comes before I even have time to think.

'Of course we have.'

Tanya looks at me, stilling now.

'We?'

I hesitate as she keeps looking at me.

'Don's seen it too.'

Tanya doesn't reply, just closes her eyes as I plough on.

'He's the head of governors. Anyway, he was there when Nia and Al came to the school.'

She keeps her eyes closed. I can almost feel the humiliation etched on her eyeballs. Which is when I finally give voice to the question that's been going round and round my head all night.

'Has Ethan...?'

Tanya opens her eyes and looks at me as I struggle for a moment.

'Has he ever said anything to you? Anything that even hinted at anything like this?'

'No.'

'You haven't noticed him looking at you or anything?'

Tanya shakes her head, impatient again.

'Of course I have, and just about every other boy in his year and most of the boys in all the other years too. Throw a stone, every teacher in the school has at one time or another, male and female – you know that.'

She looks at me, helpless again.

'It's just kids. It's normal.'

'But Ethan in particular?'

Tanya looks out of the window again, struggling for a moment, then she takes a quick, deep breath.

'I have been paying him a bit more attention lately.'

I look back at her, waiting.

'He's been going through a bad patch. You know that – you were there at the parents' evening with Nia.'

She takes another deep breath.

'And yes, I've been taking extra pains with him. I even dropped off a DVD for him the other night. His grades used to be good, really good, and to watch them dip like that has been heart-breaking.'

Then Tanya shakes her head, absolutely firm on this.

'But he has never, ever, said or done anything that's even remotely crossed any sort of line. For God's sake, I'd have come straight to you if he had.'

Then, and just as suddenly as her defiance flared, she's back to looking and sounding helpless again.

'So far as I was concerned, he was just a normal, sweet kid.'

I stay silent for another long moment because I simply have no idea what to say.

Half an hour later, we're pulling up again, this time a hundred or so metres away from the school.

If Tanya notices that we haven't actually driven in through the gates onto the yard she doesn't say. Maybe she's already begun to accept the suddenly changed world we're all living in.

Which is when she comes out with it.

'Do you believe me?'

Tanya hasn't asked up to now. But it's a question that's been hanging heavy between us, something I've been expecting right from the start, and dreading too. Maybe the fact she hasn't asked it so far has lulled me into some false sense of security. Maybe that's why the question ambushes me.

I look back at her, and all I can see are her eyes, desperate again, and on her face is the plea that I'd have on mine were our roles reversed.

'Please, Megan, I need to know.'

Then we hear them, a group of Year 11 boys heading into school. I don't know how long they've been standing there. I'm not sure if any of those boys even see me or care I'm there. There's only one object of their attention on this street this morning.

'Hey, Miss.'

Tanya stares across at them. It's the sort of greeting each of us hears a dozen times a day, in and out of the school. But today's different, of course. That changed world again.

The voice belongs to Aidan Mulville. He's not a bad boy – mouthy, liable to kick off under even the slightest provocation, in other words a totally normal teenager. We've hopes of his going on to college after the summer.

Aidan nods at Tanya as she keeps staring back at him.

'Will you do me too?'

To both sides of him, his friends crack up at what's obviously the single most hysterical thing they've heard in their collective lifetimes.

Tanya looks at him for a moment longer, then she gets out of the car and, without looking back once, walks away.

DI MCCARTHY – THE COP

'THERE'S no CCTV in the girls' changing rooms, obviously.'

We're in the school office, a map of the building on a large table in front of us. The two secretaries have been told to take a break. As a precaution that's probably way too little too late, given the rumours that are already sweeping the school and the town, but procedures still have to be followed.

'But you've cameras outside?'

Don, the head of governors, nods back at me. Megan, the head, isn't in yet so he's been deputed to look after me.

'And along most of the corridors.'

'Most?'

He shrugs. What can he say?

'Cuts.'

I nod back. 'Nuff said.

I checked up on him before I came over from the station. Like most of the people in the town, like the head herself in fact, he was born here, but this is his first year in his new role. His first few months of his first year, in fact. He probably thought it would just be handing out prizes on sports day. Something like this must have been far from his mind when he threw his hat into this particular ring.

'And this here?'

I tap an image on the map in front of us.

'At the rear of the yard. Do you have any cameras covering that?'

Now he looks at me curiously. He obviously knows some of the story by now, but he doesn't know it all. But by the look on his face, another piece has just slotted into place.

'That's just a storeroom.'

He keeps looking at me, now even more curious. Then he leans closer to the map, trying and failing to make his next question sound casual.

'So, is that where this is supposed to have taken place?'

He keeps his eyes trained on the map of the school in front of us, trying and failing again to keep his tone from sounding defensive as I stay silent.

'Well, you've not actually established that anything has happened yet, have you? One way or the other?'

He keeps looking at the map.

'So, either Ethan's told you it happened there because he knew no one could say it didn't.'

In truth, that hasn't taken all that much working out, but he still sounds pleased with himself.

'Or?'

And now that pleased tone falters, and now he's looking less like the amateur sleuth and more like a hard-pressed school governor facing the most unholy mess any school could face.

I finish it for him.

'Or Mrs Adams took him there because she knew they couldn't be seen.'

Then we both turn as a voice sounds behind.

'Guv.'

Gee, standing behind me, inclines her head slightly, a private word required. I move across to her and she hands me a single sheet of paper.

JOEL – THE HUSBAND

Lucy, the union rep, arrives mid-morning.

Tanya's still not home from wherever she's gone. Whether that signals good or bad news I have no idea, which is par for the course right now. I've no idea about anything anymore.

But Lucy's arrival is still like some hope. So far, aside from that one letter from Tanya's school, no one's been in touch with us. Now it feels like some kind of cavalry's arrived at least.

I fuss over her, making her coffee. I know she's in a tricky position, that anything she has to say to Tanya and vice versa should be confidential. It's a professional thing, so I try not to press her. I manage some small talk about Danny's birthday and the bouncy castle still waiting to be inflated in the back garden. We even talk about a tiny sprinkling of soot that's appeared overnight in the fireplace, a small bird attempting to nest maybe.

But in the end, I can't help myself. As Lucy sips her coffee and I check for the umpteenth time whether Tanya's responded to my texts telling her she's here, I come out with it.

'What can she do?'

Lucy hesitates in turn, and I backtrack straight away.

'Sorry – I know. Just tell me you can get this sorted.'

Lucy smiles, quickly, a smile that isn't really a smile at all.

'I've found out everything I can for now.'

I wait for her to continue, but she doesn't.

'And you can help?'

'I can explain.'

'Explain what?'

But then the door opens behind us and Tanya comes in. She looks at Lucy for a moment, then barrels across the room into her arms.

'The school can't do anything till the police have finished their investigations. At the moment their hands are tied, but that doesn't mean ours are.'

We've been sitting together for the last ten minutes. Most of that time has been spent with Tanya going over and over the whole thing from the very first appearance on our doorstep of that copper last night. The start of the nightmare we've been living through every second of every minute of every hour since.

I'm by her side, listening, grim. Tanya's told Lucy that anything she has to say to her I can hear too. Sometimes I stand, pace the floor as everything that's happened just pours out of her. Sometimes I just hold Tanya's hand. I have the feeling I'm going to be doing a lot of that for the next few days. Pacing the floor. Listening in grim silence. Holding my wife's hand.

'I know the police have only done a preliminary interview with you for now and there's been nothing under caution as yet, but I think we should go and see them together, get your side of the story out there right from the start.'

Tanya and Lucy have been friends since college. They'd both intended to go into teaching, and Tanya had – and at the earliest opportunity, too. She'd become the youngest head of department out of her intake that year. Lucy's career took a different path, but they've always remained close. Thank God, as events have turned out.

'And when the police do finish these investigations?'

Lucy looks at me as I roll on.

'When they decide that this is the total shit we all know it is – what then?'

'How do you mean?'

'Then Tanya can go back to work, yes?'

I look across at Tanya, who's staying silent now, but I can see it in her eyes. She already seems to know it's never going to be as simple as that. Just like they can both see in my eyes that I don't remotely understand why it shouldn't be.

Lucy takes a quick, deep breath.

'No, she can't, I'm afraid.'

I already know the world has gone totally fucking mad. The last day or so has proved that. Some random kid makes a wild accusation, and suddenly, all our lives are put on hold. But this should be the start of the fight back.

'The school will still have to conduct its own inquiry.'

'Even if the police drop all the charges?'

'The police are looking for evidence to prosecute. If they can't find any—'

I cut in.

'Which they won't.'

Lucy nods. We're in total agreement on that, it seems at least.

'Then yes, they'll drop the case.'

Then she glances across at Tanya.

'But so far as the school's concerned, that may not mean there isn't a case to answer.'

I stare at her, now even more bewildered.

'Maybe an actual offence hasn't taken place – nothing that merits any sort of police action anyway. That doesn't mean that something might not have gone on that shouldn't.'

Lucy hurries on. I probably look as if I'm about to explode.

'I'm just trying to explain the way any future inquiry might work, that's all.'

Then Tanya cuts across with one of the few direct questions

she's asked during the whole of this. Maybe I haven't let her get much in the way of a word in. Or maybe she's just becoming ever more cowed as the enormity of all that's happening sinks in.

'And then what?'

Lucy looks back at her as Tanya continues.

'If the police do drop this, but the school still decide to have an inquiry, what can they do?'

'We're a long way from that.'

'But if they do?'

Lucy struggles for another moment.

'If there is an inquiry and if they find there's a case to answer, that you've encouraged this boy in any way, then that's a breach of protocol and if the breach is deemed sufficiently serious—'

'They can sack me.'

Tanya cuts across again, flat, finishing it for her. It isn't a question, and she isn't inviting an answer. It's a simple statement of fact.

'But like I said, we're a long way from that.'

I look at her.

'So how long? How long is all this going to take? How long has my wife got to sit at home like this?'

I know none of this is Lucy's fault, and I know there's more than an element of my trying to shoot the messenger here, but she's the only messenger who's even talking to us right now.

Tanya stands and moves across to check on Danny, even though he hasn't moved in the last half hour. She smooths his blankets like she always does, checking he's securely tucked in. Lucy takes another deep breath.

'We're probably talking months.'

I stare at her, hardly able to believe my ears. I could get a small estate of houses built in months, for Christ's sake.

Lucy takes another of what are fast becoming her trademark deep breaths, clearly struggling to balance the counterclaims of friendship and her professional duty. In other words, trying not to sugar-coat any pill.

'But if you want my honest opinion, it's more likely to be anything up to a year.'

Tanya just stares back at her. Neither of us respond. Neither of us can. We've not even had a single day of all this and that's been bad enough.

Tanya's eyes suddenly flash, bitter, wounded.

'And even if Ethan suddenly sees sense, even if he suddenly withdraws all he's saying, how easy is it going to be for me to go back now anyway?'

I look across at Lucy, the expression on her face already the all-too eloquent answer.

Tanya continues. 'I know how this works. You do too. The damage has already been done. We'd have a chat, me and Megan, maybe a couple of the governors too.'

Tanya leans forward.

'They'd suggest that maybe it might be best for me if I start looking for a position elsewhere – best for me and best for the school – and if I start pointing out that I haven't actually done anything wrong, we both know what they'll say too, don't we?'

'Will you do me too?'

I haven't the faintest clue what Tanya's talking about. But I can guess. Gossip is going to be rampant now. If any of the older pupils have happened on Tanya while she's been out and about this morning, it really doesn't take too much imagination to work out what might have passed as schoolyard humour.

Tanya keeps looking at her.

'It's been less than a day. And that's already where we are. It's not fair. I haven't done anything wrong.'

DI MCCARTHY – THE COP

'I've just received a report.'

There's no husband present this time, although make that ex-husband, from all I've been hearing. It's just Ethan and his mum on one side of their kitchen table, me sitting opposite, Gee standing by my side.

'Regarding Mrs Adams's phone.'

There's the same anxious expression on the mother's face, but there's a wary, uncertain expression on Ethan's face now. I let the silence settle for a moment, waiting to see who'll speak first. The guilty often talk ten to the dozen. The innocent usually have no need to say a word. It's not any sort of cast-iron rule, but it's a useful indicator. Maybe one day I should write a book.

As it happens it's the mum who's the first to break the silence.

'And?'

I take the report out of my briefcase.

'And there's numerous photos on it: Mrs Adams and her baby, Mrs Adams and her husband, the two of them out with friends.'

I nod across at Ethan, who's still just watching me.

'There's even some from a fete, a fund-raiser I understand you had in the school.'

I look back at Ethan, holding his stare.

'But there's no pictures of you, Ethan.'

He keeps looking back at me.

'None at all.'

'She must have deleted them.'

His mum cuts in, nodding at Ethan as she does so, part reassurance, part something else. I've never had kids. Probably now, I never will. But even I know it's something parents do the world over when their kid's in trouble – nod at them like that, trying to tell them that everything's going to be OK.

'The tech boys have been all over it. If any photos had been deleted or if there'd been any attempt to delete any, there'd be a trace.'

I turn to Ethan.

'But there's nothing. Nothing at all.'

Ethan leans forward, passion inflaming his eyes.

'She took pictures of me. Three or four. She showed me. I saw them.'

I just look down at the report in my hand again.

'We also took a look at your phone, Ethan.'

And now a different expression begins to creep across his face. Now he doesn't look wary. Now he's starting to look hunted. By his side his mum glances at him again. She has no idea where this is going, but she probably already knows from the expression on her son's face that it isn't going to be good.

'There wasn't just that one picture of Mrs Adams on there, was there?'

I reach into my bag, extracting another file. One by one I spread a series of printed stills out on the kitchen table.

'You've taken pictures of her jogging to school, pictures of her out on the playing fields. She takes PE from time to time, I understand.'

Ethan keeps his eyes firmly fixed on the succession of photos that are now appearing before him. His mum doesn't even give them a second glance. All she's looking at is her son.

'And some of these are obviously taken from a fair distance away, and if you look at the dates on the bottom...'

I tap them, pointing them out.

'Some of these go back weeks, if not months.'

I keep my eyes fixed on Ethan.

'So, you seem to have been interested in her for some time.'

Ethan just stays silent.

I glance up at Gee, who's maintaining her own silent brief. She's a good copper, wasted in uniform, which was one of the reasons I co-opted her onto this investigation. It isn't just the fact she's local and can give an outsider like myself some useful pointers. She knows when to keep her mouth shut, to watch, observe. It's good to have a partner who can pick up on things when you're focusing on asking the questions.

Nia cuts in again.

'That's not exactly a crime. And you know he's been interested in her; so has she in him. None of this would be happening if she wasn't. The point isn't what Ethan's done, it's what she's done.'

Ethan keeps his eyes trained on the floor. Gee keeps her eyes trained on him as I tap his phone again, not exactly ignoring Nia but not responding directly to her either. The truth is the mum's just a bit player in all this, the onlooker, no matter how keenly she might feel involved. She's like us all right now, trying to fit together the pieces.

'And I don't want to embarrass you in front of your mother.'

I pause, waiting for Ethan to flinch, which he duly does, and Gee notices. Like I said, she's good. She'll go far.

'But we found something else on your phone as well.'

Again, I let the silence stretch a little. Give him time to see the train as it speeds towards him. Anticipate the crash.

'On at least ten occasions in the last week alone, you've visited porn sites, haven't you?'

By his side, Nia shoots a quick glance at him.

I keep on. 'Nothing illegal, actually. Anything but.'

Nia looks back at me, puzzled now, the question clear in her eyes. What the hell's that supposed to mean?

A tell-tale flush is now starting at the base of Ethan's neck, creeping up towards his face.

'Your taste seems to be for the more mature sort of woman.'

That flush spreads and keeps on spreading. Within another few seconds the young boy looks as if he'll burst into flames if it travels much further.

Now I'm not looking at him, and Gee isn't either. Now we're both looking at his mum, and we both see it at the same time.

For the very first time as she glances sideways at her son there's a flicker, just a tiny flicker, of doubt in her eyes.

KATE – THE NEWBIE

THAT LOOK on Ethan's face is all I can think about. The look he gave me as he was walking away from the site those two days ago. I just can't get it out of my mind. I haven't since a shell-shocked Al came back and told me what had happened with Ethan's teacher.

Or what Ethan is telling us happened with his teacher, although that's a fine distinction I really can't make with Al right now.

Ethan and I have seen each other since the split, of course. Al's tried to bring him round now and again, get him used to this new situation, which is totally understandable on his part, no matter how excruciating it's occasionally been, and I've tried to play my part too. OK, I've left them largely alone when he called, because it seemed better, less awkward that way, but I haven't shied away from him either.

But each time it's been tricky. Not that Ethan's been offensive or anything, but there's still been something in his eyes, something behind the quick darting glances he gives me when he thinks I'm not looking. Something calculating – I can't put it any other way. As if he's biding his time, trying to decide what to do next. And it was the most pronounced of all that day.

I know this sounds crazy, because what can he actually do? The break-up's happened; me and Al are together now – none of us can turn back time. Apart from the fact that's exactly what's happening. Al's up at Nia's most of the time now, and of course he is, with everything that's going on. Like he's always said, he chose Nia all those years ago and now he's made another choice, but a child isn't a matter of choice – a child's there for ever, and I understand that, I really do. If anything ever happens, if your child is in any sort of trouble, you have to support them.

Which still leaves him spending all that time with his ex-wife.

It could just be an inevitable consequence of all that's happening, but every time I close my eyes right now, I keep seeing Ethan's eyes looking at me like that.

Careful.

Considering.

And that's when they race through my mind, all those thoughts I daren't give voice to, everything I can't say.

All the upset of the last few months and yes, all the pain and angst Ethan has got to be feeling right now, is that all coming out in some weird way? Is this some sort of payback? The world has hurt him, and big-time, lately, so is he hitting back? Which sounds mad again, I know. Who'd construct such an elaborate charade just to do that?

I can't stop thinking it, though. Because is this the game? Create a massive crisis, something that makes everyone stop in their tracks? Force his mum and dad back together to try and sort it out? And if he can do that, force them back together to do that one thing, maybe he can get them back together more permanently.

In other words, are we all being played? That's the one thought that keeps hammering away inside, even as I'm supporting Al as he supports his family in turn, telling him that of course he has to go and see his ex, of course he has to go and spend the evening with his son.

Which means, if that's right, then all that's happening to

Tanya right now and to Joel is collateral damage. They're paying the price for everything Al and I did all those months ago.

AL – THE DAD

NIA CALLED me just after the police left. I got there ten minutes later. Ethan looks bruised, and no wonder – the poor kid must feel as if he's been put through a wringer.

'It doesn't mean a thing. And whatever you've got on your phone doesn't make any difference to what you're saying either.'

Nia cuts across, agitated.

'That copper seemed to think so.'

'A teenage boy's got a few pictures of an attractive female teacher on his phone, so what? I bet most of his mates have too.'

Now Nia stays silent. I know what's much more on her mind right now, and I know the longer we don't mention it, the bigger this particular elephant is going to grow.

'And a teenage boy's been looking at some porn sites.'

Ethan flushes. I would have done too. In fact, I'd have died if my parents had suddenly started talking about stuff like this in front of me.

'I'd be worried if you hadn't. Talk about a late developer.'

I stare at him, trying to force him to look up at me.

'In my day it was top shelf of a newsagents, but we all did it – me and all the rest of my mates. It didn't make us liars.'

That flush is beginning to recede from Ethan's face a little now.

'And it doesn't turn you into one either.'

And then, slowly, he looks up at us.

'There's something I need to tell you.'

NIA – THE MUM

For a moment there's just silence. I don't speak and neither does Al.

Then I lean forward.

'What, Ethan?'

He struggles for a moment.

'What do you need to tell us?'

Then out it comes.

'She didn't know.'

We stare at him as Ethan falters. He doesn't say anything else for a few moments. I keep staring at him, as does Al.

Then I lean forward again.

'Who didn't know what?'

'That picture.'

A cold feeling begins to spread through me.

'The photo on my phone.'

Ethan hesitates again.

'She didn't know I'd taken it.'

By my side, Al just keeps staring at him too. You could have heard the proverbial pin drop.

'She told me not to, but after she took those pictures of me, I didn't see why not.'

Then Ethan looks at us, a shadow of the defiance we saw last night, when this whole story broke, back on his face.

'But everything else is true, I swear.'

I don't say a word. I can't.

Al stays silent too.

AL – THE DAD

McCarthy takes his time coming down from his office. We must have sat in the small reception just in front of the main desk for fifteen minutes, maybe more. Other officers come and go, all of them shooting quizzical glances at us. Who we are, isn't an issue. Everyone in the town knows each other anyway, and the events of the last day or so have well and truly guaranteed that no one's now going to forget Ethan in a hurry.

But I can see it in all those eyes. What are we doing there? Has there been some new development? The curiosity's almost naked.

Then the door opens, and McCarthy comes out to meet us. Nia tells him that Ethan has something to tell him, something to do with the case. For his part, Ethan just keeps his eyes fixed on the floor. Then McCarthy turns and leads us into an office.

Once we're inside, he seats himself on one side of the desk, while we flank Ethan on the other. For a moment no one speaks, then Nia takes the lead.

'Ethan needs to…'

Nia hesitates, stumbling over exactly how to phrase this.

'He needs to correct part of his story.'

McCarthy stares at Ethan.

'Correct?'

I nod, trying to back Nia up, but not exactly making the best job of it.

'Change.'

'Ethan wants to change his story?'

Nia hurries on.

'He's still saying that he and Mrs Adams…'

She looks at him. Ethan's cheeks are burning. Even to my eyes, he looks exactly what he is right now. A young boy who's been caught out. Now we have to convince McCarthy this really is just a single error of judgement, that this isn't the sort of stain that spreads from one small corner of a picture to blot out everything else.

'But that photo he took of her…'

Ethan, finally, cuts across. 'She didn't know.'

I didn't think he was going to say a single word. I thought we'd have to spell out the story between us in fits and starts. But to his credit, and yes, I'm aware it's probably only myself and Nia who'll actually give him any credit right now, he starts to speak.

'She didn't know I'd taken it.'

McCarthy keeps his eyes fixed on him.

'You're saying you took that photo without her knowledge?'

'Yes.'

'Or her permission?'

'Yes.'

'Just as Mrs Adams has maintained all along?'

We can see it. Ethan must be able to see it too. The foundation on which he's built his whole story slowly beginning to crumble before his eyes.

Ethan hesitates.

'Yes.'

There's a long pause as McCarthy keeps eyeing him, and Ethan keeps his eyes fixed on the floor. Nia hesitates too, waiting, in case Ethan wants to say any more. Then she turns back to McCarthy.

'This isn't something we found out for ourselves. This is something Ethan's told us of his own free will.'

McCarthy switches his silent stare towards her.

'It's the one part, just the one part of this whole story that didn't happen as he told you.'

Nia takes another quick, deep breath.

'And when we found out, we decided you should know too.'

'Why?'

Now we both look at him, puzzled. Why did we decide he should know? Is that seriously what he's asking? But McCarthy's still staring directly at Ethan.

'Why did you lie in your original statement, Ethan?'

Ethan stays silent, but McCarthy rolls on anyway.

'Because you knew how it would look if you confessed to sneaking into a changing room and taking a picture like that without Mrs Adams's knowledge or permission?'

Ethan doesn't hesitate this time.

'Yeah, I knew exactly what you'd think. And I didn't understand why she wouldn't let me anyway, I still don't. After everything that had happened, after she'd taken pictures of me…'

Ethan breaks off.

'And I know you didn't find them, and I don't know why. Maybe your computer people aren't as clever as they think. Maybe she deleted them, and they can't work out how – I don't know.'

He pauses, helpless.

'But she did. I swear.'

McCarthy keeps eyeing him.

'You swore, in your statement, that she was wholly aware of the naked picture you took of her too.'

Nia cuts in again.

'And now he's telling you that was wrong.

'No, now he's confessing that it was a lie.'

This is going every bit as badly as Nia and myself both privately feared, and it's all down to that stain again. That stain in the corner spreading wider and wider.

'Mrs Adams says she took no pictures of Ethan, and we find no pictures on her phone. She says she had absolutely no idea that Ethan took any pictures of her and now Ethan tells us she did not. She tells us she never slept with him, but Ethan is still saying she did.'

Ethan cuts in again, desperate.

'She did.'

Once again, DI McCarthy just looks at him. We seem to have had a lot of these looks in what can't have been that long an exchange, but one that already feels like it's gone on forever.

Then he nods at Ethan again.

'I'll need to caution you as you've now admitted to taking a photograph without permission, but before I do, is there any other part of your statement you'd like to change or correct?'

Ethan just stays silent.

I look across at Nia, who looks back at me,

That stain?

Now it's covered almost everything.

MEGAN – THE HEADTEACHER

I WATCHED a video once of a tsunami that engulfed a holiday resort. It was one of the eeriest things I'd ever seen; there was total silence for a moment, almost as if the world was holding its breath. Then you saw it. Dimly glimpsed at first, an unstoppable tidal wave on the horizon gathering in intensity and ferocity all the while. No possibility of escaping its implacable flow. Nothing to do but watch the onset of total destruction.

All right, compared to that we've got off lightly. The walls of the school are still standing, and no pupil or member of staff has been actually swept away. But there's still that same sense of being overwhelmed by forces impossible to oppose. Everywhere we look right now an approaching tide seems to be swamping us.

Not that the vast majority of the kids see it that way. Most of them are delighted right now, exultant even, and for good reason. They're in on the ground floor of a story that's going to run in our small town for years. Generations of pupils will grow up in the shadow of this – time and again, successive intakes will ask the pupils who were there to tell them the story of all that happened, and these lucky few are actually watching that story unfold.

As well as helping it along a little.

Don and I stare at the pictures on the screen.

'It was on the main computer feed as I logged on.'

The office computers are set up so any reference to the school on social media automatically appears in our news feed. These references aren't automatically disseminated into the wider world. All sorts could be and has been posted about any school, but it's still a useful tool to pick up the exploits and achievements of former pupils or any references in the press to school initiatives.

Or the alleged exploits of one of our teachers and a fifteen-year-old pupil.

A video is on there too with a soundtrack. And there are other images, doctored images of Ethan and Tanya in all sorts of compromising poses, the couple artfully arranged courtesy of some computer trickery to make it look as if they've actually been caught in the act.

'Take it down.'

Don looks at me, but we both know it's too late. We can and will take it down, but it's already out there on almost every pupil's phone, iPad or laptop. By the end of the day, it'll have spread to every other school in the area and beyond.

From there it's always going to be the shortest of steps to some journalist or other. All it will need after that is a slow news day in the wider world and that implacable tide will be roaring ever closer as we stand in its path, blinking at its approach, totally unable to run from it or hide.

NIA – THE MUM

It should be mine and Ella's Chinese night later, something we've done for years. A weekly get-together, a chance for the two of us to demolish a bottle of cheap red wine from the local Bargain Booze, pig out on sweet and sour, special chop suey, boiled rice, chicken curry, extra hot, and chips, obviously, then put the world to rights.

Ella always moans about school. I moan about Ethan, or lately, almost exclusively Al. We do an increasingly giggly character assassination on just about everyone we know before she stumbles home, usually in the small hours, and I tumble up the stairs to bed or just pull an old dressing gown over myself and grab a few hours on the sofa. Since the split, that weekly ritual has become even more important. A chance for me to let go a little, I suppose. Kick out at a world that's turned strange and cold.

I've tried so hard with Ethan since Al left. Putting on the bravest of faces, never letting down my guard. And if I did, I never really gave way, never did what I wanted to do, which was scream and shout, then scream and shout some more. I was always only too aware that he's every bit as fragile as I am. The last thing he needs is to try and prop up a disintegrating mum at the same time as dealing with a flake of a dad.

In recent weeks, these nights have been different. Sometimes I hardly speak, but that doesn't matter. We still demolish the take-away, and by the end of the night that bottle of cheap red vino joins the empty trays in the bin. On those nights, I just want companionship, not conversation, someone to sit with, and Ella, bless her, is always happy to do that. She's been with me through all the crises in my life – George Michael coming out, to name but one. Now she's with me through this one, too.

This is different, though. Very different. Marriages break down all the time and it's hard, especially when kids are involved, but it isn't exactly unheard of. It's unfortunate, of course, but sad to say these days it's almost routine. But something like this, what's happening with Ethan right now, has simply never happened before in our town, or if it has it's very definitely been swept under the carpet.

For the last hour, since she first called in, we've just hugged our coffees. We haven't mentioned Chinese night once.

'Is it…?'

Ella starts, then stops.

I look at her.

'What?'

She struggles for a moment longer.

'It's just something I can't get out of my mind, that's all.'

Then she takes the deepest of deep breaths, aware she's crossing a line here but knowing she has to say it anyway.

'I keep thinking, OK, Ethan might have said something stupid on the spur of the moment, but why would he keep on lying about it if it isn't true?'

Which is when she finally comes out with it. And, like everything else in our lives right now, all roads, even this one, lead back to Al.

'Then I keep thinking, his dad did.'

I look at her.

'You asked him, you told me, time and again, if something was going on.'

She drains the last few drops of her coffee as I keep staring at her.

'He looked you in the eye. Just like Ethan. Swore blind every word he was telling you was true.'

JOEL – THE HUSBAND

We get the call to go to the police station just before six in the evening. Or rather Tanya gets the call to go to the police station, but no way is she going alone. I still can't believe I let myself be persuaded not to sit in on that first exchange back in the house.

What the hell was I thinking? I prowled around the kitchen, like some pathetic kid, while my wife went through just about the single worst experience of her life. So, this time I don't give a flying fuck what any copper might say. I'm going to be at Tanya's side whatever happens. Every step of the way.

Although that is a decision made a little easier by another phone call I received a few hours ago. A phone call that saw me heading away out of town, driving up onto one of the mountain roads and pulling up in a layby behind an unmarked police car.

I step from the van at the same time as Gee steps from that unmarked car.

She doesn't waste time. She clearly wants to get this over and done with as quickly as she can.

'You didn't get this from me, OK?'

I nod back, stealing a quick glance round as I do so. I know how this will look if anyone sees us. So does Gee. No, this is not the way things should be done. But lots of things happen that shouldn't. Like a fine teacher's career being threatened with destruction because of one stupid adolescent. So far as I'm concerned, that puts this strictly unofficial chat into its proper perspective.

I look down onto the town. Tanya told me she'd driven up onto one of the mountain roads with Megan. Maybe it was this one, and maybe they'd stood in this exact same spot looking down like this too.

'It's what you said. Last night, when we first called.'

I keep looking down onto the school, the bridge behind us, looking down on us in turn. Last night already seems like a lifetime ago.

'You know my dad. You went to school with my brother.'

Then she pauses, clearly conflicted even at this late stage.

'Gee, whatever help we can get right now, we're grateful, believe me. Tanya's in bits.'

She struggles for a moment longer as I look at her, waiting for her to speak.

'We've found some more pictures on Ethan's phone. Not just the one from the changing room, other pictures too – dozens of them, all of Tanya.'

For a moment, fear grips me like a vice. What pictures, for Christ's sake? Gee must have seen the expression on my face because she hurries on.

'Out jogging, in the town, even some with Danny in the shops and the park. He must have been following her for weeks, months.'

Darkness began to spread inside me, replacing the previous vice-like fear.

Gee hesitates.

'And other pictures too. Not of Tanya.'

Now I stare at her.

'Other teachers?'

She shakes her head.

'Lots of other women though. From all sorts of places.'

She pauses again.

'He does like his naked flesh.'

For a moment neither of us speak. Neither of us need to. Then she looks at me again.

'This conversation hasn't taken place. I'm trusting you, Joel. This is my job.'

I nod. Of course.

'But there's something else as well. About the picture that started all this in the first place.'

Then she tells me all about an exchange she overheard in the nick just a few hours ago.

Gee had seen Nia, Al and Ethan leaving.

She could see from their body language that it hadn't exactly been an easy encounter. Then again, meetings with McCarthy rarely were. He hadn't been in his new post long, as she'd already told me, but it was obvious he intended to make his mark. When cases arrived on his desk, he had one intention and one only, to get them off that desk and as quickly as possible.

In his book, and it was an oft-repeated mantra, cold cases were for fridges. They had no place in a busy nick, especially his busy nick. Allegations were investigated, lines of inquiry were pursued, decisions were made, and conclusions were reached. Preferably within the same half hour.

OK, that might have been overstating it, but it was very much deal with one case, then onto the next. And from the phone call Gee had just overheard, the conclusion he was reaching about the one case that was preoccupying everyone right now was all too obvious.

She didn't deliberately linger outside that office door. Then again, she didn't need to. It's a small station and the walls are thin, meaning it wasn't easy to have any sort of confidential conversation.

'So, there's no CCTV footage of them together in the school that we've found so far.'

Gee didn't know who McCarthy was talking to at first, but it was obvious who he was talking about. Everyone had been agog ever since that unhappy trio had arrived earlier in the day. Everyone knew they hadn't been called in, meaning there were no new developments on the police side that McCarthy needed to discuss with them. Meaning there had to be some sort of development on their side instead.

So, what had happened? As usual, he was playing the whole thing close to his chest, so thank God for that small building and those thin walls.

'And there are no photos of Ethan on Mrs Adams's phone.'

Gee guessed he was either talking to the ACC, the Assistant Chief Constable, currently in headquarters in the county town some forty or so miles to the south, or he was talking to the Crown Prosecution Service. Someone fairly high-ranking had called that morning wanting an update. And the ACC had been on a few times too.

McCarthy cut across again as Gee lingered outside. Behind, she became conscious of other officers pausing by water coolers, studying notices pinned on walls, each and every one doing exactly what she was doing right now in fact – listening in, all keen for an update too.

'And now the boy's saying she didn't ask him to take any pictures of her – and she didn't know about the one he did take.'

Gee and all the other listening officers stared at the door. This was new. This was a massive change in the story. And it was, equally obviously, why Ethan, Nia and Al had called in.

How McCarthy reported it was also a neat touch. How he'd just described Ethan. The boy. It spoke volumes for his attitude towards him all by itself. McCarthy was fast losing patience with this particular witness. Innocent people stating an honest testimony don't tend to change their story, the guilty are the ones who twist and turn, proffering stories that become more convoluted all the time. A little like Ethan's story was becoming right now.

From the other side of the door there came a sound that was a cross between a sneeze and a snort as McCarthy reacted to something his unheard and still-unidentified caller had obviously said.

'Insufficient evidence? There's no fucking evidence here at all.'

Behind Gee, her Duty Sergeant was now at the water cooler too, also making no pretence that he was doing anything other than listening in right now. And Gee realised that McCarthy must be talking to the CPS. Her new senior officer and the ACC got on well – he'd been one of the great man's personal appointments, by all accounts. But McCarthy would still have observed the protocols. The language would have been toned down along with the traditional courtesies of 'Sir' in his case or 'Ma'am' in the case of the actual Chief Constable. Which meant that this wasn't an official update. This was McCarthy chewing the fat with an opposite number in the Crown Prosecution Office.

Then Gee heard McCarthy's voice float through the thin partition door once again.

'And the longer it goes on the worse it's going to get for this poor bloody teacher.'

That was when Gee had moved on and the Duty Sergeant and all the other coppers moved on too. They'd heard all they needed to hear. They all knew now why Ethan and his family had called into the nick. It was also equally clear that this investigation was now on the home straight. The first chink had been breached in Ethan's story, and the whole thing was now creaking badly.

Why he'd lied about the photo wasn't the issue. All that mattered was he had. So how many more lies would follow?

How many more times would his story change before this case would join the rest of those speedily solved investigations in McCarthy's filing cabinet?

From the tone of his voice, according to Gee, not long.

'A thousand trees.'

I look across at Tanya as she suddenly speaks. We're in my 4x4 outside the house. I'd expected her to tell me to get going, as in straight away. All down the street small knots of people have gathered again, too many to be just neighbours, meaning our home seems to have become sort of unofficial tourist attraction. Dotted in among the faces are some kids too, maybe some from Tanya's own school. The frisson of excitement in the air as we came outside was palpable.

But Tanya is just looking out of the window at the knots of onlookers, all of whom are trying to make it seem like they aren't looking back at her.

I look at her, quizzical, some dim association sounding, but I can't pin it down.

'What are you talking about?'

For a moment Tanya doesn't answer. She just keeps staring out of the window, but she doesn't seem to be looking at anyone or anything – she just appears to be in a world of her own. Then she looks back at me.

'It's a poetry module I run. We look at all sorts: limericks, graffiti, songs.'

The different knots of people are being augmented all the while by new arrivals, the news that she's out of the house clearly spreading like wildfire.

'That one's all about how gossip does the rounds.'

Dimly, a memory does now return, an old song floating through my head, the lyrics coming back in fits and starts.

'It only takes one tree. To make a thousand matches.'

And now I have it. All it's taken are those few words by way of a prompt and suddenly I not only have the words in my head, I can hear the music, the pounding beat, the raw, seemingly unpolished vocal of the lead singer driving it on. And I have another image in my head now too, the pair of us a few years ago at a party, belting out that exact same song in a karaoke session, friends cheering us on, the whole world about to open up before us, our whole life together ahead. It was one of those magical nights when everything around you feels rich with every kind of possibility.

I contribute the next line.

'Only takes one match.'

Tanya nods back, her eyes still on the street and the onlookers.

'To burn a thousand trees.'

We both fall silent, looking out on the street again. I've no idea if she's seeing the same pictures I'm seeing now, whether those few lines of that song are sparking the same memory. Maybe that was just another night to her. There were lots of parties back then.

Maybe it's just the contrast, then and now. That image of hope captured in the memory of that one night, compared to the stark example out on the street before us showing how it can vanish so quickly. How dreams can crumble so speedily into dust.

We're still at the start of all this. The fight's still very much to be fought. But despite Ethan's change of story, despite all I've just learnt from Gee, was Tanya right in all she said to Lucy? Casualties are always going to be created whenever something like this happens. Is she, irrespective of what might happen next, going to be chief among them?

I look out of the window again.

That one match.

Those thousand trees.

Then I put the 4x4 into gear and drive us both past the swelling knot of onlookers to find out.

But for a moment, as I turn at the bottom of the street, it's right in my eyeline. High above us, that ancient bridge, the devil's offering to the town.

And for that brief moment, before I turn out onto the main road and head for the police station, I'm back there all over again.

DEVIL'S BRIDGE – TWENTY YEARS BEFORE

JOEL

I'd seen her a week or so before in school.

A few of the other boys had noticed her too, but she hadn't been looking at them, she'd been looking at me. The first couple of times I thought maybe I was imagining it. Couldn't believe my luck, I suppose. She was hot, as in seriously hot. She hadn't been a few months before, but even at that age I'd seen it time and again. You could pass someone on the corridor at fourteen without a second glance, maybe at fifteen as well, but then, when they get to sixteen, all of a sudden something happens.

On the way out of school that afternoon, she was with her little sister and some of her mates, heading home. I was with a few of my mates. I didn't actually invite her, as in single her out. We just stopped as we passed on the way out to the yard, just a group of boys talking to a group of girls, and I mentioned the party.

It was all kicking off later. Up by the bridge. The usual sort of stuff – booze, music, whatever. The whatever always got a cheer from the rest of the boys and knowing smiles from the girls. But not from her. Nia just stared back at me, a long, almost appraising look. And suddenly there it was, that pounding in my chest. That strange flush beginning deep inside.

Later, at the party itself, it was all I could do to concentrate on even the simplest conversation. My eyes kept scanning the new arrivals all the time. Then, just as I was sure she'd bailed out, that maybe that look wasn't what I thought it was, just a seventeen-year-old's hopeful imagination, she was standing in front of me, that same appraising stare on her face again.

I moved towards her, a couple of bottles in hand, necking mine as I made my approach, praying she wouldn't notice the slight shake in my hands. I didn't say anything, just held out the other bottle. She looked at it, then asked if I had anything stronger. Every other girl was well into their fifth or sixth bottle of that cheap lager by then, but not Nia. She was different.

I turned to hunt out some vodka. I was sure I'd seen some, but then I stopped as a voice cut in from behind, telling us to try this.

We both stared at a boy who had just approached from across the bridge. He was about my age – maybe a little younger, maybe a little older. But he was a stranger, not from our school. Maybe he was from the one in the next town along the coast – those kinds of parties always attracted all sorts. In his hand were some pills.

I looked at them, then looked at Nia. I couldn't read the expression on her face. Was she up for this or not? I looked back at the boy with the pills, who was just standing there, challenging me almost. It was a challenge I didn't want to duck, but who was he and what were those pills, for fuck's sake?

Then, behind the boy, I saw him approach. Shambling, as he always did, as if apologising for his existence, the way he did in school too. A soft groan started from some of the girls as they caught sight of him, because Terry always had that effect on people. It didn't help that by way of some sort of strange compensation he always had a puppy-dog desire to please, which was even more of a turn off.

I looked at the boy with the pills, then at Nia again. She'd seen Terry by now too, and it was as if she could read my mind, because now she gave me a small smile and I smiled back. No words needed. Making me even more sure there really was that connection I'd sensed back in school.

I turned back to Terry, beckoning him over, and he approached, a smile widening on his eager face all the while.

DI MCCARTHY – THE COP

I'M NOT PAID to speculate. In my world, I deal in facts. What can be established, what can be proven, both inside and outside a court. My job is simple, or it should be. Gather evidence, collate statement.

'So?'

Joel seats himself next to his tense, staring wife, the pair of them across the table opposite me.

'Has he seen sense? Is he dropping all this?'

He keeps his eyes fixed on me. Gee takes her usual place at my side. Right away I sense that something's changed, and I can't quite work out what. Joel just seems surer of himself, more confident. He looks totally convinced that his wife is about to be vindicated, which is much as Ethan's mum and dad looked just a few hours ago in this very station. Despite everything, despite all Ethan had told them, I could see on their faces the same total trust and faith I can see now on Joel's face too.

It's the single biggest puzzle in this whole thing. Everyone around the two main players in this case is so clear, so sure. And now I'm looking at Tanya much as I looked at Ethan that short time ago too, because trying to get a handle on the two people at the heart of it all is still proving almost impossible.

I don't look at Joel, just at Tanya. She looks just how she's appeared from the start of all this too. As if she's landed on some distant planet somehow and has no idea where she is.

Again, I don't bother with any sort of preamble.

'Do you know a Luka Miller, Mrs Adams?'

Tanya looks up at me, puzzled. By her side, Joel pauses too, equally puzzled. That question has obviously come from way out of left field for them both.

Tanya hesitates, then nods back.

'Yes, Luka's in Year 11.'

'Your class?'

'Not mine, no, but the same year as my class.'

I steal a quick glance across at Joel. I checked on him at the start of all this like I checked on everyone else. He employs quite a few people locally, and like most businessmen he's probably developed a knack of reading people. Sussing the way the wind is blowing. Maybe that's why he's growing wary now too. Or maybe it's something else.

'Luka called into this station with his mother half an hour ago to make a statement.'

Joel looks across at his wife, growing more puzzled by the moment.

'Luka told us that he'd also had a relationship with you, a relationship that began around three months ago and lasted approximately four to five weeks.'

Now, and much like in our very first interview, Tanya's eyes aren't leaving mine.

I look down at my notes.

'According to Luka, you told him you were ending it to protect him, that it was for his own good.'

I look back up at Tanya. Now she doesn't look lost on some distant planet – she looks as if she's been blasted into a totally alien universe where nothing makes sense.

'He now believes you finished your relationship with him to begin a new one with Ethan.'

Joel cuts in again, increasingly agitated.

'They're in this together. That slimy little shit's just backing up his mate.'

I look down at a file on my desk, pick up a photo and slide it across the table. It's another photo of Tanya, but this isn't in the school. There's no time stamp on this one either, which we're looking into. This is out in the hills, the bridge clearly visible in the background. She's naked once more. And this time she's smiling straight into the lens of the camera. Smiling at the unseen figure taking the picture.

For a moment no one speaks. Not myself, not Joel, not Tanya. By my side, I sense rather than see Gee's stunned reaction to all this too. She hasn't seen this photo before; she was out of the station when Luka and his mother came in, meaning this is the first time she's seen and heard all this, and she seems as poleaxed right now as the couple sitting opposite.

'Luka's mother found this on his phone. It's why she marched him in here in the first place.'

Joel's face twists again, his voice now a snarl.

'He's mocked it up, photo-shopped it, for fuck's sake. Jesus Christ, this is ridiculous.'

I nod back. It was the first thing that occurred to us too.

'I sent it straight on to our tech boys. If necessary, it'll be sent to a more specialist lab. But the early report I've received from them is that this image appears to be genuine.'

And suddenly it's like stepping back in time. All of a sudden, I see it, and Gee sees it too – I can feel it in the way her body tenses at the same time as mine.

Suddenly it isn't Tanya either of us are focusing on; we're both looking at Joel. And I'm seeing in Joel's eyes now what I saw in Nia's eyes back in her house.

For the first time, the very first time, as he glances sideways, almost involuntarily at his wife, there's just a tiny flicker, maybe even more than a tiny flicker, of doubt in his eyes too.

DEVIL'S BRIDGE

THEY CAN'T SEE A FACE, just that body rotating above them, impaled on that high branch. But they can see the neck is at a really strange angle to the rest of the body, clear evidence, if any more were needed, that he, or she, is dead.

They also know now where that first scream came from, and why it suddenly stopped like that. It had to be that poor soul falling, the scream cutting short as the body hit the tree. And it's been suspended there ever since.

No one moves. No one can. Everyone just stares upwards, almost holding their breath. Watching, waiting. Which is when another more intense gust of wind whips the figure around, and this time the branch loses its tenuous grip.

And as the horrified teens watch, the body falls from the tree to the ground.

For a moment they all just stare at it, now slumped on the floor a few metres away, still facing away from them. Leaves begin to cover and uncover the inert form as they dance backwards and forwards in the wind.

Swiftly, and for want of anything more constructive to do, the boy who dealt the blow looks round, checking his companions in case they missed someone. Had one of their party wandered off earlier, maybe decided to go home, then had that encounter with the figure up on the bridge?

Meanwhile, the girl who first screamed checks her phone but there's no signal.

There never is any up there and never has been – it's always been one of the attractions of the place. No one can reach them so there's never any risk of over-anxious parents gate-crashing the party by proxy with insistent phone calls demanding that their offspring return home.

The boy turns back to the body. So far as he can tell, everyone's still here. So, this isn't a friend – it's someone they don't know, and he doesn't know if this makes it better or worse. It means that they've become caught up in something that's not their business, only now it seems to be very much their business. The silent accusation that's the corpse before them is making that all too clear.

Then the boy, some sixth sense at work, looks behind, and a moment later wishes he hadn't.

Because the figure from the bridge, looking as large and as terrifying as before, is now down from the bridge and is heading straight for them.

PART THREE

When the Devil lies, he speaks his native language, for he is the father of lies.

John 8:44

BEX – THE WANNABE

THE RUMOUR MILL had gone into overdrive.

You couldn't keep anything quiet in that town anyway. The police station was on the main street, and there was only one door in and out, so even the geography didn't exactly lend itself to confidential assignations. The sight of Ethan and his mum heading in there, hurrying along to avoid any prying eyes, both looking tense and wracked, and then coming out a short time later looking anything but, was always going to fan the flames. But that didn't matter, because by that time everyone knew why they'd been in there anyway.

I don't know how the story broke. The police would probably have tried to keep it under wraps, but could Nia deny herself the satisfaction of an odd word in a stray ear? Or his dad? Or Ella? She was our dinner lady in school.

I didn't know Luka well. He wasn't in my class for starters, but even if he had been I doubt I would have been close to him. He was one of those boys you were aware of without ever really realising he was there. A loner, I suppose, but not in the way some boys are, the ones who have something about them that marks them out as different, so you take notice. He just seemed to merge into the background, someone you'd hardly look at if you passed him in the street or the corridor.

Of course, when the story broke everyone wanted to look at him, but there was no chance of that. He was very much being kept away from everyone then, the front door of his small links house, on a local new-build estate a few streets away from my own front door, resolutely closed to all callers.

It was weird, though – everyone agreed on that. If you'd had to put money on the kind of boys who would have been targeted in this way, then you'd have chosen two very different ones to Luka and Ethan.

All right, there were no Greek gods in that school but there were the jocks. Older kids, more confident, with more developed bodies; boys who could actually have some sort of conversation with you and who seemed to know what they were doing when it came to the opposite sex. Yes, I fancied Ethan, but I was his age back then. He was an unlikely choice of lover for a woman like Tanya. And if Ethan was, then Luka was even more so.

But if everything everyone said back then was true, then cases like these were never actually about sex anyway. They were all about the exercising of power over the lives of weaker souls. A different, but no less damaging form of rape, I suppose.

But it all led to one of the biggest questions of all in our small town. Had Luka opened the floodgates? Up to then it had been just Ethan that had come forward, and while it remained just Ethan the tide was always going to be against him. But two boys and a second photo made even the most diehard sceptic pause for thought. So, would another one now come forward, and then maybe more as well?

As we walked down those school corridors, everyone was looking at everyone else with the same unspoken question in their eyes. Girls looking at boys, boys looking at other boys. Who'd be the next name in the frame, the next boy to scurry along the main street towards the police station, frogmarched by another anxious parent? It was like the whole school, the whole town indeed, was holding its breath.

But I remember something else as well, and that was this hollow feeling inside as if I'd just been kicked in the guts. It was a feeling that hit me the very first moment I heard about Ethan and about what he'd done, or, more accurately, what Mrs Adams had done to him, and it hit me again when I heard about Luka. I had this sense of falling into some kind of bottomless pit. Every now and again I'd hit what I thought was the bottom and feel a momentary sense of relief that it was over, only to keep spinning down through space.

So, what was that?

Love?

I didn't know back then.

All I knew at the time was how I felt, but, as with so many things, I soon found out.

JOEL – THE HUSBAND

The knock sounds on the door at nine-thirty the next morning.

There's been no phone call, nothing to prepare us. But there's no need, apparently, because this is just a routine visit, or so she tells us. As if there's anything routine about a social worker calling round unannounced, the day after your wife's been accused of sleeping with a second fifteen-year-old boy.

The social worker's in her fifties and female. She asks to speak to Tanya alone. Actually, she insists on speaking to her alone and this time I don't protest. Then she wants to speak to me and to see Danny as well.

He hasn't been well these last couple of days – just a sniffle he can't seem to shift, nothing serious. But I still can't help worrying, and I know Tanya is too. Is he picking up on something? We've been trying to act normally around him, but it hasn't been easy. So, is this some sort of reaction, is he unconsciously trying to grab back the attention he must know has been elsewhere lately? We don't know, which is the story of our lives right now. We don't know anything anymore.

While the social worker's with Tanya in the next room I go on the net, trying to find out all I can about why she might be here, what we may now be facing, most particularly why she wants to see Danny, for fuck's sake.

Within moments, extracts from various sites float across the screen in front of me.

Within one working day of getting a report of concerns about child abuse, a local authority social worker should make a decision about what action is needed in respect of the wider family.

I scroll down, not wanting to read any more, but totally unable to stop myself.

Once an investigation has been carried out, the social worker may simply monitor the situation to offer on-going support, or they can call a child protection conference.

Now I really should just close it down.

A child protection conference?

I stretch out a finger, but still can't exit the screen. Like some sad masochist, or a junkie unable to keep away from a drug he knows will kill him, I keep on reading.

In the latter case they could apply to court for an emergency protection order to remove the child from where they are currently living and take the child into the care of social services.

And now I do finally turn it off, but the damage has been done, because my head's pounding and my heart's thumping. Tanya's still in with the social worker. I can hear their low voices on the other side of the door. Danny's in his buggy, just dropping off to sleep. I look at him for a moment, and, if my heart was thumping before, now it feels as if it might burst.

Even the thought of it. Someone taking away my precious little boy on the say-so of two evil little bastards with over-active imaginations.

That second photo is a fake. I know it is and it'll be revealed to be a fake once the proper tech boys examine it, not those Mickey Mouse small town tecchies who've looked at it so far.

I go to the door to get some much-needed air and move outside, keeping the door open behind me and making sure I keep Danny in sight all the time.

The problem being that other people are in sight now, too.

AL – THE DAD

I START the car to drop Kate off at work.

I'm still not going to work myself – it's that same old problem, working for a man whose whole world has been so spectacularly torpedoed by one of my own. Not that I'm saying that this is Ethan's fault, but it's not Joel's fault either. Whether we'll ever be able to square that particular circle only time will tell.

The route down to Kate's garage takes me past the yard. A couple of the lads see me passing. Some nod, but most turn away, not in hostility I don't think, but embarrassment probably. What are they supposed to do or say? I wouldn't have known, and I don't blame them not knowing either. If I'd seen one of them in similar circumstances, I'd probably have suddenly found something infinitely more pressing to attend to at the other end of the yard as well.

For my part I just do what I've done the past few mornings, drive past – or at least I intend to.

'Oh, Jesus.'

Kate sees it first. I glance through the window, then stare along with her as we see the van. There's usually three or four parked outside, the name of Joel's company stencilled along the side of each one. But there's something else daubed alongside on one of them too. Picked out in big, bold, red letters.

The first word is 'Sick'.

The second word is 'Paedo'.

There's other words too, but I don't see them. By that time, we're down the road, and short of turning round and heading back again I'm not going to see what they are.

But I don't need to. I've heard dark mutterings, and Kate has heard more at work as the town pronounces on the latest development in the scandal that's engulfed the place. Now it seems those dark mutterings have started to translate into dark deeds too.

I pull up at a set of traffic lights further down the street. Via the rear-view mirror, I can see Terry coming out from one of the huts at the far end of the yard, a bucket and sponge in hand. As I keep watching he throws the full bucket of water over the side of the van. Nothing happens for a moment, then the soaked paint starts to run down the bodywork, russet red streaks inching their way down to the road, making it look like the whole vehicle is bleeding.

Kate looks across at me and I can see the unspoken question in her eyes. How do I feel? Is this good? Am I gratified that at least some people in the town are starting to take Ethan's side, if the evidence of that vandalised van is anything to go by?

But I just feel like I've felt since the moment this whole thing started. Numb. Just like Joel's going to feel in all probability when he sees that van. Numb and powerless. As if we're both at the mercy of events totally beyond our control, steeling ourselves as best we can for whatever's going to happen next.

I drop Kate off at work a few moments later. We haven't spoken for the remainder of the journey. I should turn the van round and go home, but I don't.

I've something to do instead.

JOEL – THE HUSBAND

THE NEIGHBOURS ARE STILL CONGREGATING in clusters outside. They've done that since that very first night, the night of Nia's visit. And it's not just neighbours again – all sorts of visitors are still rocking up too. It's become something to be endured as well as ignored, and up to now I've managed to do both.

I haven't had to endure or ignore any similar treatment at work, as I haven't been in all that much, so I don't know if it's the same story there, although all logic tells me it probably is. There's only one topic of conversation in this town right now and that's very much my wife and what she may or may not have been getting up to with various pupils in her charge.

But today something's different. Maybe it's that second boy coming forward. Maybe it's emboldened people in some way. Because I sense it from the moment I step outside – something new in the air, a change in the atmosphere. Or maybe it's that social worker's car outside our front door. Maybe she's been recognised or something.

Whatever it is, those small knots of people seemed infused with a different spirit. As if this new development has suddenly given them some sort of permission to do and say anything they want.

It's only a few words I pick up, followed by a snorted explosion of laughter and eyes that are very much picking me out at the same time. I can't make out exactly what's being said, but that doesn't matter. I hear Tanya's name and that's enough. I can almost physically feel the waves of contempt and hostility wash over me as that laughter rolls up the street, and before I know what I'm doing, and definitely before I can fully register the door opening behind me and Tanya and the social worker emerging from inside, I'm striding down the small street to one man standing there who's laughing the longest and loudest of all.

No words are said. He doesn't get chance. I've moved way beyond that. I snake out a fist, and that single blow fells him to the pavement. I'm about to follow up with another when someone grabs me from behind and I wheel round to see a shocked Al standing there.

'Joel, for God's sake!'

Everyone's staring at me, hushed. For a moment I have no idea what to say. Then, suddenly, Tanya's in front of me too. For a moment longer we just stare at each other as the equally shocked social worker takes in what's so obviously just happened, and the owner of the mocking laugh, who's very definitely not laughing now, begins to stir on the ground.

Still staring at me, Tanya just tells me to get back inside, now.

I expect all sorts.

The biggest tongue-lashing I've ever had from her is the bare minimum, and there's been a few of those over the years. In school and out of it, Tanya can be the strictest disciplinarian when she wants to be, and when someone displeases her, she has no hesitation in letting them know. And laying out one of those lowlifes whose principal sport right now is to congregate outside our door was always going to send her into orbit irrespective of the provocation.

So, as she steers me back into the house, and Al and the social worker join the small knot of onlookers huddled around the bloke I've decked, I steel myself. Briefly, I wonder what the hell Al was doing there anyway, but there's no time to ponder that now. Because what happens next floors me, but in a totally different way to anything I was expecting.

'Do you trust me?'

I stare at her. What the hell's she talking about? Tanya doesn't say anything else, but her eyes don't leave mine for a single moment as she waits for an answer.

'Do you, Joel?'

I all but explode.

'Of course I fucking do!'

Tanya gestures outside towards the street.

'Then what was that all about?'

I carry on staring at her for a moment.

'Why let a total dickhead like that get under your skin?'

Tanya nods at me again.

'Unless he caught you on the hop? Touched a nerve? Put into words something you've been thinking yourself?'

I still don't speak.

'Because that's what every saddo out there is going to say when you do something like that – lash out like a complete idiot, at a man you hardly know, and I'm starting to wonder too.'

I pause, putting my hands up, Tanya's point finally beginning to get through.

'I trust you.'

'Don't tell me, Joel. Don't just say it. Look at me. Look into my eyes. I want to see it, I want to see it in your eyes. I want to see the answer – I don't want to just fucking hear it.'

For a moment there's silence. I've no idea what to do. I can't do anything aside from look back at her as her eyes almost drink me in. But she can see it. She has to. No matter how much I might have let myself down just now, there's absolutely no way that I have ever had the slightest doubt about her, which is also why I've never kept anything from her. I even told her my darkest, deepest secret about the bridge, for God's sake, and what happened up there all those years ago.

And Tanya must have seen that as I stare back at her, because after a moment or so she nods at me.

Which should have been enough. Irrespective of what's going to happen in the aftermath of that single blow out on that street – and even at this stage I know there has to be repercussions – the only thing that matters is Tanya and our family. I made a mistake just now, but I seem to have repaired it so far as she's concerned.

It's just a shame that before I really know what's happening, before I even really know what I'm doing, I've fucked up again.

NIA – THE MUM

ETHAN'S hardly been out of the house since the story broke. But now Luka's come forward, everything's changed.

How he's been up to now is hardly surprising, I suppose. Everywhere I go right now, eyes swivel my way, and I've found that hard enough. Al hasn't said much, but, from the little he has said, I know it's been the same for him. Even Ella's been swept up in it all. People either target her openly and ask her questions or try to steer an ever more tortuous conversation round to exactly the same set of questions. No wonder that, to a greater or lesser extent, we've all done a Greta Garbo these past few days.

I don't know what to expect when I suggest it. I wouldn't have suggested it at all if it hadn't been for Luka. But since he made his statement, some small semblance of normality has begun to descend on the house again. Last night, we even managed to have a meal together. Up to now I've been ferrying trays upstairs to Ethan's room, retrieving them largely untouched an hour or so later. We also caught up on the latest episodes of a box set I'd ordered, which, pre-Tanya – everything these days seemed to be pre- or post-Tanya – had become our nightly ritual. We used to have tea, then settle down to watch a couple of episodes. Last night we actually managed to do that again.

'Let's just grab a coffee somewhere.'

'We've got coffee in the house.'

I urge him along.

'A change of scene. A walk along the front. Check out what's on in the cinema.'

Ethan struggles, which is an advance in itself. If I'd even mooted the ghost of such a possibility before, it wouldn't have got to first base. But now he's considering it, at least. And the quick glance he shoots towards the front door as he does so tells me that not only is he considering it, but deep down he really needs this as well.

Ethan needs to walk out of that door, just as he's done a thousand times before. He needs to walk down the street, call in at a café, say hello to any passing friend. Just do some normal, everyday things for a change. All this, our post-Tanya life, hasn't gone on that long – just a couple of days - but it's long enough.

And there's something else here and we both know it. Because this isn't going to be just a simple, hopefully restorative, walk. This is going to be a statement, too. The fact that we both feel we can do this, that we can invite all those eyes to swivel our way, that we can run the gauntlet of what we both know is going to be all that open curiosity is going to tell our small corner of the world that we don't care how they look at us, that we don't care about the hushed exchanges we both know will dog our every step.

And we don't care, because Ethan isn't the guilty party here, as he's always said and as Luka's statement has just made crystal clear. He's an innocent caught up in something he hadn't understood, and innocents have no need to ever hide away.

I don't know what stage Ethan has reached in his own struggle to understand his feelings towards his teacher. I don't know whether he still feels that it was something genuine and real, or if he's beginning to suspect the truth we knew all along, that he's been used for reasons none of us can even begin to fathom. But all that's to come. For now, what matters is taking all this one step at a time, and the first step is persuading him to do what he obviously now wants to do and walk outside that front door and down the street.

Ethan, finally, nods and I try to keep my answering nod calm, even though inside I'm feeling anything but. I tell him to find Sami's lead – we'll take him too. As he turns away, with a small but definite spring in his step now, my heart dances.

Then Ethan reappears in the doorway.

'Not down to town.'

I stare at him.

'Let's go somewhere else.'

I nod, cautiously. People, cafés, streets, are obviously still too much for him, but getting out somewhere, anywhere, would still be something.

'Let's go up to the mountain. Up onto the bridge.'

I keep the same, fixed smile on my face. My brain tells my head to nod, and it does. But as Ethan heads away again, that fixed smile wipes.

Because I can't help it. Even now, after all these years, all anyone has to do is talk about it, all I have to do sometimes is just to look up and see it, and I'm back in the last place I want to be, back there again up on that bridge reliving all that happened.

Then comes the banging on the door.

DEVIL'S BRIDGE – TWENTY YEARS BEFORE

NIA

Terry was harmless enough, although no one I knew ever felt too easy around him. Partly that was because of where he lived, up on the mountain, well away from the town. His parents farmed an inhospitable smallholding on the other side of the bridge. It was remote, unapproachable, and by all accounts so were they, and he was their only child. Maybe it was inevitable he'd come across as isolated and strange.

Each day he'd walk across the devil's bridge and come down to the school. Each night he'd walk back along the bridge home. He made both journeys alone, which was how he remained most of the day as well. Alone, and friendless. A boy apart.

He'd try to join in with things, take part in whatever was going on, but it always seemed to go wrong for some reason. Everything he said just seemed to fall flat, and every attempt to reach out to some group or other fell flat too. Dark mutterings soon began to sound branding him a weirdo, which only made him try even harder, of course. So, when he appeared from the other side of the bridge that night, the night of the party, there was an almost audible groan. But not from Joel.

Nothing had happened between us up to then, and I was unsure if anything would. Yes, I'd caught him looking at me, and, yes, there'd been that invitation up to the bridge for the party, but I didn't know if I'd been one of a long line of girls he'd invited. Joel was never exactly short of female company. But since we'd got there, he'd definitely singled me out. It wasn't just the bottle he held out to me as I arrived, and didn't I put a lot of effort into looking as if I'd already moved way beyond bargain basement lager, when in truth I hadn't moved beyond anything at all. It was something else. Something in the way he smiled at me. Something that made me want to make him smile even more.

I don't know who the other boy was, the stranger who brought the pills. He didn't matter anyway; it was more what he'd brought with him we were interested in.

I stood by Joel's side, looking at those pills in his hand. I had no idea what they were but had no intention of asking. I also had no idea what they'd do and was already beginning to brick myself at the thought of finding out. I could sense Joel's hesitation too, but neither of us wanted to come across as a frightened kid.

Terry must have thought the tide was finally beginning to turn, that things were going his way at last. Usually, he'd just encounter a succession of turned backs and choked conversations.

But tonight, he stopped, surprised then delighted, as Joel held out the bottle of cheap lager I'd just declined, then one of the pills.

JOEL – THE HUSBAND

I DIDN'T REALISE what I was doing till I found myself outside Nia's door. Or maybe I just didn't want to admit even to myself what I was doing. Deep down, I knew it was totally stupid, but I could no more have not marched round there than stopped breathing, even if I didn't know what the hell it was supposed to achieve. And yes, I know that sounds totally mad, but that's probably because I was.

And looking back there's something else going on too, of course. Look at the world I live in – I do things, I make things happen. My whole life is spent achieving something tangible, even if it's only putting one brick on top of another. But for the last few days all I've been able to do is whirl around in circles, not able to do anything about the single biggest crisis that has ever hit my family.

And, yes, I admit there's an element of the caveman in all this too. Tanya's a modern woman, we're a modern family, and I wouldn't have it any other way, but I'm still the product of a small town, and maybe part of me still inhabits that small-town mentality. Somewhere deep down there's something in my make-up that needs to protect my wife.

Which is even more crazy. Tanya's the head of her department, and while she's never going to be able to buy any Caribbean islands on her salary, she still brings home more than her fair share each month. But I still want to take care of my wife and child, and maybe that blow I landed outside our house a short while ago has opened the floodgates, because what I'm scenting in my nostrils right now is blood lust and I want, more than anything, to spill some more. And no prizes for guessing who's in my sights.

'Joel?'

I can see it in Nia's eyes as she opens the door. She doesn't need to ask what the hell I'm doing there because she's done it herself. What's just propelled me through those few streets from my house to hers is the same impulse that propelled her on the reverse journey those few nights ago. Which means that maybe all this is nothing to do with my being a caveman. Maybe this is just about loving someone, and it doesn't actually matter if you're a six-foot-four-inch brick shithouse of a builder or a five-foot-two-inch slip of a woman. It can turn you into a raging bull irrespective of height, sex or weight.

'Ask him.'

Nia just stares back at me.

'Look in his eyes.'

Behind Nia I can see Ethan hovering in a doorway. No matter how lunatic his actions have been lately, at least he's having the good sense to stay where he is right now. He has a small dog at his feet and the dog looks the same – nothing could have dragged him to join Nia on that front doorstep right now either. Who said animals were dumb?

'Look in his eyes and make him swear to you, make him swear on your life, on Al's life, on that fucking dog's life if you have to, that what he's telling you is true. And don't listen to what he says – look at him, look in his eyes and then tell me you believe him.'

But Nia hits back immediately.

'What do you think I've been doing? I haven't been doing anything else.'

And now it's Nia's turn to move closer to me.

'He's telling the truth, Joel. He's telling the fucking truth.'

Which is when I do it too. I look deep into her eyes, just as Tanya looked into mine. And what do I see? It's like looking into a mirror. I see total honesty and I see total transparency. It's like looking straight into her soul, and I can see from the expression on her face that she feels exactly the same way as she looks back at me.

I believe her. I believe every word she's saying.

And she believes me. She believes every word I'm saying too.

I look beyond Nia towards Ethan in the doorway, or at least where Ethan was a moment or so ago. Only he's not there now. There's just the ghost of his presence somehow, still hanging there.

Then I turn to see the copper who first called in on us that night, DI McCarthy, pulling up by the kerbside.

MEGAN – THE HEADTEACHER

WE'RE CHECKING the CCTV recordings again, over and over.

All the advice we've received in the last day or so from various professionals tells the same story. Boys don't talk. If anything like this has happened to them either in the present or at some time in the past, it usually has to be dragged out of them. So, we can't just sit back and wait; we have to be proactive in uncovering any more possible abuse ourselves.

The truth is that at this stage we're into Brownie points. The school's already going to be facing a massive investigation. Anything we can do to demonstrate how co-operative we've been might just help in some way.

There's no camera covering the storeroom – Don's already told DI McCarthy that – but there are plenty covering the corridors and the classrooms. So, is there any incautious moment captured on camera we can find for either of the two boys who've come forward so far, and Tanya? Or anyone else?

It's the very last thing we want to find. But if there's more to be found we have to. This is like a cancer; we have to get to its root and cut it out it once and for all. At least then, in some way, although none of us can see quite how, we might just move on.

But so far there's been nothing. We're even spending funds

we don't have getting in some tech people to put a trace on any images of Tanya. Like some sort of sub-James Bond spook, she's being tracked through all the tapes on which she appears.

We see her walking from the staffroom to her classroom, pausing to talk to a dozen different people each time – other members of staff, pupils, supply teachers and teaching assistants, each encounter exactly like the last. Light, friendly, absolutely nothing untoward.

We watch her out in the school yard and out on the playing fields. Again, there are plenty of encounters to observe, but again there's absolutely nothing odd about any of them. And all this covert viewing is leaving me feeling grubby again, as if we're sad voyeurs, which I suppose, in a sense, we are.

The one thing it doesn't uncover is anything remotely grubby about Tanya. She seems to sail through her working days, and sometimes her working evenings as well when there's some sports event to supervise. She's the same woman everyone in the wider school community has always known. She's warm, friendly, supportive – the model teacher, in fact. If that is a mask, there isn't one occasion when we see it slip.

And we never once observe her alone with Ethan or with Luka, let alone having with either of them the sort of hushed conversation that might lift a lid on anything. It's one of the remaining puzzles in a total conundrum. Their paths simply never cross in all those hours of CCTV footage.

So, then we put the same trace on Ethan. The surveillance software we're using might seem state of the art to us, but it's always possible it hasn't tracked Tanya quite as efficiently as the tech guys promised. It's possible there are times when she might have slipped under the radar, so it makes sense to do the same sort of check here too. Follow Ethan and see if it leads us, however fleetingly, to Tanya.

Feeling more and more like detectives from old B movies, we track him as he arrives in school in the morning and leaves in the late afternoon. We watch him as he heads along corridors and walks into various classrooms. Is he betraying any uncharacteristic excitement? If all he's claiming is true, he'll soon be seeing again a new and very exotic lover, after all. So, will he hang back once the other pupils leave to go to their different classes to talk to Tanya alone? Will he spend more time than normal out on the playing fields? A quick check on the school logs revealed that Ethan never seemed to have much interest in team sports, so if he's suddenly started haunting those playing fields when Tanya was taking lacrosse or netball, that would be something.

But again, there's nothing. Sometimes he's a little early into his form classroom in the mornings, but not spectacularly or suspiciously so. Sometimes he's a little late in leaving, but there's never an occasion when he's actually the first into the classroom, nor is there a time when he's the last to leave, meaning there's no time he's alone with Tanya and the pair of them have that classroom to themselves. So, there's no point at which we can see what they're like with each other when there are no prying eyes or ears around.

But the fact we see nothing doesn't mean there is nothing, of course. If all Ethan is saying is true, then they'd both have been well aware of the CCTV cameras, and the last thing either of them would want to do was ring any alarm bells. Frustratingly, the absence of evidence doesn't mean there isn't any, and it doesn't invalidate the claims of either side. It just means we're being led down what seems to be yet another dead end.

So, then we try the same technique with Luka. We use the same software, employ the same tracking mechanism.

Which is when, all of a sudden, everything changes.

DI MCCARTHY – THE COP

MY GRANDFATHER on my dad's side had been a copper, so when I first joined the force there were lots of wry comments about apples and trees. My dad was a welder, and even though he probably made more than his old man ever did pounding his largely rural beat, he never really moved out of his shadow somehow. He always felt second best by comparison, so when I started my basic training, it was like some sort of circle had been squared. At last, someone in the family had, literally, picked up the baton.

Police work in my grandfather's time had been very different, of course. Most of it wasn't policing at all, in truth – he was effectively judge and jury. More often than not he'd administer a clip round the head to some light-fingered local, along with a stern admonishment to give back what he'd just lifted, and woe betide him if he was ever caught again. Disputes between neighbours were resolved in similar fashion. He'd sit both parties down and bang their heads together until reason dawned and a compromise was reached.

Which is what I'm doing right now. I've got Joel on one side of the desk, the wannabe joker who uttered the not-so-funny joke about his wife on the other. For his part, Joel looks tense, and no wonder. The last thing he or his family needs or wants right now is more trouble. His victim looks equally tense. He's been on the wrong end of Joel's temper once before today and his bruised face is telling us both that he has absolutely no wish to endure a repeat performance.

'So how are we going to do this?'

From out of the ether, I can almost see my old grandfather smiling down at me. Because that is just what he would have done. No formal charges or courts or fat cat briefs. Just three men in a room working out a deal.

'Because it seems to me we've got a choice here.'

I nod at Joel.

'Joel, you put your hands up and get a rap on the knuckles. It gets entered on your record. Or you don't just get a rap on the knuckles, this goes to trial, then the pair of you get dragged through the mud and the whole thing takes up months of your lives, not to mention the wholesale destruction of a couple of rain forests for all the newsprint that's going to be written by all the local hacks about it.'

I hunch closer to them.

'Or nothing happens. I tell one of you to watch your mouth in future. I tell the other one not to be the kind of knob who lets himself get wound up by a loud-mouthed prat. We write this whole thing off as one of life's more regrettable, and soon-to-be-forgotten, experiences.'

I nod at them both.

'So? What's it to be?'

And actually, I'm intrigued. I have absolutely no idea which way this is going to go. In a sense, it's all down to the idiot Joel attacked, I suppose. Which way will he go? Will he push this or not?

'I've got no problem with that.'

But it's Joel. He's the first to speak, the first to crack in a sense, which surprises me, I have to admit. Joel carries clout in this town. And by the look of the still-angry purple bruise on the face sitting opposite me, that's with a capital C. But Joel seems to be the first to want to make peace.

I nod at the man with the angry purple bruise.

'And you?'

An immediate nod comes back across the table. I hesitate a moment, then stand, this interview, if that's not too grandiose a word for it, at an end. A total flouting of all protocol and procedure, but a victory for common sense. Joel stands and follows me to the door, but the other party to this unofficial agreement holds back a little so he's keeping his distance. If I'd been him, I'd have done the same.

As I open the door, Tanya looks up at us up from the small waiting area where she's been sitting for the last half hour or so. Briefly, her eyes fix on Joel, and I can almost see him visibly wilting, and looking at her right now I don't blame him. He might pack a literal and metaphorical punch, but from the little I've seen of Tanya so far, she's no shrinking violet herself. She probably couldn't be, given her job. Maybe it was why she gravitated to Joel in the first place – maybe it's a case of like attracting like. Personally, I've never subscribed to the notion that opposites attract.

Because Tanya's clearly feisty and her partner is clearly the same. Why, in that case, she would even think of looking at the likes of Ethan or Luka when she's got a soul mate like that at home is beyond me. Unless I'm wrong about opposites attracting, of course. Unless deep down Joel isn't feisty at all, because he certainly caved in pretty quickly just now.

Joel nods at her, a silent signal exchanged and understood. Everything's good, he's OK to go. Tanya nods back, doesn't even look at me or the shifty character behind, who seems to be currently trying to set a world record for the longest time taken to travel three metres across an interview room floor to an open door.

They both turn and head for the entrance to the nick, which is where, as the door's opened by Joel and Tanya steps outside, she comes face to face with Ethan.

NIA – THE MUM

It's the first time we've seen each other since that face-off outside her house.

I know she's been seen in the town. The local grapevine buzzes every time and that always seems to find its way back to me somehow. Courtesy of the same local grapevine, I also know she's been up to the school, although she's not supposed to set foot anywhere near the place. Then again, simple things like rules don't seem to apply to the likes of Tanya Adams.

For a moment I'm tempted to just steer Ethan away. There's nothing new I can say to her, and definitely nothing my son should say. I don't even register for a moment that they've obviously just come out of the police station. But then Ethan turns to face her.

And suddenly, time stands still. For that moment the whole world shrinks down to two people, just Tanya and Ethan. At the same time the whole street seems to hush. It's like that moment in all those old Western films when two gunslingers face each other across a dusty street.

Joel puts his hand on Tanya's arm, maybe some silent signal not to do anything, just walk away. Or maybe it's a gesture of support – again, I don't know. All I do know is that, and without my even realising it, I've moved closer to Ethan too. And for that moment, which now seems to be stretching a hell of a lot longer than just one single moment, we wait for the shooting to start.

'Why are you doing this?'

Tanya should speak first by rights. She's the grown up, the one who's supposed to be the more calm and collected. But it's Ethan.

'Why are you saying all these things?'

But if Tanya is momentarily lost for words, it doesn't last long. Because she hits back, and she hits back hard.

'Ethan, what's happened to you?'

She leans forward, looking, even though I hate admitting it, like the caring and concerned teacher who was on view what seems now like a million lifetimes ago, at that parents' evening. For a moment I half-expect her to start talking about his essays again.

'I don't know how all this started, I don't know how long it's been going on in that head of yours, but that's where it is. You know that, and I know that – this isn't real Ethan, none of it.'

Ethan cuts across.

'What we did wasn't real?'

'We've never done anything.' Tanya's eyes suddenly flash in anger. 'The first I knew about any of this was when the police showed me that photo.'

I look at Joel, who looks back at me. He must want to step in every bit as much as I do, but he doesn't, and probably for much the same reason. This exchange should not be taking place. It's off-limits on almost every level. But it is taking place. It's happening, and before our eyes. And both of us, more than anything, want one party to this exchange to crumble, to put their hands up and roll over. So, I stare at Tanya, willing her to do that, while Joel stares at Ethan, willing him, no doubt, to do the same.

'You know what happened.'

Now it's Ethan's eyes that are flashing back at her, a sudden surge of anger taking over inside him too.

'You know what we did. You can't take that back, and why would you want to anyway after everything you said?'

And now I'm screaming inside. Ask her about Luka! But I don't, and he doesn't either. Maybe that's just all too raw for him. Ethan's built an instance of sordid abuse into something akin to Doctor Zhivago – he probably can't bear the thought that he's one of a now-lengthening line.

Tanya leans closer, her voice lower now, more desperate, more urgent.

'Please, Ethan, just tell the truth.'

But Ethan leans close in turn, his voice lower now as well, equally urgent.

'I am.'

Almost involuntarily Joel and I look at each other. I see it in his eyes at the same time as he sees it in mine.

All of a sudden, the two of us are a long way away.

A long way away and in a different time.

DEVIL'S BRIDGE – TWENTY YEARS BEFORE

JOEL

For the first time in his life, Terry was the sole focus of attention. For the first time he looked as if he belonged, and he almost seemed to grow before our eyes.

I'd never realised it before, but up to then he'd always stooped as he walked, almost as if he was trying to occupy the smallest possible space, apologising somehow just for being there. But now, when Terry started laughing, reassured schoolmates started laughing too. A couple of the boys even clapped him on the back. And, within moments, there was a small crowd around me and Nia, wanting some pills too. I still had a good few in my hand.

We had a quick whip round. The boy, the stranger who'd brought them, was waiting patiently some short distance away just up on the bridge. I paid for the pills, and he told me there were plenty more where they came from. I tried asking how we could find him, but he told me he'd find us. I looked at Terry, still in the very middle of a laughing, joking gang. Then I looked back towards the boy, the stranger, but he was gone.

I heard the weird gasp as I made my way back a moment later. Then I saw Nia staring down at her feet. I couldn't see what the problem was at first, as she was blocking my view.

Then, quickly, she moved to one side, and on the floor, fitting, a thin, white drool of spittle oozing from between his clenched lips, was Terry.

MEGAN – THE HEADTEACHER

We wouldn't normally have checked that particular tape.

Tanya had already been suspended, albeit unofficially for now. She wouldn't even have been in the school at the time that tape was running, meaning hers and Luka's paths couldn't cross, so there could be no words or looks exchanged, nothing we could freeze-frame, replay, examine. That tape should have been another dead end in an extended viewing that had already packed in more than its fair share of those already.

But then, just at the edge of the frame, I see it.

Luka has paused before heading out of the school. Another boy, obscured by Luka initially, is with him, and an animated, very animated, even angry exchange seems to be taking place. The CCTV can pick up words and images, but the boys are too far away for the former, although the latter are sharp enough. Then another gang of boys barges past and Luka has to step to one side.

The boy Luka was talking to grabs him by the shoulder and pushes him out of the gates. We still can't see who it is. But we watch him as he propels Luka along the street, pushing him all the while towards the entrance to a small complex of storage units, which is when we see who that other boy is.

Don and I exchange looks. As well as the school, he looks after the accounts of the owner of those units, and he's way ahead of me. Before I can say anything, he's taking out his mobile to contact him.

NIA – THE MUM

THE CALL COMES out of the blue and it's short and to the point. DI McCarthy wants to see Ethan.

I call Al to find out if he knows what this is all about, but only Kate's home. I leave a message for him to get down to the police station as soon as he can, struggling as I do so. The fact I need to leave a message with another woman for a man I still regard as my husband, actually, a man who still is my husband until the divorce is finalised, still feels wrong. Maybe it always will.

All the way down to the station I conduct an animated inquest with Ethan, although the animation is more on my side than his. As he has been all the way through this, a few brief moments aside, he still seems to be locked away somewhere inside. But a call like this means there has to be a development. Nothing has changed so far as Ethan's concerned, so if there has been any sort of development it has to have come from Tanya.

So, has she finally decided to come clean? Has the double whammy of Ethan's and Luka's accounts finally opened her eyes to the impossibility of maintaining what, up until now, has been her stonewall defence? It has to play better in any subsequent trial if she presents as a contrite woman seeking to atone for the error of her ways. Meaning that maybe, just maybe, this nightmare might finally be nearing its end.

Which doesn't mean the end of our trials, of course, because I haven't even dared to think what happens after this. We're definitely going to need specialist counsellors for Ethan to try and repair some of the damage she's done. Maybe the school will provide them. In my book it's the least they can do for harbouring an abuser among their staff.

DI McCarthy meets us in the reception area. He doesn't say a word as he leads us past the front desk and into the rear of the station. I tell the Duty Sergeant that Al will be arriving at any minute and he promises to send him through. Then we're led into a small interview room where Luka and his mother are waiting.

And now I'm feeling even more hopeful. Luka and Ethan are fellow victims here. Whatever development has taken place has to involve both boys, so it's only right that both boys and both sets of parents should hear it.

For a moment there's silence. Ethan and Luka glance towards each other. Then I become aware of Luka's mum looking not at Ethan, but at me. There's something in her eyes, and much like Ethan those few days ago, I can't work it out at first.

But then I do. She looks as if she hates me.

Still, no one speaks. I'm about to turn to McCarthy, who's standing to one side as if content to just watch whatever might happen next. What the hell is this, why have we been summoned down here and why is no one saying anything?

But I don't get chance to speak. Because then, before any of us can do anything to stop him, Ethan suddenly launches himself the couple of metres or so across the concrete tiled floor of that small interview room and attacks his friend.

AL – THE DAD

I ARRIVE TEN MINUTES LATER. Ethan's been taken into a different room by then. Gee's with him. Luka's been taken away by his mum.

There's been no real damage done, thank God. The whole thing seems to have been little more than a playground scuffle, and it's pretty unlikely any charges are going to be pressed. Apart from anything else, Luka is going to be in a fair amount of trouble right now, too. Not as much as Ethan admittedly, and there do seem to be mitigating circumstances, so far as he's concerned, which is putting it mildly. But the last thing on his mind right now will be plunging headlong into more of the same.

DI McCarthy shows us the CCTV footage that has been sent over from the school. The footage that provoked that attack on Luka by Ethan in the first place.

The cameras first pick them up just outside the school. Ethan must have been waiting for Luka as he left. Nia had no idea Ethan had even been out of the house at the time – so far as she was concerned, he'd been up in his room just as he had been on every other day since this whole thing started. Only he wasn't, of course. The images we're watching are ample evidence of that.

The exchange is hissed, intense, and caught not on the school CCTV but one a little further along the street. Ethan is doing almost all the talking. Luka tries to get away, but Ethan follows. What happens next is picked up by another CCTV camera, mounted at the back of a storage unit on a small industrial estate nearby. I recognise it straight away. Joel and I had put in the footings.

There isn't any sort of intense debate going on this time. Ethan is beating Luka up. We can't hear what's being said, but we can see that Ethan's yelling something at Luka. I watch for about two minutes, which is roughly one more minute than Nia manages. Then we walk back into the small anteroom a few moments later, where Ethan himself is still waiting.

DI McCarthy didn't say anything as we viewed the tape. Maybe he felt as if he didn't need to. Ethan doesn't look up, just keeps his eyes fixed on the desk in front of him. And despite all we've just seen, despite all the emotions and questions that are whirling away inside me right now, my heart breaks for my son.

Nia takes a seat next to him. For a moment she doesn't say or do anything either. Then she reaches out, put her hand over Ethan's.

McCarthy breaks in.

'Were you scared, Ethan, was that it?'

We both look up at the copper, but Ethan doesn't.

'Could you see the way it was going? No one believing you?'

Ethan struggles to lift his eyes from the floor.

'So, you thought, what if someone else said something too?'

Then, suddenly, Ethan looks up.

'Everything else I said...'

He looks at McCarthy before continuing.

'That's true.'

He pauses.

'Everything that happened, me and Tanya, I'm not lying about any of that. I don't know why she keeps saying I am. I don't understand.'

We all just sit there, waiting for a moment longer. Ethan keeps looking at the watching copper, but he doesn't say any more.

I just keep looking at him as his mum keeps holding his hand. Across the room, McCarthy stays silent. Gee does too.

All I can think is – this is the second one. First, there was the lie about that picture he said Tanya told him to take. Then it turns out she didn't know anything about it. Just as she'd said.

And now this. A second boy coming forward with exactly the same story as Ethan's, a story it seems Ethan forced him, beat him, into inventing.

Lie number two.

KATE – THE NEWBIE

Al doesn't speak for the rest of the night, just retreats deep inside into a place where I can't reach him.

He told me what happened when he first came home. The bare facts, as in Ethan seems to have persuaded his friend to make up his story. That was the word Al used anyway. Persuaded. After he let slip details of that violent-sounding assault it's not the word I would have chosen.

All I could think was, what kind of kid does that? The only answer I can come up with is a seriously deranged one. But, like so much these days, I keep that very much to myself. As to why Luka in particular should be targeted like that, it seems that he's something of a computer nerd. The police are working on the theory that if anyone could mock up a convincing-looking photo it's him. Ethan hasn't confirmed that one way or the other.

What the hell did he hope to achieve? More than anything right now, I want to talk that over with Al too, but again I daren't. Did Ethan start to hate Tanya, where before he believed he loved her? Did he now just want to destroy her because she wouldn't fall in line and support his sad little fantasy? I know Al is still clinging to the hope that he was simply panicked into doing something stupid, but all I can see is a teenage boy lashing out against the world. A damaged kid intent on causing as much damage as he can in turn.

And more and more the same fear's growing inside. We've been together for less than a few months, and everywhere we look right now there's the shadow of Ethan. Sometimes it's as if he's actually in the same room. What he's done, what he hasn't done, what he's said, hasn't said – every day there's some fresh crisis to deal with and it's having its inevitable effect. At a time in our relationship when we should be as close as can be, I feel Al and myself slowly drifting further and further apart as the weight of all those unspoken words presses down on us and the pressure of all those unaired exchanges becomes heavier all the time. Sometimes I think it would just be better to have those exchanges. Can anything we say be more corrosive than this silence?

And in the wake of that thought comes that other one, the same one I've had before. Al is round at Nia's even more now. Sometimes it's like he's actually living there. OK, he comes back to me at night, but every single waking thought on his part revolves around his old home, meaning even if he isn't actually in the house with his ex and his son, he might as well be.

And now there's all this with Luka. Ethan manipulated him. Terrorised him, even. He set in train a scam, a con, and he might have seen it through too if his friend had been made of the same stern stuff as himself. And I'm becoming more and more convinced that this is all part of a very different kind of scam, a very different game. A game that right now Ethan seems to be winning.

So, can anyone blame me?

I mean, really?

Compared to what Ethan's getting up to with his mum and dad right now, what I'm doing is pretty small-scale stuff.

It's just one little white lie, that's all.

MEGAN – THE HEADTEACHER

I CALL A GOVERNORS' meeting and Don chairs it. Among the nine other members on the school's governing body there isn't a single absentee.

I talked to McCarthy an hour or so ago. So far as any official investigation is concerned there are still two options.

Tanya is a manipulative abuser.

Ethan is a delusional fantasist.

So far as Tanya is concerned, nothing much has changed. She comes across in much the same way she's come across throughout.

So far as Ethan's concerned, it's a very different matter. He could still be telling the truth, of course, about the main matter anyway. He could still be what he claims to be, a boy who panicked and made a stupid mistake in trying to strengthen a genuine case. Having come clean about one lie he felt he had to do something to counterbalance it, making things ten times worse along the way. That makes him foolish, but not necessarily anything else.

Or he could be a manipulative kid, spinning ever more lurid stories and creating ever more mayhem for anyone unfortunate enough to be caught in his web of vicious untruths.

So, whose side is McCarthy on? It's a question I know he's being asked more and more, both inside the police station and outside, this case still being very much the only show in our town.

But he doesn't actually have to answer that question in any professional capacity now anyway, because as he's just made clear in our phone call, the whole thing has been taken out of his hands. In the light of the Luka development, the CPS has decided not to pursue any charges against Tanya. In their view, Ethan's lie regarding his friend has fatally compromised any chance of a conviction. They simply can't put a self-confessed liar in the dock when so much of this case rests on the word of one party against the other.

So that's it from a police point of view at least. End of story. But what about the school?

In one sense it's good news, even though we still need to carry out our investigation. The fact the CPS has dropped all charges means this isn't going to become the nightmare we all feared daily. A court case would have meant the rat pack descending in their hordes, but any reporter will now have to tread very carefully for fear of libelling one or other of the two parties involved. So, as I tell that uncharacteristically packed meeting of the school governors, the maelstrom in which we've all become enmeshed these last few days seems to have passed over.

The update over, Don and I go from the meeting back to my office. I open a drawer and take out a bottle of our traditional toast to good fortune, a single malt Penderyn. I splash generous measures into two glasses and put them on the desk, but I don't pick mine up. Neither does Don. He's quite obviously struggling with all this every bit as much as I am.

'It's no resolution at all, is it?'

'It is for the school.'

'I'm talking about Ethan and Tanya.'

I look at the amber liquid in my glass, the light from the desk lamp giving it a warm, mellow glow, which is about the only thing that does feel warm and mellow in this office right now.

'This must be the definition of purgatory. Can you imagine Ethan just walking back into his classroom and getting on with his lessons? Even if he's strong enough to do that, to face everyone down, imagine the rest of his class? No one's going to let this go for months.'

But it isn't just Ethan, of course. I pick up the glass and take a sip, but hardly taste it.

'The same goes for Tanya. Imagine her walking back into her old classroom, trying to pick up where she left off. Imagine what the kids are going to be like the minute they see her.'

Don hesitates.

'Meaning that Tanya's career is wrecked, and Ethan's school career destroyed anyway?'

It isn't really a question. It's a simple statement of fact. And I still have no idea, so far as Tanya and Ethan are concerned, what the hell is going to happen next.

JOEL – THE HUSBAND

No man's land.

It's all I keep thinking on the way back from the police station where we were summoned to hear the news about the CPS dropping the case. Yes, there's now going to be no court case to face. No, Tanya's school record will not show any black marks in respect of any unproven allegations. But we're so far from being out of the woods here, it's laughable. We're both still well and truly in limbo. That no man's land.

Everything Lucy said the first time she came to the house is swirling around inside my head, and if I'm turning all that over time and again, I know Tanya's doing exactly the same. It's obvious in the way we're not even talking about it.

And I do it again within minutes of returning home, as Tanya goes to relieve the babysitter and check on Danny. Why the hell I put myself through it, I've no idea, but I just can't seem to help myself. Moth to a flame – I go back on the net again, access all those sites I've accessed before, all those helplines, not that they've exactly been much help so far.

Once a student makes an accusation, it is highly unlikely that the teacher will ever be able to work at the school again. Even if they are found not to be guilty, the damage to their reputation and the school's reputation would be done and it would often be too difficult to have them back.

I keep staring at the screen.

Often, the teacher will be harassed on Facebook and other social media platforms. There are also likely to be Facebook groups and abusive WhatsApp groups created targeting the teacher, who often becomes isolated and scared to go out in the local community.

At one point Tanya comes in behind me to collect some food for Danny, but I just keep staring at that screen, although I do make sure it's facing away from her.

All this takes a huge toll on staff. Nearly all accused teachers lapse into depression. It takes a big toll on their family too, and if they have children themselves, they are often bullied and teased.

I keep staring. So, is this what we've now got to look forward to as well? Depression? Harassment? Children being bullied?

In other words, this has all been bad enough, but are we actually only at the start? Are the really bad times about to begin?

Which is when my mobile pulses with an incoming call.

NIA – THE MUM

Sometimes you really can have too much information.

I thought it was supposed to be empowering. The more you know, the better prepared you are; the more knowledge you have, the better able you are to plot a way forward; but if that's the theory it really isn't working.

I've checked the sites before. Advice lines and the like. There's so much stuff out there – all you have to do is google a few key phrases and out it rolls across the screen, case after case of teachers becoming inappropriately involved with their students, detail after detail of all that happened or was alleged to have happened between them.

But I'm searching for something specific now. Something that's only relevant to Ethan's case, because I'm terrified and I know Ethan is too. We haven't discussed this openly, but we don't need to. I can see it in his eyes. The CPS has dropped the case against Tanya, but what about the case against Ethan? Is he going to end up in court charged with making a false statement under oath or something? And even if the CPS decides it isn't going to prosecute, that doesn't mean Tanya or Joel aren't going to bring some sort of civil action against him.

I visited a legal help forum last night. Posing as a student needing research for a paper, I sketched out a scenario and asked for advice. As I logged back on there were three or four replies.

The first swam in front of my eyes.

A student stalking or taking photos of a teacher is an offence in itself, and the police might also investigate whether the student had been sharing the photo anywhere or using it to blackmail the teacher.

I click on the next reply.

If it was found that an accusation was deliberately false and that there had been collusion between two or more pupils, this would be treated extremely seriously as it is an attempt to pervert the course of justice. The student or students could potentially be cautioned or prosecuted.

At which point I decide I don't want to read any more. I turn off the computer and do some long, hard, uninterrupted and unaided thinking instead.

Ethan knows he's done wrong. And he doesn't have any defence apart from the fact that he panicked. Looking back, he can see how stupid that was, and he understands only too clearly the damage it's done.

The first lie can be written off as a bit of teenage bravado. The second is something that I still don't believe for a second cancels out all he's said. What happened between Ethan and his English teacher did actually happen – I'm still totally convinced of that.

The key issue now is that Ethan can't go back, and he can't move forward. His old school's still closed to him and may be for good, and it's difficult to imagine another school welcoming him with open arms. So, what can be done? What can anyone do to try and rescue something, anything, out of all this? I've got one card to play now, just one, and maybe it's not much of a card, but it's all I've got so it's got to be dealt.

I go outside. I don't use my mobile. For what I now have in

mind, I don't want to leave any sort of trace. I walk down the street to a nearby phone box instead, one of the few remaining in the town, passing various neighbours along the way, none of whom approach me or say a single word.

Then I close the door, pick up the handset and make a call.

JOEL – THE HUSBAND

I didn't even know she had my mobile number, although thinking it through, Al's been with me since I started the company – he was one of the first people I took on. Over the years I've probably taken quite a few messages on his behalf from Nia. Just routine stuff – Al's going to be in late today, Al's delayed on his way somewhere – messages I received and mentally wiped. But there's nothing routine about this call, and this message isn't going to be wiped.

I put my mobile away as Tanya comes in after settling Danny. He's wired again, meaning he's definitely picking up on the tension in the house. Kids, even kids Danny's age, aren't stupid. They can sense an atmosphere as well as the rest of us.

Tanya slumps in a chair and picks up a magazine, one of a dozen she's picked up lately then discarded. As she flicks, unseeing, through the pages, she asks me who was on the phone. For a moment I hesitate, but then I roll on quickly before she notices, and I lie to her.

I can't believe I'm doing it. The words are out of my mouth before I even realise I'm saying them. I tell her it's a work thing, an issue on site that needs sorting out, nothing serious, but if I don't do it tonight, they won't be able to make a start in the morning.

I don't think she even hears me. She nods in all the right places and makes all the right-sounding noises, but if I asked her to repeat what I've just said she would probably just look at me blankly, and no wonder. She does have other things on her mind right now, which makes me feel even worse that I've taken advantage of that to pull the wool over her eyes.

Nia hasn't asked me to keep our meeting a secret, but she hasn't needed to. All she said was she thinks it's time for the two of us to talk – no tricks, no agenda, no games. Just myself and herself to see if there's any way out of this unholy mess. So, while she hasn't specifically excluded Tanya from this strange-sounding summit, the message is clear enough. This is private. An attempt, away from the two people most intimately involved in all this, to see if we can do something about it all.

What we can do I have no idea, but there's a desperation in Nia's voice I understand only too well, because she's wallowing in as deep a morass as we are. Meaning this meeting could be a monumental waste of time, yet another dead end in a sorry tale that's already produced more than its fair share of those already. But if I don't go, I won't find out.

It doesn't help the strange sense of dislocation I'm feeling right now that another storm seems to be brewing outside. It's been threatening for hours, with all the tell-tale signs in place – leaves rustling, the wind picking up, the sky darkening. In truth it's no evening to be out and about.

But I still collect my keys and coat and head for the door, maybe because it affords me at least the illusion of activity, when all I've been doing for too long now is trailing along in the wake of events I've been powerless to influence or alter.

But no matter how hard I try to rationalise it as I walk out of the door, I'm still hiding things from my wife.

NIA – THE MUM

I've never been big on spy movies. All those moody shots of strange-looking men in hats and long coats staring into the distance. Mist swirling around a couple of other shadowy figures in the half-light in the background. Everyone looking as if they're either searching for someone or really should be somewhere else right now. So, it's all a bit ironic really, because here I am starring in the middle of my very own.

Or maybe I should make that co-starring. Because there are two of us and we're both looking as shifty and uncomfortable as the other.

A couple of intrepid dog walkers are out and about, but that's it as the weather's really not great. But we're at the far end of the gorge with the bridge above us. Not too many venture down this way, because it's so far off the beaten track. It's the kind of place kids might head for at the end of a night, well away from prying eyes, and I can hear a group of them right now messing about closer to the bridge itself. But here and now, it's just myself and Joel.

'So, what is all this?'

Which is a good question. It must be, because as Joel keeps looking at me, I don't really have an answer. Everything I said to him on the phone is true. I just want to meet. No tricks, no traps, no hidden microphones, or cameras, even if I knew where to get hold of them and how to use them. Back to that age-old aversion to spy movies again. Maybe I should have paid more attention to the TV on the few occasions an old John Le Carré flick washed before my eyes.

So, I know what this isn't. I just don't know what it is yet.

I take a deep breath.

'When you called round.'

Joel shifts uncomfortably, clearly as proud of that as I am of marching round to his house, door-stepping his wife and shouting the odds in front of all his neighbours.

'I'm not having a go. That isn't what this is all about, I promise.'

I struggle for a moment as Joel doesn't respond, just waits.

'I understand why you did it and I know I did the same. I couldn't help it and neither could you.'

I nod at him.

'Someone you love is in trouble. Same on my side.'

Joel hesitates, then nods back.

'And that someone I love is in even more trouble now. Maybe the same goes for you. Ethan's still in this right up to his neck and so is Tanya. Forget the rights and wrongs for a minute – that's the situation, we both know it, and right now we can't do a single thing about it.'

'But you do think there's something we can do? That's why you called?'

'Maybe.'

'Go on.'

I take a deep breath.

'Ethan wouldn't have said all that unless it was true.'

And now Joel starts to still as I continue.

'I know my son.'

He cuts in.

'And I know my wife.'

'Joel, please, I'm just asking you to keep an open mind on this for a minute.'

'An open mind?'

His face is mottling all the time.

'As in entertain, for one single minute, that my wife is some kind of abuser, is that seriously what you're saying?'

He rides on, doesn't even give me time to answer.

'You're not here to talk anything through at all, are you? You're here to get me to say Tanya's everything Ethan's saying she is.'

I look at Joel, already feeling helpless. He looks back at me, already looking the same.

Is it being here? In the shadow of the bridge like this? On a night much like that night, the wind picking up just like it did back then? I don't know, but suddenly, and from nowhere, out it comes.

'Have you ever thought?'

Joel looks at me, puzzled, as I stop.

'What?'

'That all this…?'

And now I'm really struggling.

'That it's some weird sort of payback?' I nod at him. 'Me and you?'

JOEL – THE HUSBAND

NIA'S SUGGESTED this meeting for one reason and reason only – that's clear enough by now.

She wants me to persuade Tanya to come clean. Which should make me angry, but actually it doesn't. Not as in white hot anger anyway. Because, and even though I haven't realised it till now, that's exactly what I'm doing too. I've agreed to meet her because I want Ethan to come clean too. To admit that all my wife is saying is right, that all this has been the twisted product of an immature imagination.

Looking at Nia right now it's like I'm standing outside my own body, seeing the two of us a few feet apart in the mist that's beginning to gather, another harbinger of that approaching storm. And I'm seeing the two of us as we both truly are right now too, bit-part players in a bigger drama but every bit as much as marooned in it as Ethan is on her side and Tanya is on mine, and we both already know we're going to remain that way for months, if not years, to come. But that doesn't mean I'm about to dance to her tune any more than she's about to dance to mine. I'm not about to budge a single inch on this and neither is she.

But then she says what she says, gives voice to what's become, over the years, the unsayable.

And I don't need her to say another word, because the minute she says it I know that I've been thinking exactly the same.

DEVIL'S BRIDGE – TWENTY YEARS BEFORE

NIA

SUDDENLY, Terry was back on his feet. Just as suddenly – that pill working through his system maybe - he started lashing out. The next thing I knew I was on the floor, my head ringing from one of the blows he was landing, my dress ripped, my legs scratched from where I fell. Then Joel caught a stray punch full in the face.

I don't think he meant to retaliate. He was more protecting himself than anything else. But he lashed out too. A big fight developed, which was no fight at all in truth, not when it came to Joel and Terry. But Joel kept on even though Terry was putting up less and less of a defence. Then, suddenly, a last huge punch from Joel caught him, and Terry plunged over the side of the bridge.

For a moment we all just stared at each other. We couldn't hear a thing. Not a scream, not a yell, nothing. We hadn't even heard any impact, although later we'd discover that the soft moss below had cushioned his fall. Then I looked over the side and screamed. A moment later Joel, who suddenly seemed to recover his senses, was running like the wind back into the town to get help.

The paramedics were there in twenty minutes. One look at Terry told them all they needed to know. The deranged druggie and all that. Joel didn't enlighten them. Neither did I. Nor did anyone. The pills we gave him were never even mentioned and neither was the fight. The whole thing was just an accident, that's all.

Terry was never quite the same after that. The hospital believed there might have been some brain damage sustained along with his other injuries. He was certainly a lot meeker and milder from then on. Maybe that's why he never said a word about what really happened that night. And why, those few years later, he took up Joel's offer of a job and came to live in a small flat Joel also found for him down in the town. Maybe he thought Joel owed him.

I tried to never go back to the bridge, but that wasn't just because of Terry. I never told anyone, but just as we were all leaving that night, after the police had gone and the paramedics had taken Terry away, I saw him. Standing on the other side of the bridge – that boy who'd brought those pills. Which was when that old story floated before my eyes, about the stranger who'd return from time to time in different guises, each time dragging disaster in his wake.

I was about to call out, telling everyone else to look too, but by the time I turned back again he'd gone.

NIA – THE MUM

WORD FOR WORD, almost as if I'm reading it from some sort of invisible crib sheet, I repeat to Joel what Ethan first said to me and to Al.

I must have memorised it or something. Even though all he said seemed to wash over me at the time, I must have buried it deep inside, because it's all coming out again now.

Then I break off and appeal to Joel, who's just staring at me.

'That's what he said. That's what Ethan told me and Al. Detail after detail, places, times.'

I break off again.

'He even told us the make of phone she used to take those pictures of him, for God's sake.'

I spread my arms wider, appealing, but Joel's just standing there looking at me, still silent.

'He wasn't making all that up. He couldn't have been.'

For a moment, just a moment, there's something in his eyes. For that moment I think I might just have got through to him in some way, that there is some point to this crazy meeting after all, that I'm going to go back to my foolish, but not deceitful son and give him some small hope at least.

I lean forward, ever more energised.

Time to play that card now.

'And there's something else too. Something I've only just seen.'

I hunch even closer.

'All that with Luka.'

Slowly, Joel seems to come back to me as I press on.

'According to that copper, Ethan bullied Luka into making his statement.'

'Which he's admitted.'

'But look at him. Look at Ethan's face. He's in torment. Whatever was happening there, it wasn't one boy bulling another.'

Joel just stares at me, his eyes giving nothing away.

'I don't think Ethan was trying to persuade him to make a statement. I think he was beating him up because he was jealous, because he couldn't bear the thought that he was one of a string of young lovers.'

Joel's still not speaking. For a moment he almost looks as if he's not with me at all, and momentarily I curse myself for making that stupid crack about payback. Maybe he's not looking at me at all now, maybe he's looking back at our teenage selves that night instead, at what we did.

But I'm wrong. Because now Joel starts talking. And once he starts, he doesn't stop.

At which point that faint hope I've been clinging to inside vanishes.

JOEL – THE HUSBAND

I WIPE EVERYTHING ELSE. I focus on the one matter of the moment: those photos, the photos Ethan insisted Tanya had taken of him. One of the very first things he said in that initial statement to the police. The statement that kicked this whole thing off in the first place.

What Nia's saying about Ethan and how he looks on that tape, I don't even give the time of day. If she hadn't been so desperate, she probably wouldn't have constructed such a crazy theory anyway.

Because you could, maybe, explain all the other things away. You could, maybe, explain away his lie that Tanya knew about the photo he took. You could just about argue that it was the act of a besotted boy unable to understand why this new love of his life wouldn't permit him a memento of an event that had to be the most extraordinary of his life so far. You could just about understand his attack on his friend as the panicked act of a teenager desperate to shore up a story that was almost visibly disintegrating before his eyes.

But how the hell can you explain those missing photos? The photos he insisted Tanya had taken of him. Ethan still hasn't retracted that part of his story. He still insists those photos exist.

In which case, as I now point out, keeping my voice low, my tone reasonable, where the hell are they?

The police have been through Tanya's phone time and again, and her computer, both work and home. She has the use of an iPad in school, and that's been requisitioned too. Every electronic device she's so much as looked at in the last few months has been sent away to all sorts of state-of-the-art labs, who've performed all sorts of tricks trying to find any trace of anything that might have been deleted, and they've found absolutely nothing. It's inconceivable she could have taken the pictures that Ethan was alleging had been taken and then left absolutely no footprint at all.

All the time I keep my voice low and my tone reasonable, and it's starting to have its effect too. That's only too obvious in the way Nia's shoulders are beginning to sag, the worry lines around her eyes seeming to etch deeper all the time. It's the one part of Ethan's story she can't explain, because there is no explanation. It's a story that's been tested and found wanting, and despite that, Ethan's still insisting it's true.

And I keep talking. I kept hammering away at that one point like a prize fighter who's worked out the weakest point in his opponent and is now pounding away at it over and over without mercy.

But it doesn't do it. It doesn't even begin to stop the scream I can hear inside my head, a scream that's building all the time, because I can see in Nia's eyes that she isn't going to let this go. She's going to go down to the police station and rehearse with them this new and insane story of hers, get them to go over that tape again probably, maybe even try and get some lip-reading expert in to try and reconstruct what the two boys were actually saying.

And then what? Is this whole thing going to blow up all over again?

AL – THE DAD

NIA PHONES and I take the call outside. She's in a state, really raving – the worst she's been for a long time. It's going to take a while to try and calm her down too, I know that from the off, and I don't want a hovering Kate listening in while I try. I know she finds this sort of contact difficult, and I don't want to cause her any unnecessary angst.

Out of the barrage pouring from the other end of the phone, I try piecing the story together. Something about Joel and a meeting and that CCTV footage with Ethan and Luka. We've been given copies of it by the police, but I haven't looked at it since. Why would I want to watch footage of my son beating up a mate? But Nia obviously has, and she wants me to watch it too – in fact she's insisting I do, something about how Ethan looks and how we have to try and find out what exactly he was saying to Luka.

Which is when Kate appears at my shoulder, coat on, bag in hand, on her way to the shops. She moves past, the look she shoots my way as she gets into the car telling me she really does not appreciate me taking what looks like secret calls like this. Sometimes you just can't do right for doing right.

But then Nia goes off again on another rant and I tell her, OK, OK, give me a minute, I'll go and load that tape onto our ancient laptop.

JOEL – THE HUSBAND

I've got to find Tanya, tell her what's happened. Yes, that means telling her about my meeting Nia, but that's very much a minor issue right now. The much more major concern is what Nia may do next. The aftermath of the whole Ethan saga is proving bad enough, but we both thought the police interest in all this was finished, at least.

But she's not home right now. She's left a note to say she's gone out on another of her runs and has dropped Danny with the childminder. She's doing that more and more these days, going on longer and longer runs, and the reason's simple enough. Running's always been her way of blocking everything out, encasing herself in some sort of protective cocoon, I suppose.

I drive the van from home towards the childminders' house, but I don't get there. Because suddenly I see her.

I stand on the brakes, staring at the familiar figure running just a few hundred metres ahead. I'm about to call out, but then I stop again as I see her suddenly take a left, meaning she's not about to do what I expected her to do – take a right at the end of the street and head back towards home. Taking that left fork instead means she's heading up towards the bridge.

And equally suddenly this chill feeling hits me. I can't help it

– it's not just what happened with Terry all those years ago, it's something almost imbued in everyone in the town from birth. That unshakeable conviction that something bad will always happen up there, that it's somehow ordained.

And now, and equally impossible to shake, a new fear grips me too. Has this all become too much all of a sudden? Is Tanya going up there not to continue a simple, if now extended, regular run but for a much more sinister reason?

Which is ridiculous, I know. Tanya's simply not the type. But the sort of pressure she's been facing could send the hardiest soul under, so I get out of the van quickly and follow her along the rough track.

AL – THE DAD

I'VE JUST TURNED on the laptop and loaded the USB stick into the port when I see an icon at the side of the screen. I click on it to close it down, but all that does is bring up the last file that's been opened, the file Kate must have been working on.

I assume it's work stuff at the start. She often brings home files from the garage to work on them in the evening, get a head start for the next day. But this is nothing to do with work. These are poison pen letters we've been receiving, all grouped in that file together.

I stare at them stupidly for a moment. Why would Kate have scanned and loaded them into a file like that? It makes no sense. Then I see that some of them look more like working drafts than the finished notes we've received.

Which is when I realise she hasn't scanned them and she hasn't loaded them. She's written them.

JOEL – THE HUSBAND

I GET to the bridge just a minute or so after Tanya. For a moment I think she's going to keep running, disappear into the mountains on the other side, but then she stops.

For a moment she just stands there. For some reason I stop too. I don't know why – it's as if I'm taking my cue from her somehow.

Then she crosses to the very middle of the bridge and approaches the parapet.

I spring forward, all my nameless and formerly baseless fears now not so nameless and very much not so baseless, ready to wrestle her back if need be.

But then I stop again.

Because Ethan now approaches from the other side.

DEVIL'S BRIDGE

THE FIGURE'S getting closer all the time.

None of the teens is moving. None of them can. The only route away from the advancing figure is past the dead body on the path, and none of them can even contemplate moving towards that.

Besides, there's something about the metronome-like progress of the approaching figure that seems to be draining them of the ability to do anything.

But then the boy who dealt the blow tenses. Because he's starting to pick out more of the approaching figure's features, and suddenly he realises he knows him.

He knows exactly who it is who's drawing ever closer all the while.

JOEL – THE HUSBAND

I CAN'T MOVE. I can't even make a sound. All I can hear is the sound of blood roaring in my ears.

But then slowly, dimly, as if it's coming from the other side of the world – and maybe it is, because the voice I'm hearing now belongs in no world I know – I hear faint snatches of an exchange that can't be taking place.

It's Tanya's voice, but it isn't Tanya. Because she can't be standing there, just inches away from Ethan.

And now Ethan says something. I can't make it out, but the tone's unmistakable. He's sorry, contrite. Moonlight, stealing out from behind a cloud, illuminates his face for a moment, and I step back into the shadows. Has that brief shaft of moonlight illuminated me as well, the watcher as well as the watched?

But Tanya just continues talking, and now I catch something about that photo, the one on Ethan's phone, and then I catch something else. My ears straining, I hear her telling him how stupid that was, and can he see that now?

And suddenly I turn away. Suddenly I can't do what I know I should do – approach, confront them.

Then I just catch Ethan again.

'Joel's here.'

Did I actually hear that? I can't, again, be sure. I can't even be sure I'm not hallucinating all this in some way.

Then I catch Tanya's response, and once again I don't know if I can trust the evidence of my ears, or maybe I just don't want to.

'I know.'

DEVIL'S BRIDGE

HE'S DRAWING CLOSER ALL the while, and now everyone knows who he is.

It's not just the vans emblazoned with his name that power up and down virtually every street of their home town most days and sometimes well into the evenings. It isn't just the building sites that also boast his name on large hoardings advertising some new development or other. They would have by-passed most in that loose group of teens. How they all know him is down to something else.

It's that story. The biggest scandal ever to hit their small town, at least in living memory. Not that anyone still knows the full facts, which is what's given the whole thing its ultimate appeal. It's still unresolved, unfinished business. And so it remains of eternal fascination.

The boy and his friends watch as the large local builder looks beyond them towards the stricken figure, twisted on the ground behind them. He hardly even seems to realise they're there. And his eyes look empty, as if they've had all the life drained out of them.

Just as he must have robbed that figure, lying just a few metres away, of all life too.

BEX – THE WANNABE

THE TOWN IS JUST as I remembered it, which isn't the same as saying nothing has changed.

On the surface, it's still pretty much the same and probably always will be. The main shopping centre is still grouped around the same ramshackle collection of winding streets. The ever-present soundtrack of gulls out in the bay still underscores every conversation. The same faces, or, at least the same sort of faces, still patrol the same streets at roughly the same time every day – the early morning road sweepers, the fishermen returning from an overnight trip out on the water before haunting the greasy spoon that's served heart attacks on a plate for as long as anyone in the town can remember and will most likely continue to do so long after most people I'm walking among right now have lost all capacity to remember or forget.

In among them I glimpse a few familiar faces – old school friends dimly recollected who, from the fleeting look on their faces as we pass, might dimly recall me too. Or not. Maybe they just register a strange looking twenty-something woman shooting them a quizzical glance as they pass on the street and wonder who she might be, trying to put a name to a face that hadn't meant too much to them even when they did know me, and which must mean even less now.

I don't see any of the old teachers, or, at least none that I recognise.

Quite a lot of them left in the wake of the whole Ethan and Tanya saga anyway. Up to then the school had done pretty well in a middling sort of way, but that whole episode soured things for a lot of them. The moment any of the staff mentioned to other teachers in other schools in other areas, or to prospective employers, exactly where they were teaching, the questions started, and a lot of them quickly tired of the notoriety by association. Some probably also feared being tarred by whatever brush had inked out the relative former rural innocence of the place. Suddenly, from a solid if unspectacular place of learning, our former school wasn't a place to boast about when its name appeared on a CV.

Quite a lot of the pupils found that, too, when they applied to colleges or went looking for jobs. The minute prospective interviewers saw the name on the application form before them, a look crept over their faces and the same questions started all over again.

People just can't help being curious, I suppose. What had we seen, what had we heard? Few believed that anyone in that school could have been unaware what was happening. Someone must have seen something – they had to have done. And there were only so many times teachers and pupils could tell the truth and expect to be believed. And so, inevitably, many of them simply washed their hands of the place.

I climb up the steep hill that leads to the actual school itself, but that isn't where I'm heading right now. The local hospital squats on the very top of that hill too. Rumour had it the building used to be the town's mental asylum after performing an equally heart-warming role as the local workhouse. Money was spent on it over the years to try and make it more appealing, but, in truth, what was the point? Who was ever going to wake up counting their blessings that they were going into hospital that day? I'll bet Ethan never did.

From the dwindling number of reports I've read, he's still there and is expected to remain there for some time to come. The initial danger to his life has passed, but that's a very different thing to his being out of any danger at all. The threat is still all too real. Whether that's because of the injuries he's sustained or the fact that deep down he just seems to have given up, those same reports don't say, which is one of the reasons I've made this trip. To see if I can find out.

There's precious little security I can see as I turn in through the main entrance and follow the signs to Ethan's ward. But then again, Ethan's biggest enemy, as recent events have proved all too clearly, is himself. Who else is the hospital supposed to be protecting him from?

Then I see his mum.

She's just sitting along the corridor. Someone, I don't see who it is at first, is handing her a coffee from the machine. Nia smiles quickly, cupping her fingers round the cardboard mug. She doesn't look down the corridor towards me, but, like a lot of the people in the town, I don't think she'd recognise me anyway. Time's moved on and she never really knew me that well anyway. Not as well as I wanted her to know me back then.

It was probably always a standing joke in the school, my hopeless pursuit of her son. I'd tried playing it cool, but it wouldn't have made any difference. I've always had that kind of face – it always gives me away. I wear my heart on my sleeve, as my old Gran used to say, and she was right. Mum and Dad just stayed silent whenever she said it. They had their own opinion of me, of course.

Then Nia's companion turns, and all of sudden I see it's Ella, her sister, our old dinner lady. I press back against the wall of the corridor, studying the notices pinned up there. They must have had some old pupils popping in over the last few days, some old friends of Ethan's, or at least I hoped they had. But for reasons of my own I very much don't want anyone from the family to see this one.

After a few moments, I risk a look back down the corridor. Ella's now nowhere to be seen, but Nia's still there, fingers cradling the coffee, something telling me it's destined to remain untouched. Then, suddenly, she looks my way.

Because the movement is so unexpected, I just freeze for a moment. For that instant our eyes connect, but there's no sudden spark of recognition on her part, no moment when the mists clear and comprehension dawns.

But something is there in those eyes.

I was never sure about instinct or intuition. The sudden sense that springs from nothing you can see or hear or even describe. That sudden knowledge that you're in the presence of someone who holds some sort of key to something.

But that's what I see in Nia's eyes as she stares down that over-lit corridor towards me. She seems to know that I can help her. That it's in my gift somehow to lift a burden from her shoulders, and that scares me. It scares me more than I want to admit, and suddenly I want to get the hell away from here, but I can't. I just don't have the strength or the will or the capacity – I don't know which – to break that stare and come out from under that spell. I just stand there, rooted, as Nia keeps staring at me for a moment longer.

But then her eyes dip. Whatever it is she's sensed as she looks at me must have been only a fleeting sensation. She looks down instead at the still-untouched coffee in the cardboard cup in her fingers, and I'm finally able to turn, the spell now broken, retrace my steps along the corridor and go and do what I should have done at the start of all this, before this ill-advised detour to a hospital to visit a boy I was never actually going to see anyway.

It's time to go and see Joel.

AL – THE DAD

I DON'T KNOW what the hell to do.

I just keep staring at that file, those letters. Until I hear our car returning half an hour so later.

Kate walks back in. The letters are still open on the laptop, and she goes quiet, very quiet, when she sees them.

But then it all comes out even before I really get chance to ask her anything – all her pent-up frustration about Ethan, her fears as to the game he might be playing, the web that she felt he was weaving, the trap we were all falling into.

None of it makes much sense to me. And none of it even begins to explain why she should be sending poison pen letters to herself, but the way she explains it, or tries to explain it, it was her way of trying to hit back. Create some sort of siege mentality, I suppose. The two of us against the world. Her way of trying to keep us together when my first-born son was trying, in her head anyway, to force us apart.

It sounds crazy, and what makes it even more insane is that it didn't even begin with the whole Ethan and Tanya story, apparently. It began before that, when she'd catch him looking at her, when she saw something in his eyes.

I don't know what to say.

I still don't.

JOEL – THE HUSBAND

It's like going back in time. All I have to do is open the door, see her standing there on the doorstep and everything floods back.

While she was living here, she didn't really register. She was just one of many local kids – nothing to single her out from the crowd, just another of Ethan's schoolmates. That changed, of course. And the reality is I'm not really seeing her right now as she stands before me, I'm seeing someone else. And by the knowing look on her face, she knows exactly who that is. I don't need to say a word and neither does she – it's just something that passes between us, a common recognition of a shared experience that's still reaching down through time. And as she and I know only too well, continues to consume the major characters in that years-old drama who are still trying to deal with it all.

I glance behind her, can't help myself, towards the bridge, high up on the mountain in the distance.

Or, in Ethan's case, so it seems, not dealing with it at all.

I look back at her, still just standing there, still just looking at me. The house is much as it would have been back then, and the street is much the same too. Some of the neighbours have left, some new ones arrived. A couple of trees have been planted, some fences painted, the usual day-to-day changes you'd expect to see anywhere. But something has changed, of course, and we both know it.

In a sense we should never again be facing each other at all. That was always the understanding, so why the hell is the adult Bex back now? But that's only a fleeting thought and it's soon superseded by all those pictures, banished, but not, flashing before my eyes. Exchanges consigned to memory as much to protect myself as anyone else, now being re-created once more.

And all that happens in an instant. The moment I open the door, and everything comes back in such an onslaught it feels as if it might actually knock me to the floor, because suddenly there I am.

That evening.

The evening I returned from the bridge.

The evening that changed everything.

The house looks like it's been hit by some kind of whirlwind. The contents of every cupboard, every drawer, upended onto the floor, files and papers everywhere.

Up in the bedroom, our bedroom, it's the same story, only this time it's piles of clothes that are scattered all over the place. Even Danny's bedroom is a scene of devastation. If we'd come back to find the house in this sort of state, we'd have immediately been onto the local police to report a particularly aggressive break-in. Only nobody has broken in. All this is down to the householder, or at least one of the householders.

I haven't found what I'm searching for, though, and I look round the sitting room again, increasingly frustrated. Which is when I see it. Another small, almost invisible sprinkling of soot in the fireplace, probably caused by that one stray bird I'd already mentioned to Lucy, looking for a place to nest before deciding there's more hospitable places elsewhere.

Or is it?

I bend down to the fireplace and reach inside. We've been in the house just over three years, and in all that time I don't think the chimney has ever been swept. And when I bring my hand back out, surprise, surprise, it's filthy. But that's all there is. My soot-encrusted hand, nothing else at all. Certainly not what I've been looking for since that meeting with Nia by the bridge.

And seeing Tanya and Ethan up there that short time later.

Which is when the door opens behind me and Tanya herself walks in, just returned from the childminder's, pushing a sleeping Danny in his buggy.

For a moment she just stands in the doorway, looking round at the mess. Then, always the first to recover her wits, she turns to Danny, performing her trademark check on him, smoothing the blankets, making sure he's settled and securely tucked in, before wheeling him towards the kitchen, but suddenly I'm not looking at her. I'm looking at Danny.

Equally suddenly, images flash before my eyes of Tanya performing exactly the same ritual a thousand times before, those same checks on the sleeping Danny, even if she's only been away from him a few moments, making sure he's safe. I've never given it a second thought before, but I'm giving it that second thought now.

And almost before I know what I'm doing, before that half-formed thought inside my head has time to take full shape, I cross the room and bend down to Danny's buggy myself. Then I reach underneath him and bring out the phone that's been concealed there all the while.

I stare at it, unable to move for a moment, unable to even think. And for that moment I just want to throw it away. Not open it up, not look at it. And definitely not think about who might be on it and why Tanya might have hidden it away.

I keep staring at it. My phone isn't exactly state of the art, although it is packed full of gadgets and gizmos. Running my own business more or less demands it. But my phone's positively

Neanderthal compared to this one. This one is straight out of the box, totally cutting edge.

I look up at her. I still don't trust what I saw and heard up on the bridge between my wife and Ethan. I still can't believe I saw and heard any of it at all. Maybe that's why I've blocked it out, have plunged, displacement-style again, into a manic search for a phone Tanya can't possess despite Ethan identifying to his mum the type and make, a type and a make I know Tanya doesn't own.

But she does own it, and it's in my hand right now, and no wonder a fifteen-year-old kid noticed it – every boy and girl in the school would have lusted after a piece of kit like this.

Standing by the buggy, Tanya just keeps staring at me.

DEVIL'S BRIDGE

For a few more minutes he looks down at the figure on the ground.

Then the large local builder looks up at the teens, as if he's seeing them for the first time.

Then, finally, he speaks.

'Call the police.'

As one the loose group of teens look back at him.

'Now.'

JOEL – THE HUSBAND

TANYA'S still just staring at me. Not at the devastation all around us. Not even at the phone I've retrieved from Danny's buggy, which is now on the table. None of that seems to register at all.

And there's something in that stare I don't understand, but then suddenly I get it. She's annoyed, angry even. As if she can't believe I'd dare check up on her like this. She isn't remotely fearful as to what I've just found. She doesn't seem remotely concerned as to what I might say. She just seems seriously pissed-off that I appear to have overstepped some sort of boundary. This robs me of speech for a moment, but only a moment, as I gesture down at the phone.

'Tanya…?'

But she just cuts across.

'Hush.'

I stare at her again as she bends down to Danny. Unhurried, unconcerned still, so it seems, she loosens the blanket she's put on him, as carefully as ever so as not to wake him, before wheeling him gently on into the kitchen. If she's panicking inside, she gives absolutely no sign. It could be a totally ordinary day with a completely ordinary exchange taking place between us. And looking at her right now is like looking at a total stranger.

I glance back at the phone as she settles Danny, reeling ever more now. Whatever I might have expected, it wasn't this. However I expected her to react, it wasn't like this.

Tanya returns to the sitting room, almost but not quite closing the door behind her, leaving just a small opening so we'll hear and see Danny if he wakes up. Again, her movements are calm and precise.

'For fuck's sake—'

I stop, at a total loss what to say next. Tanya just keeps staring at me. I have absolutely no idea what's going on in her mind right now. Her face is alabaster.

'Say something, for Christ's sake.'

Even at this late stage, in what I now know is some sort of end game, I'm hoping for some kind of reprieve. For her to proffer some sort of explanation, to say something that will make some sort of sense of all this, even as I know there's nothing she can say, no explanation she can give that will even remotely make any sort of sense of it, or at least none that I want to hear.

And now too I know that was no hallucination. That was Tanya up on the bridge. Telling Ethan he was an idiot for defying her and taking that photo. As well as telling him what they now had to do, I have to assume. Just as I know that if I open up that phone, I'm going to find those photos, the pictures she swore she'd never taken, the pictures she insisted never existed. The pictures of Ethan she swore blind were a complete fantasy.

'So, it's true?'

Tanya just looks back at me, the same weird nothingness in her eyes. As if she's already slightly bored by all this.

'Everything he said?'

It's a redundant question of course – everything Ethan has said is obviously true, the very existence of that phone alone makes that clear enough. It's as damning as could be. Not that Tanya looks as if she's in the slightest danger of becoming damned. Again, and just as she was up on that bridge, which is something else I still simply can't get my head round right now, she seems in total control.

'You took him into that room and...?'

I stop, can't say it, all self-control and composure suddenly deserting me as I tail off.

For her part and moving in the same unhurried way all the time, Tanya turns back to the kitchen, makes a quick silent check on the still sleeping Danny, then she looks back at me.

'Now what?'

I keep staring at her. Because that's it. No explanation, no excuses. There's just a brisk, almost curt acceptance of a changed situation and then that one simple question. And if I thought Tanya had turned into a stranger before, that's nothing to how I'm feeling now.

And suddenly there's no more questions, none at all. Over the past hour or so, since I came down from the bridge, since I embarked on that crazed search, all I've had inside are a multitude of questions, one after the other, each pounding away until I thought my head would burst. Now it comes to it, to actually facing Tanya, they all seem to evaporate.

Why? Cowardice? Is that what happened up on the bridge too? Was that why I just turned, walked away like that? Was it all just too much? Or is it the sight of Danny still slumbering peacefully in his buggy, totally and completely unaware of all that's happening just a few metres away? Maybe some protective instinct is already kicking in. Or maybe I'm just already doing it. Maybe I'm already trying to find excuses for the inexcusable.

'If this gets out, we're finished.'

And for the first time there's the flicker of a reaction. For the first time something flashes behind those eyes. For the first time I seem to have surprised her.

I carry on.

'You are, yes, but so am I, so is Danny – we are all one hundred per cent fucked.'

Tanya keeps eyeing me, her tone wary.

'Go on.'

I take a deep, deep breath. Where's all this coming from? I genuinely have no idea. Was it percolating inside all the time I was walking back down that track? Or did it crystallise somehow the moment I found that phone? But all that's for later. For now, all that matters here isn't any sort of inquest, but what we do next.

'You've already seen the damage this has done. And nothing's happened. There haven't even been any charges. If the police see this...'

I tail off and gesture at the phone again before continuing.

'Find out what's on it.'

I stare towards the kitchen again, Danny stirring a little now.

'If Social Services get hold of it.'

For a moment, Tanya's eyes flicker again towards the partly open kitchen door and Danny. And for that moment, albeit all too briefly, she looks like the Tanya I know, the Tanya I married, the mother of our child. Only she isn't and maybe she never has been.

'It's not only you that'll be finished – it'll be all of us. Our lives here. Our family. What the hell will they do? What the hell will happen to Danny? They might think I was in on all this, for fuck's sake, and even if they don't, they might decide to take Danny away just to be on the safe side, I don't know.'

I break off, anguished, starting to rant now, and I know it. So I take another quick, deep breath, battling to get back under control.

'So, this is what we do.'

Even as I'm saying the words, I can hear that other voice in my head. What the fuck am I doing? I've only just stumbled across all this; I've only known about it for a matter of minutes and already I'm talking deals.

But this isn't just me and Tanya, is it? Not anymore, and maybe that's why I'm moving into survival mode. Because this is now for that little boy, not stirring any more, but sleeping again. So, I don't care how all this sounds, because we're playing for the highest of high stakes now.

'I'll keep quiet.'

I stop for a moment and nod at her.

'But you leave. Now. You pack a bag, and you leave the house. You walk out on me, on our marriage.'

Now my eyes flicker almost involuntarily towards the kitchen and the still-slumbering Danny. But that quick sideways glance, far from sabotaging me, sets a new sense of resolve coursing through my veins. One part of me envies my small son his unaware state. Another part of me is becoming ever more determined that it's exactly how he'll stay. Totally unaware. Totally unknowing as to the truth.

I look back at Tanya.

'You walk out on Danny.'

Her eyes remain fixed on mine, her stare level. Again, nothing, as in absolutely nothing, seems to be happening inside. No momentary flash of any emotion, even at the mention of our child. Like everything else, this seems to be all just washing over her.

'I'll tell everyone it was the pressure. All that has happened these last few weeks. You couldn't hack it anymore, the comments, the looks. The school had as good as said you were finished there anyway, so you decided you were finished so far as the rest of the town was concerned too. I tried to persuade you to stay but you weren't having it. You needed time away. Time to think. You told me you'd be in touch once you'd done all that, once you'd got your head straight.'

I nod at her and plough on.

'People'll understand. Who wouldn't? A month'll go by. Then another month. Then a few more. Then this'll become old news. And after a while people are going to stop asking me what's happening, they'll lose interest. You'll be what you should be.

History. By that time, Danny will have forgotten he even had a mum.'

'And if I don't?'

Finally, there's a response – bare, but a response, nonetheless. I ignore it and continue.

'I'll bring Danny up. I'll have lots of support, single dads always do, especially in a town like this. Especially with everything that's happened with you. Social Services'll be falling over themselves.'

But Tanya just repeats herself.

'If I don't?'

This time I stare back at her.

'I keep this.'

I nod at the phone, her second phone, the phone she affected never to possess.

'I'll make a copy of everything that's on it. I won't keep it or the copies here, I'll put them somewhere for safe keeping. Maybe in the bank, I don't know.'

Tanya keeps staring at me.

'If you don't agree to all this, or if you do and then you ever even try and make contact with either me or Danny again, I send this phone and everything on it straight to the police.'

'And when they ask you why you hadn't sent it before?'

'I'll tell them I only just found it.'

Inspiration strikes from some dark, subterranean place.

'I started doing some renovations on the house. Finally got round to my own place after years doing up other people's. That's when I found it, hidden away.'

I pause, the blood racing in my ears again. Where that has also just come from, I again have no idea. It's always been a standing joke that I was never that good at thinking on my feet, which only goes to show what you can do when your back's against the wall.

Tanya keeps looking at me. Then she glances once again behind me towards Danny, who's turning over now in his sleep. He's still at least an hour or so away from waking up. Plenty of time for Tanya to act on all I've just said to her. If she is going to act, that is.

For a moment I stare back at her, some silent battle taking place, but it's one that's already lost, and she knows it, I can see it in her eyes. For once, and I'm only just starting to realise how unusual this is in our relationship, I hold all the cards. I push my point home.

'I'm not doing it. I'm not having you taking us down with you.'

I pause for a moment.

'I'm thinking about our family, which is more than you've been thinking about.'

She doesn't even flinch. And if I intend that last crack, and maybe I do, as some sort of challenge, an attempt to get her to at least try and explain what the fuck this is all about, she doesn't rise to it either. Her eyes also don't flicker again to Danny. It's as if somewhere in that head of hers, a head that might as well be on some other planet, I'm that far away from understanding it right now, she's already computed the options, made her choices, and they don't include a family we've spent the last few years building, a home we've spent the same amount of time creating, a life I'd envisaged going on forever.

'I'll give you an hour to pack. I'll take Danny to the park. By the time we come back I want you gone.'

Which is when she cuts across again.

'That's not quite the full story, though.'

She nods at me.

'Is it, Joel?'

BEX – THE WANNABE

I THOUGHT he might need some sort of explanation. What the hell am I doing calling on him like this? But it's as if he knows from the very first moment he sees me just why I'm here.

Maybe he's always known more than we realised. Maybe he's even been keeping tabs on Tanya all these years. It wouldn't have been that difficult; she hasn't reinvented herself or gone to live on some tropical island somewhere. Why should she? So far as the rest of the world's concerned, hers is a totally ordinary story. She was married and now she isn't. The break-up was all down to some trouble at work. Not many people in Tanya's new life know too many details, and even if they did, it might not have excited too much in the way of comment. It was one of those crazy little interludes lots of people endure. A life gets knocked off course and then rights itself. Happens all the time.

So, Joel might well have been aware of all that's happened in her life lately. I can just picture him late at night in front of some computer, googling images of a former wife, picking her up every now and again in the usual places and via the usual means, a colleague's pictures of some evening out, Tanya tagged along with a whole lot of other colleagues, that sort of thing. And, of course, I'd have been in some of those pictures too. So, if

I'm right, if that's what he has been doing, it would explain why there's no puzzlement in his eyes now as he stares out at me.

But then I realise there's something else there too. Because it's fear I can now see as well. And that's what's telling me, more than anything he could ever actually say, that he's already well across the next step in what I suppose you'd have to call this ongoing tale. The rest of our small home town might think it all ended all those years ago, but of course it didn't. Tanya knew that. Joel knew that, and I know it too. What Ethan has just done, his fall from that bridge, either by accident or design, has made sure of it.

And that fear I can now see in his eyes tells me something else too. He hasn't changed. Joel might have always been a big man, physically, but underneath he's always been weak. No one who knows him would ever have suspected it, but when it comes to the really big challenges, Tanya was right. Give him a building site and some arsy builders and he'll mix it with the best of them. Give him anything more difficult and he folds. Shrinks inside. As he did all those years ago.

Which is so far so good. But the question now is, has anything changed? Has all that's happened to Ethan brokered any kind of shift? There's been precious little reason up to now for him to poke his head above any parapets, the toys I can see behind him dotted around the hall being ample testament to that. Plenty of people, Tanya included, have a lot to lose if he did, but Joel has a lot to lose too, and he knows it. And the more years that pass and the older Danny gets, the higher the stakes become.

But people can still surprise you. As the old saying has it, even worms have been known to turn. So, is Joel going to perform an about-turn too? Is this the time the edifice he's so carefully constructed over the years comes crashing down?

I keep looking at him as he stands there, staring back out at me.

The next few moments will tell.

JOEL – THE HUSBAND

I STARE BACK AT HER.

Not quite the full story?

What the hell does that mean?

But Tanya just keeps eyeing me, and now she almost looks amused.

'I know the way your mind works, Joel.'

She nods towards the front door, the street outside.

'Like I knew what was behind you laying out that idiot like that. I reckon that copper did as well.'

She nods at me.

'That wasn't about me. You didn't suddenly see red because he'd made some stupid crack about your wife.'

I keep staring at her. I genuinely do not have a single clue what she's talking about. Maybe I'm reverting to type. Not quite so quick on the uptake again.

'Yes, you want to protect Danny. No, you don't want all this coming out. But there's more to this than that, a lot more.'

She hunches closer.

'What about you, Joel? What would people start saying if it did? And even if they weren't saying it, you'd know they'd be thinking it. Everyone on this street, everyone in this town, all the boys you've got working for you, all the friends you still go out for a drink with.'

Tanya nods at me.

'You'll see it everywhere you look. Every conversation you have from now on, they'd be looking at you thinking, why would she do that? Why, when she had you at home, would she go for a fifteen-year-old?'

I cut in, desperate for an answer to that myself.

'And?'

But Tanya rides on as if this is a speech she's rehearsed many times before, and maybe it is. Maybe she's seen this coming for a long time.

'You'd burn with shame; you know it and I know it. It'd eat you up inside, and even if you managed to get over that you'd still have Danny to contend with. You'd still have all those same questions when he's growing up, those same looks, particularly when he gets to that age and starts looking round at his friends and then starts looking at you.'

I don't reply because I can't. Is it because I simply can't believe she can even think like this? Or because, deep down, I know that at least part of what she's saying is true?

'Saving your family? Saving you and Danny? Maybe. But you're saving face too – at least be honest and admit it.'

I hit back, or try to.

'And what about you? What about you being honest?'

I appeal to her again.

'Why, Tanya? For pity's sake, why?'

But she just looks at me, and if there is any pity in that soul, I can't see it right now. Once again, I can't see anything, just that same chilling blank stare.

'So, is it just him?'

She just keeps looking at me.

'Is it just Ethan? Or is it Luka too? Is that why the police can't work out how he mocked up that photo, because he didn't?'

She takes a step closer and instinctively I back away. Maybe

I'm already sensing something here I've never even suspected before. Evil, where previously I believed none existed.

'Take him out, Joel. While he's sleeping. Take Danny to the park, wherever.'

She nods at me.

'I won't be here when you get back.'

For another moment I just stare at her. She's about to walk out on her husband and her son. On a child she's carried inside her. On a life she worked so hard to bring into being. And it's as if she's going out to the shops. I don't understand.

But I understand something. As I keep staring at her, as I keep, despite everything, trying to find even a trace of the woman I married, the woman I love, I know that at least part of all she's saying right now is true.

Yes, I'm acting in my family's best interests, reprehensible as that might sound in terms of any sort of justice for the now-clearly wronged Ethan. I'm putting Danny above him, and for that I accept blame, but what parent wouldn't? In the end it's always going to be you and your child against the world.

But part of this is for me too. The idea that this might come out is simply too much to bear. It isn't just the fact I've misread someone who's been so close to me for so long, it's the humiliation.

So, I go to collect Danny from the kitchen, still sleeping in his buggy. I pick up my keys and I walk out of the house and my life with her, leaving all those questions unanswered.

And I know as I do so that Tanya will already be heading for the stairs to start packing without even a backward glance at myself, at Danny, or at the life she's leaving behind.

NIA – THE MUM

ETHAN HASN'T SPOKEN for the last half hour.

All we've done is walk. Around the park and past the small lake, before skirting the children's playground and back again. All in complete silence.

I had thought of telling him about Joel, about our talk up under the bridge, but what would be the point? Nothing came out of it in the end. Nothing will come of it despite all I said about that tape and the date on it, because deep down I know that's a busted flush too. If I did go to him with all that, McCarthy probably wouldn't even give me the time of day.

Joel will go back to however normal a life he can live right now and so will we. Tanya will get a job in some other school somewhere; it doesn't need to be too far away. Plenty of people commute out of Devil's Bridge in the morning, return at night.

As for Ethan, I don't know if these silent walks we've started to take together help or hinder. Are they giving him space, time to think, absorb, maybe even start making plans? Or are they just filling in the empty hours and the even emptier days?

Then, suddenly, out of nowhere, a memory flashes in front of my eyes. I've no idea why – maybe it's because we've just turned by the lake and the bridge is now in full view.

We went up there again, years later, me, Al and Ethan. Usually, I avoided it like the plague, but Ethan was at the age when he wanted to explore. He was going to the big school, as he called it, in a year or so's time, and playing up and around the bridge was like some sort of rite of passage for all the kids in the town, just like it had been for us. So, we all went up there one Sunday. I made a picnic, and we were going to make an afternoon of it.

Quite a few local families were doing the same that day, along with the usual sightseers and tourists. And someone else was up there too, someone I wouldn't have expected to see there either, given everything. Joel was standing at one end of the bridge talking to someone, but I couldn't make out who at first. Then he nodded across as he saw us, and I saw a young woman standing by his side.

I spread the picnic out on a patch of grass, then stole another glance back at them. They were walking across the bridge back towards the town. Al followed my look and, leaning close and keeping his voice low, told me it was Joel's new girlfriend, someone he'd met a few days before, apparently, and that she was starting at the school the following term, teaching English.

Then Al smiled, looking across at Ethan, now playing with a few friends a short distance away. She might even be teaching Ethan one day, he said.

I kept watching as Joel and his new companion continued across the bridge. I didn't even know her name back then, but that was my very first sight of Tanya. Up on the devil's bridge.

And the next morning was the first time I woke with those scratches and bruises on my legs and my shoes all muddied. The first time that strange sleepwalking started, and I woke in much the same state I'd been the morning after that party all those years ago. The morning after Joel had smashed Terry from the bridge.

I keep looking up at it, but then I realise Ethan's doing the same. I glance sideways at him, but he doesn't even seem to notice. He just keeps staring up at it.

BEX – THE WANNABE

It was just a chance meeting, years later. One of those moments when all of a sudden everything just falls into place.

I was living in London, had been for a couple of years. It was the usual story, or at least my usual story. Moving from job to job, flat to flat, relationship to relationship. Sometimes the flats were a house share; sometimes it was just a spare sofa. The jobs and the relationships were about as rootless and unsatisfying too.

I was trying to fool myself that I liked being in perpetual motion, not putting down any sort of roots, but deep down I knew the truth. It was aimless, pointless. If things had kept on like that, it probably wouldn't have been too long before I did what countless other émigrés from our small town had done before me. Spread my wings all too briefly, only to come crashing back down to the ground, at which point I'd have packed my bags and headed home. Picked up where I'd left off all those years before, lived out the rest of my life wondering why I'd never found whatever it was I'd left home to look for in the first place, even if I'd never quite known what that was. As well as confirming my parents' opinion of me at the same time. I'd have grown older and a little more bitter as the years passed and as I watched others set out to do what I'd done, only for most of them to reappear those few years later as well.

That day I was taking the tube from Bermondsey to Green Park. The Jubilee Line, no changes. It was a regular trip; I'd picked up some temp work in a solicitor's practice in St James. It was just low-level filling in for a woman who'd gone on maternity leave and who was due back in a couple of weeks. There'd been noises about making the post permanent, but I knew that was just to keep me turning up on time. The moment the new mum came back, flashing pictures of her new-born, was the moment the stand-in was going to be booted out of the door.

But that morning felt different somehow. Later, I put it down to some sort of premonition, which was nonsense of course. All logic told me it had to be just a chance encounter. But logic didn't come into it.

The tube doors opened, and I waited for the press of people to stream out before I followed. But then, before the last of them exited, she walked on. I knew who she was the moment I saw her. It hadn't been that many years, but even if it had been decades, I'd have known her anywhere. She carried herself in exactly the same way. She always seemed to almost glide through any space.

As she came up to me, she paused. Maybe it was because she registered my stare; maybe it was something else. Again, it hardly mattered. She looked at me looking at her, and that's when it happened. That's when I knew.

I'd hated her for so long. Ethan had become a stranger to me after all that had happened or not happened, and I blamed her for that. I blamed her for taking him away from me, even though we'd never actually been together in the first place. But in that moment, standing on that tube train, I suddenly realised what it was really all about.

I didn't hate her because she'd come between me and a boy I'd fancied all those years before.

I hadn't hated Tanya because she'd chosen Ethan.

I'd hated her because she hadn't chosen me.

And from the slow smile that started to spread across her face as she kept looking at me, it was obvious she knew exactly what I was thinking.

JOEL – THE HUSBAND

It's only the second time I've been here in all my time living in the town.

The first time was all those years ago on that late summer evening when I walked out of the house leaving Tanya to pack. I came to the park then too, pushing Danny ahead of me in his buggy. Maybe it's some default reflex or something, because now I've ended up here again.

That first time I came here I saw Nia and Ethan. They didn't see me; they were on the far side by a small lake the council had once earmarked for pleasure boats, before the inevitable cuts, and the equally inevitable health and safety regulations, put paid to it all, condemning it to become just a rank, moss-covered mess.

I turned away the moment I saw them, but for some reason kept them in sight. Why, I don't know.

Guilt?

Something else?

The pair of them were huddled together. I assumed Nia was telling him all about our meeting, her last throw of the dice, her final attempt to rescue something out of an even bigger mess than that foul-smelling patch of water. Which turned out to be just like that lake in the end, of course, just another doomed endeavour.

Only it wasn't, was it? It had actually unlocked everything in a way, only Nia didn't know that, and neither would Ethan. No one would ever know it, save for myself and Tanya. She may have set this whole thing in motion, and I still couldn't even begin to get my head round either the fact of that or the reasons behind it, but at least I'd made sure it had stopped with no one else any the wiser.

I remember that, as I watched, I saw Ethan lean forward and his mum put her arms around him, and instinctively, almost involuntarily, I looked down at the still-sleeping Danny, couldn't help myself. All I could think was, how would I feel? If I was Nia and Danny was Ethan?

What I was really asking was, how could I do this? How, as a parent myself, could I put Nia through all she was now going through? How, as a father, could I put Ethan through all that too? But it was precisely because I was a parent and a father, as I'd already realised back in the house. This was all about preserving everything we still had. Did I blight Danny's life, or continue to blight Ethan's? And that choice, once I put it in those terms, became no choice at all. Which was why I remained on the other side of that small apology for a lake, making no apology either, in actuality or even in my own mind, for not doing anything to relieve what I knew was going to be their crushing burden from now on.

But even as I turned away, I paused once more. As I made to wheel Danny out of the park, I slowed.

It was already blindingly obvious what the whole of the town was thinking. It was already crystal clear just what kind of future Ethan now faced – if he even stayed around, of course. Fingers would be pointed at him for the rest of his life, whispers would shadow his every movement, and not just among his former friends and contemporaries. This would reach down through generations.

As a story it wasn't exactly going to rival the fable of the young woman and her trick on the devil that had given our town its name, but it was still going to take its place among the more prominent of local tales. The story of how one crazy teen destroyed the life and career and marriage of a much-loved local teacher.

A salutary lesson to others perhaps not to tell tales.

Or an equally salutary lesson not to speak out when a genuine injustice had been done to them.

I remember struggling for a moment longer, looking down at Danny again. Then I looked back towards Nia and Ethan once more, but by then, and just in the last few moments, they'd gone. So, I walked home, pushing Danny, trying not to think about anything.

I came home to find Tanya had gone. I remember walking round the house for the next couple of hours, just moving in and out of every room. Then early the next morning I dropped Danny off with the childminder and went to the yard for pretty well the first time since the whole story had broken and began to get on with life without Tanya.

Now I'm standing by the lake again. It's much the same as it was back then. Still no pleasure boats and still no prospect of any. But this time there's no Nia and no Ethan, yet someone's here, I can sense it. I did when Bex was talking to me. Some instinct settled over me. I couldn't pin it down at first, but then I realised.

Tanya's back.

A shudder passes through me, and it's nothing to do with the sudden chill that's crept into the air as the rain that's been threatening all day begins to fall. I really should go home, but I don't. I stay as a brief shower hammers down, momentarily obscuring the bridge high above me in the distance.

I stand stock still like an animal sensing its prey, trying to work out where she might be.

And what I do.

NIA – THE MUM

THE CALL CAME THROUGH HALF an hour ago. Ethan's coming out of hospital at the weekend, which is good news. So why doesn't it feel like it?

I walk out into the garden, where everything's still. Too still. I look up towards the hospital on the hill, the school squatting in its shadow, the bridge towering over them both.

And I know why the call I've just taken isn't good news of course. Because Ethan's safe where he is. He's cocooned, cosseted. The doctors and nurses know where he is every minute of every day. All that ends the moment he takes his first step outside and comes home.

I can't keep those sort of tabs on him and he'd never let me. Within a couple of days, we'll be back to the same old routine. I leave for work in the morning praying that I find him safe, sound and at home when I get back at night.

What he was doing up on the bridge in the first place he's never said. The police think it was an accident; he'd been seen drinking in the town earlier in the day. And I might have accepted that, had it not been for that place, the bridge. Because everything always seems to come back to that, and yes, a lot of it's down to all that happened all those years ago, I know. I'm always going to have a blind spot so far as it's concerned.

But I can't help it. Joel and Terry, even my very first sight of Tanya, for God's sake. I've always tried as subtly as I can to tell Ethan to avoid it, to not go near, but he didn't avoid it, he did go near, and far too near that night. And I know he just fell, I know no one else was involved, but I still can't get out of my head the weird conviction that the bridge was responsible somehow.

That in some way it drew him up there.

And that once he's out of that hospital it'll draw him up there again.

BEX – THE WANNABE

I STAY around for another hour or so. Just long enough to call in at the hospital and make a final check on Ethan.

The gossip I overhear from a couple of the nurses in the canteen is reassuring. Everyone seems confident there'll be no ill effects, but as one of the nurses points out, they can't guarantee there won't be complications in the future. As she also observed in a cutting aside to another of the nurses, you can't guarantee anything with a character like that.

They know the story as well as anyone in the town. Look at all the trouble he caused just those few short years before. The devastation he wreaked on that poor teacher and her family. So far as that nurse is concerned, and her friend seems to agree wholeheartedly, this is just the latest in a long line of curses, mostly self-imposed, that have afflicted him and his family, and it probably won't be the last.

I see Nia again and I'm bolder this time. She arrived a few moments ago and now she's in her usual spot on the corridor outside Ethan's room. She's just doing what she was doing the first time, maintaining a silent vigil. Last time I froze as she looked my way, but this time I don't. Maybe I'm more emboldened after facing down Joel. Tanya always told me it was like a drug and she's right. Once you challenge yourself like that and come through the other side, all you're looking for is the next hit. It's what separates out people in the end. People like Tanya and people like Joel anyway.

I stop Nia in the corridor as she gets up to go to the vending machine. I ask an innocent sounding question, checking the way to some ward or other. She doesn't even bat an eyelid as she points the way down a corridor. Nothing in how I look, or my voice clearly gives her the slightest hint that she knows who I am. If there is any almost telepathic awareness of the kind I sensed before, there seems none now.

But that was all probably just in my imagination anyway. I'd been unaccountably nervous stepping back in time like this, but that's gone now too. Now all I can feel is a strange thrill. To be in such close proximity to her feels like tasting forbidden fruit. But all I really want to do now is finish what I've started and then get the hell out of here, go home. With the waiting Tanya, who texted me just an hour or so ago.

On the way out of the hospital I see Ethan's dad. He's being dropped off by his new squeeze. Not that she's that new a squeeze now, of course. In the back of the car and in a booster seat I see a kid. More local gossip picked up by the usual grapevine already told me they'd had a new addition to the family and that Al's working for himself again. I don't know if that's his choice or something forced on him by Joel. More probably it's one of those tacit accommodations, something that doesn't really need stating anyway. He's still fairly toxic, courtesy of his connection to the still-disgraced Ethan, but he's also cheap and competent, and so he just about picks up enough local work to scrape by.

But I'm wasting time now and I know it. I've already seen and heard enough. Nia and Al and Kate aren't really the matter of the moment. Even Ethan is irrelevant. That main matter of the moment is and always was Joel.

Will he crack? Will this be a tipping point? He didn't make

waves before, Tanya saw to that, but after what's just happened to Ethan, will the floodgates open? There was always that risk, as Tanya pointed out. But it's obvious by now that it isn't going to happen. Yes, the incident with Ethan must have twisted the knife in what's always going to be a painful wound, but it isn't going to change anything, particularly as Ethan himself has now recovered. Maybe if he hadn't, things might have been different, which is another reason for me to make that final check on him in the hospital. Maybe, if anything happens to him again in the future, I'll have to return once more to maintain another watching brief.

But for now, it's clear there's no need. Things will go on much as they have these last few years. Life in Devil's Bridge will go on too.

I look round the hospital one last time, see Nia and Al now in a concentrated huddle.

Then I stand and head away.

JOEL – THE HUSBAND

It's madness and I know it. But when I see her waiting by the front entrance to the hospital I don't hesitate, I swing the van alongside.

The moment she sees me, the same mocking half-smile appears on her face, the same smile I saw earlier that day as she stood on my doorstep. But that wipes the moment I sweep her off her feet and bundle her into the back.

The heavens open immediately. Is that a blessing or a curse? Is it a sign the gods are on my side, because with everyone scurrying for shelter right now no one actually sees me? Or are those heavens pouring curses down on me? I don't know, and by now I don't care.

Half an hour later we're up there. I've got Bex's phone, and I've already used it to text Tanya. A gang of kids is somewhere down in the gorge having some sort of party, but they won't bother us.

All those years ago the devil came to this very spot, so they say, to make his trade, to do his deal. Is that why I'm here now? Again, I don't know. But suddenly I tense, that same instinct at work again maybe. Which is when I look up to see Tanya, who's just set foot on the other side of the bridge. It's only a glimpse of her I catch as she stands there, illuminated briefly in the forked lightning, but she's unchanged, totally unchanged from the woman who walked out of my life all those years ago, and in a way that chills me even more.

I take a step towards her. Then, just as suddenly, Bex appears behind me. She must have freed herself from the back of the van somehow. She's advancing, hissing at me – what do I want, what is all this? – but I keep moving across the bridge towards Tanya, who just keeps standing there.

Then, and this is almost the next thing I know, I'm back down in the gorge. The kids I could hear earlier are all staring at me. And I'm doing what I did all those years before with Terry.

I'm telling them to call the police.

BEX – THE WANNABE

WHAT THE HELL'S he doing?

Have I got everything wrong, misread all those signs? Which means Tanya's got it wrong too; she was so sure he'd never break ranks. All this was supposed to be little more than just a precaution, but if that's true why the fuck am I locked up like this in the back of his stinking van?

I finally manage to kick the back door open and clamber out, but I'm drenched in seconds. The storm's really blowing in now. I can hardly see my hand in front of my face, but I keep pressing on in the blackness, moving more by sense than anything else up onto the bridge.

And suddenly there he is. But there she is too. Lightning illuminates the path across the bridge and Tanya's standing on the other side; for a moment even I tense as I see her. It's just the storm, all that howling wind and the lightning, but for a moment there is definitely something other-worldly in the sight of that sole figure looking back across the bridge towards us.

I still don't know what Joel wants. I definitely don't know what he's going to do. But then he takes a step towards her, and suddenly it's only too obvious. All Tanya's instincts were wrong.

She has misread all the signs and so have I. Joel is seriously out of control.

I spring forward, forcing myself between him and Tanya. She doesn't move, just watches. I see Joel's mouth open, an almost-animal like howl of fury sounding a moment later, and in that moment, I realise he simply doesn't care anymore. He wants one thing and one thing only right now, and that's payback for everything – the hurt, the humiliation, the betrayal. Nothing else matters. It's taken him years, but he's going to exact his revenge and I'm going to have to stand by and watch.

I grab hold of his arm as he moves towards the still-stationary Tanya, but he doesn't seem to realise I'm there. I cling on, feeling myself being swept along, powerless to make him even break step.

I put my hands up to his face, clawing at him, my fingernails scoring his cheeks, and now he flings out his arms, smashing a fist into my cheekbone, and I feel myself spinning away.

Then spinning some more.

And then there's nothing.

Just blackness.

DI MCCARTHY – THE COP

ANYTHING TO DO with that old case always rings bells.

Partly that's because, while the official investigation was formally concluded with no further action needing to be taken, the whole thing was never properly resolved, at least not in my eyes. No action was a good thing from the point of view of our small force's clear-up rate. Yet another file to be consigned to the cabinet with a great big tick on the front.

But that question mark still hangs over the whole thing. We still don't know the full story, still haven't actually worked out exactly who was telling the truth. All the evidence pointed to Ethan as the guilty party, and the way his life has gone off the rails ever since only seemed to confirm that. But there was still that small scintilla of doubt, that niggle at the back of the mind. So, whenever something came in that had anything to do with the main parties involved, a flag was raised that was routed directly to me.

And, of course, there was the fact that Joel and Tanya had called this in themselves. Which wasn't just a flag, but a huge flare shooting across the skies. To the best of my knowledge, they hadn't been seen together since Tanya decided to call quits on her job, her marriage, and her home, and start again somewhere far away. But now here they are back together again, it seems, and as well as everything else I really have to find out why.

They'd met before apparently, and many times too, which is the first surprise. It was a regular thing. Tanya would come to the area, although never to the actual town. Memories were still too painful. These reunions would usually take place at night, with no prying eyes, and they'd just involve the three of them, Joel, Tanya and their little boy, Danny. A chance for them to catch up and for her to spend some time with him.

That night it had just been Tanya and Joel, although they weren't going to be up on the bridge for long, not in the teeth of that storm. They'd already turned to head back to Tanya's car; they had a lot to discuss, as they both told me, a big decision to make. Next year, Danny would be going to the big school, as it's always called in this town, and there was only one, which was Tanya's old school.

And Ethan's old school, of course.

So, the question was simple. Did they commit their son to that school's potentially not-so-tender mercies? Did they risk his education being compromised by what had happened all those years before, or should they send him somewhere far away from all those associations?

All of that they intended to discuss as they hurried back across the bridge in the wind and rain.

And then they saw Bex.

JOEL – THE HUSBAND

I STARE across the bridge as lightning strikes the mountain behind.

Tanya remains where she has been since the moment she first appeared. All I can hear inside my head is that piercing scream as Bex fell. Followed by the even more chilling silence that moment later as the scream abruptly stopped.

Then Tanya, slowly, walks towards me. I don't move, I can't. She doesn't look right or left. And she doesn't look down towards the fallen Bex once.

She just nods at me instead.

'OK.'

And suddenly it's like everything's turned full circle. It's as if we're back in our house all those years ago. I see it on Tanya's face, just like I could see it back then, the wheels turning.

There's a situation and now we have to work out how to deal with it. What to do.

Then Tanya starts talking, as calm and cool as ever.

And I listen.

The wind picks up, the rain drives into us harder and harder, but Tanya keeps talking.

NIA – THE MUM

A FEW OF Bex's old school friends were there, the few that remembered her anyway, and Megan's come along from the school as well. It's a nice touch, her old headteacher attending. Don's there too – he's still head of governors, although rumour has it that's more by necessity than choice. No one else seems to have volunteered in all the years since the Ethan and Tanya story broke.

Al's there too, but Kate's stayed at home with the baby. There seem to be tensions there, but I don't probe. The one thing the intervening years have given me is a definite distance on anything to do with my ex. These days I just don't want to know.

Joel's there as well, but as he's the one who found her up there that night and tried to stop her throwing herself to her death, I suppose he feels some sort of kinship.

No one knows quite what led her to that spot and in that state that night. What happened, in an eerie echo of what happened to Ethan, was probably accidental. The coroner certainly hasn't recorded a verdict of suicide anyway. She had a fair old cocktail of drink and drugs in her system, and her life since leaving the town seems to have been one low-level disaster after another. Much like Ethan again, I suppose.

Joel doesn't think she intended to go over the edge like that. She was swaying wildly when he first spotted her, but there didn't seem anything pre-meditated about it. And even though the police have cleared him of all blame, he's still obviously wracked with guilt about it all.

Should he have approached like that and tried to shepherd her to safety?

Did that spook her in some way?

Did he unwittingly precipitate the tragedy that unfolded?

But Tanya was there too, of course, and she was adamant it was just an accident waiting to happen, that the combination of a girl in that sort of state on that sort of night in that spot was always going to end in disaster.

Certainly, Megan seemed to feel something might always go badly wrong for Bex, if the aside I heard her mutter to Don as we came outside after the service was anything to go by. She'd always, it seemed, marked Bex down as trouble.

It was strange seeing Tanya again. Not at the funeral – she didn't come to that – but before, when the police were investigating, and she was in and around the town. Seeing her again was a bit like seeing Al now. It's like looking at a stranger, listening to an old story that doesn't really touch me anymore, and from the look on Ethan's face whenever her name was mentioned he seems to feel the same. Then again, Ethan doesn't seem to feel anything anymore.

One strange thing happened just before the end of the service. As we all filed out behind Bex's parents, who looked as if they couldn't get away quickly enough, I saw Terry. I didn't even realise he was there till then. But he wasn't looking at me or at Joel or at Bex's parents or the rest of the mourners. For some reason, Terry was just looking at Ethan. And as Ethan walked by, he looked back at Terry. And something passed between them.

It was like a look exchanged between two kindred souls.

As if there's some sort of connection there, one that only they and no one else could ever understand.

DI MCCARTHY – THE COP

A FEW MONTHS after we wrapped up the Ethan and Tanya case, Gee joined CID in a much larger force across the border. I always said she was good. One promotion followed within a year and then another two years later.

Whenever she came home for family visits and the like, she'd always call in to her old nick, we'd meet up, and conversation would invariably turn to the Devil's Bridge Affair, as we'd all come to call it.

I'd update her on Ethan, which didn't usually take long. He still wasn't doing all that much with his life. And so far as Tanya was concerned, she seemed to have vanished off the face of the earth after leaving Joel. He remained what he has been ever since, the boss of that same local building firm and single parent to Danny.

She wouldn't have made a special trip back for the funeral, despite Tanya and Joel's involvement. Bex was always a satellite character in that story. But something still took us both to the church that day, and I don't really know what. Maybe, in Gee's case, it was the same something that drove her through that series of rapid promotions. Some instinct working deep inside.

That's probably hindsight. But what's certain is that the simple trip unlocked all sorts.

JOEL – THE HUSBAND

He was waiting in the yard as I came out from the site hut.

It was the copper from before, McCarthy, the one who'd conducted the original investigation. The one who'd also turned up that night I called in the news of Bex's accident.

And it was an accident too; that's totally clear in my mind. OK, I did gloss over the struggle, or at least made it clear that any struggle involved my trying to stop Bex straying too close to the edge. We didn't touch on the rest of it, principally the fact that she was trying to stop me getting to Tanya at the time or the blow I landed. That was buried. As Tanya said, and she was right, we both knew what would happen if the full facts came out. I'd be arrested, and that wouldn't bring Bex back.

And so, and for not the first time, I went with the flow.

The Tanya flow.

McCarthy approached, asked for a quiet word, and steered me away from the rest of the builders, who were all now watching with undisguised curiosity. But suddenly I didn't see them, and I didn't see him either. I just saw Tanya sitting in an unmarked police car watching us. And everything else and everyone else was driven out of my mind.

Then DI McCarthy started speaking, although it took some time for me to work out what he was saying.

But then I realised he was reading me the official caution.

And telling me I was under arrest.

DI MCCARTHY – THE COP

WE'VE PARKED on the hill high above the town, just myself, Gee and Tanya. Ironically enough it was where Gee had met Joel all those years before, as she later told me, but she didn't tell Tanya that. For now, the stage is well and truly hers as she begins to speak.

'A lot of this is my fault. I take total responsibility; I still can't believe I didn't see what was going to happen.'

She tails off, wracked, and looks out over the town, up at the bridge. I wait a few moments as she keeps struggling, but then, slowly, cautiously, push this along.

'Why don't you just tell us what did happen? We can sort out the rights and wrongs of it all later down the line.'

She takes a deep breath, then nods.

'It was just one of those odd encounters that happen from time to time, I suppose. It was on a tube train, for God's sake. We actually met and started talking on the tube – who does that?'

Gee cuts in, as intrigued by this, and by Tanya's approach as we came out of the funeral, as I am.

'But you did.'

Tanya takes a deep breath and nods again.

'She saw me before I saw her. I had the impression she'd been watching me for a while, had maybe even been following me. She was nervous, I remember that, and she was obviously a lot older, but the minute she said my name I placed her.'

She struggles again.

'Which was when everything came flooding back.'

Tanya takes another quick, deep breath.

'She asked if we could grab a coffee and I said yes. I didn't really know why but looking back I was definitely curious. I'd been back to see Danny, but I'd only ever talked to Joel. I didn't know what anyone else in the town really thought about me leaving like that, so here was a chance for me to find out.'

She pauses.

'It should have just been a simple chat. A quick catch-up over a coffee, then we both should have gone on our way.'

Tanya struggles again as we stay silent.

'Right from the start she seemed fascinated by the whole story. Obsessed, almost. Straight away, she told me she believed everything I'd said, that she and the rest of the kids at the time always knew Ethan was a liar, and I suppose there was an element of relief in that. If they all thought that then maybe the rest of the town thought it too.'

Tanya pauses again.

'Then she said that the one thing no one could work out was why I'd left like that. All sorts of rumours flew around the town for months, apparently. Joel had just said it was one of those things, that it was a marriage that had run its course, but coming so soon on top of the whole Ethan thing, people did start to wonder.'

Gee and I exchange glances.

We'd both wondered as well.

'Maybe I'd been bottling it up inside too long. It wasn't just people back in the town – everyone I'd met since had been told the same story. I was married, it went wrong, I had a bit of a breakdown, and my ex kept our son. But I had visiting rights and it was all very amicable.'

Gee cuts in again.

'Are you saying that wasn't what happened?'

Tanya shook her head.

'Joel said it was impossible. That the stain of the Ethan story was always going to follow us around, and not just us, but Danny too. And the longer I stayed in the town the worse it was going to get. People were watching us all the time already and that was never going to go away.'

She pauses once more.

'So, I had to go. For the sake of what was left of my career and for the sake of our son.'

I cut in.

'Why couldn't you both go, start over somewhere else?

'Because Joel had his business in the town. He couldn't just up and leave. He'd built it up over years, people depended on him; it wasn't just his livelihood, it was all those other people too, and I believed him, at the time anyway.'

Gee cuts in again.

'But not now?'

She pauses again, then shakes her head.

'Looking back, I wonder if he was just sick of it all. That it wasn't just the people in the town looking at me and seeing all that was supposed to have happened – he was starting to do the same. The problem was that all came later. At the time I was in such a whirl, I didn't know whether I was coming or going. I did sort out how things were going to work with Danny, visiting rights and the like. We did agree on that, but then I just let myself be swept along, I suppose. Everything he was saying just seemed to make a horrible kind of sense.'

Down in the town, shouts and laughter float up to us, kids let out into the playground for a mid-morning break from one of the local primary schools, and, for a moment, Tanya struggles even more.

'Bex was really fired up about it. Looking back, that's when I should have realised this was more than simple curiosity. She seemed almost too engaged, but I couldn't help it – everything kept pouring out of me, and we stayed there for hours, just me talking, her listening. We met a few times after that too.'

Tanya pauses again.

'The next thing I knew she left me a message. I couldn't work out what she was saying at first. She was talking about some newspaper story, but then I saw it too. It was about Ethan's accident up on the bridge, which was when this really cold feeling crept over me. It was as if that was the last straw for her. She told me she was going back on my behalf, was going to get payback from Joel. I tried contacting him, but I couldn't get through. His phone wasn't connecting. Then she texted me, telling me to meet her up on the bridge. I got there as quick as I could, but they were there before me and she was yelling at him, goading him.'

Tanya stops.

'Which was when—'

She stops again. I'm about to prompt her but then she looks at me.

'That's when he lashed out. Hit her. And she fell.'

She pauses once more, struggling for another moment.

'I just stood there. Joel turned back to me. He was calm, clear-headed, just like he was the night he told me I had to leave, that our marriage had to end. And then he told me what we had to do, the story we had to stick to, that we'd found her up there, that she was in a terrible state, that we tried to stop her throwing herself over the edge, but we couldn't.'

Tanya looks at us, wracked.

'I went along with it the last time. I did everything he said, but I can't do it again.'

Tanya keeps looking at us.

'I just can't.'

JOEL – THE HUSBAND

A SHORT TIME later I listened in total disbelief to all the so-called facts as they were presented to me in court. I stared at each of the jurors in turn, silently challenging each and every one of them. How could anyone seriously believe a single word of this?

Tanya was pitch-perfect though, I had to give her that. I always knew she was the consummate actor. The way she'd fooled me, fooled all of us over Ethan and who knows how many others, was ample testimony to that. But her performance in the witness box that day was Oscar-winning. She came across as fragile but determined. A woman pushed to the brink who'd decided she'd be pushed no further.

But seriously?

Tanya?

The jurors had to see it was just an act.

And I had the proof, of course. The truth about the Devil's Bridge Affair. The truth about Tanya, that phone. The problem is that it was a smoking gun I couldn't fire, and I knew it and so did she. I think she'd always known. Because I'd have to admit to turning a blind eye to abuse all those years ago, not to mention letting the abuser walk free, condemning Ethan to his life in limbo.

And it was nothing to do with this charge anyway, so that was one defence strategy I couldn't pursue, but surely I wouldn't need to. Seated before me on those benches were twelve men and women just like me. They had to see through all this.

He was a late call. A witness brought in by the prosecution on the very last day of the trial. We were given the opportunity to object, of course, but I was in the same bind with him as I was with Tanya. There was so much I couldn't say here too.

So, all I could do was watch from the dock as Terry gave another pitch-perfect performance, telling the court that deep, dark secret I'd previously confided to Tanya. He told them about that night all those years ago when I'd lost it up on that same bridge, when I'd lashed out and hit him too, how he'd fallen but thankfully survived. And how I'd made sure through a combination of threat and inducement that he'd remained quiet about it ever since. But eventually, and as with Tanya, there's always a line that can't be crossed, as Terry made clear at the end of his simple statement. A moment when you say enough is enough.

A short time later I had the answer to my own question.

Everyone believed it.

And the jury brought in a verdict of guilty.

NIA – THE MUM

I SAW Tanya just once after that. And just like the first time I saw her, it was up on the devil's bridge.

The town's been reeling for the last few months. Ever since Tanya's testimony it's all anyone's been talking about. It's even pushed the Ethan story very firmly down the pecking order in the gossip stakes. A second Devil's Bridge Affair, some are calling it, but this one actually took place up there, of course.

I'll always hate her; don't get me wrong. But even I felt a sneaking sympathy as she re-lived the pressure Joel had brought to bear on her back then, the way he'd browbeaten her into leaving her home, and her child. He was probably right that the whole Ethan story would dog them both from that moment on, irrespective of who was to blame, but he should still never have driven her out of his life and away from the town like that. Just so he could live a life untainted by association.

He tried protesting his innocence. He even insisted at one point that the whole cover-up over Bex was actually cooked up by Tanya, not him, but that only made things worse in a way. Following that logic through it meant he was still guilty, of course, and once he grasped that he soon shut up. Joel received a ten-year sentence for manslaughter, meaning he'll be in prison for at least the next six.

And maybe longer. No one really expects him to behave that well inside, not with his fabled temper. I can still see Tanya, as we sat together in her kitchen, giving a small shudder as she reflected on the folly of anyone poking that bear.

In the meantime, Danny has to be looked after, but once they discovered the circumstances behind Tanya's earlier abandonment of her son, Social Services had no problem in agreeing to giving her custody.

All of which led to that last sighting of her with Danny as she left for the last time. I wasn't up on the bridge itself; I just saw her from a distance walking across. And, for a moment, something in the image chilled me again, but I suppose that's natural enough looking back.

I've thought of her so long as some sort of devil that the sight of her walking hand in hand with another living soul back across that bridge will always raise echoes of the legend that gave our town its name.

ACKNOWLEDGMENTS

Grateful thanks, as always, to Rebecca Collins, Adrian Hobart, Sue Davison and Jayne Mapp.

Special thanks also to Gwenno Hughes, Simon Winstone, Llyr Morus and Kelsey Richards – four great writers and producers!

ABOUT THE AUTHOR

Rob Gittins is a screenwriter and novelist. Rob's written for almost all the top-rated UK network TV dramas from the last thirty years, including *Casualty, EastEnders, The Bill, Heartbeat* and *Vera,* as well as over thirty original radio plays for BBC Radio 4.

He's previously had six novels published by Y Lolfa to high critical acclaim. This is Rob's second novel for Hobeck. He is also the author of a brand new series set on the idyllic, if occasionally sinister and disturbing, Isle of Wight. The first book in the series, *I'm Not There,* was published in September 2022.

Visit Rob's website at: www.robgittins.com

I'M NOT THERE

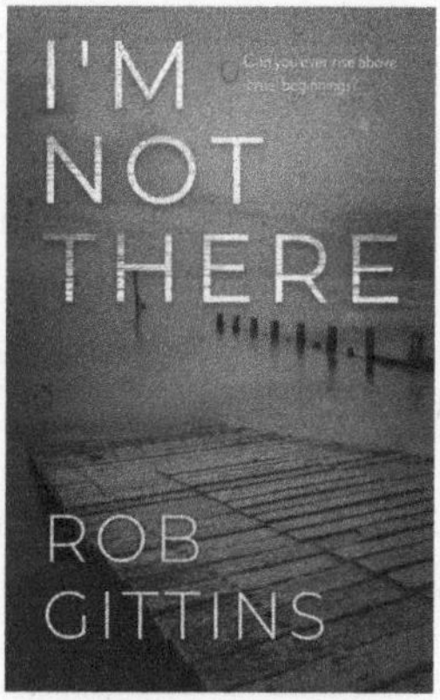

'Everything is cleverly brought together in a thrilling climax.' Sarah Leck

'It has the feel of one of those books that gets a plug and takes off to be a top ten bestseller.' Pete Fleming

'Dark, gritty, well-crafted characters and some gut-punching shocks, first rate crime writing'. Alex Jones

Two sisters abandoned
It was a treat, she said. An adventure. A train journey to the mainland. Six-year-old Lara Arden and her older sister Georgia happily fill in their colouring books as their mum pops to the buffet in search of crisps. She never returns. Two little girls abandoned. Alone.

Present day
Twenty years later, and Lara is now a detective inspector on her native Isle of Wight, still searching for answers to her mother's disappearance.

A call comes in. A small child, a boy, has been left abandoned on a train. Like Lara, he has no relatives to look after him. It feels as if history is being repeated – but surely this is a coincidence?

A series of murders
Before Lara can focus on the boy's plight, she's faced with a series of murders. They feature different victims in very different circumstances, but they all have one thing in common: they all leave children – alone – behind.

So who is targeting Lara? What do these abandoned souls have in common? And how does this connect to the mystery of Lara's missing mother?

CRIME AND THRILLERS BY ROB GITTINS

A crime series set in the hidden world of witness protection.

Gimme Shelter
Secret Shelter
Shelter Me

What's a wife, husband or partner like when you're not watching? A psychological thriller exploring the dangers waiting to ensnare those who try to find out.

Investigating Mr Wakefield

PRAISE FOR ROB GITTINS

'Rob Gittins is a highly acclaimed dramatist whose work has been enjoyed by millions in TV and radio dramas.'
Nicholas Rhea – author of the Constable series, adapted for TV as *Heartbeat*

'Visceral, strongly visual and beautifully structured... powerful, quirky characters.'
Andrew Taylor – Winner, Crime Writers' Association Cartier Diamond Dagger

'Gittins introduces the reader to a dangerous and troubled part of society, and his murky, damaged and at times violent characters are as vividly (and disturbingly) portrayed as those of Elmore Leonard.'
Susanna Gregory – crime author

'Unflinching... as vicious and full of twists as a tiger in a trap.'
Russell James – crime author

'The definitive interpretation of 'page turnability' … characters that step effortlessly off the page and into the memory.'
Katherine John – crime author

'TV writer Rob Gittins . . hits hard from the start.'
Iain McDowall – crime author

'Visceral realism doesn't come much better than this. Brilliant.'
Sally Spedding – crime author

'Noir at its most shocking.'
Rebecca Tope – crime author

'Terrifying and suspenseful, non-stop jeopardy. Just be glad you're only reading it and not in it.'
Tony Garnett – TV Drama Producer, *Kes, Cathy Come Home, This Life*

'Gittins is an experienced and successful scriptwriter for screen and radio … startling and original.'
Crime Fiction Lover

'Well-plotted and superbly written.'
Linda Wilson, *Crime Review*

'Full of intrigue and narrative twists ... powerfully written and uncompromising in its style.'
Dufour Editions

'Corrosive psychological consequences which match those in the best Nicci French thrillers.'
Morning Star

'If there's one thing you can be sure of when it comes to Rob Gittins's literary output, it is that he's not afraid of a scintillating pace … this has all the hallmarks of a cult classic and I couldn't recommend it highly enough.'
Jack Clothier, Gwales

'Well-drawn characters and sophisticated storytelling.'
Publishers Weekly

'Unputdownable … this deserves every one of the five stars. I would have given it more if I could have.'
Review on Amazon.com

"Uncomfortable, taut, brutal, it will hold you gripped right to the end. A wonderful piece of writing.'
Cambria

'Fast action, convincing dialogue, meticulously plotted throughout. Every twist ratchets up the sense of danger and disorientation.'
Caroline Clark, Gwales

'Thrilling … bloodthirsty.'
Buzz

'Gripping and exciting, fast-paced. There is something a bit different about Gittins's writing that I haven't come across before.'
Nudge

HOBECK BOOKS – THE HOME OF GREAT STORIES

We hope you've enjoyed reading this novel by Rob Gittins. To keep up to date on Rob's writing please do look out for him on Twitter or check out his website: **www.robgittins.com**.

Hobeck Books offers a number of short stories and novellas, free for subscribers in the compilation *Crime Bites*.

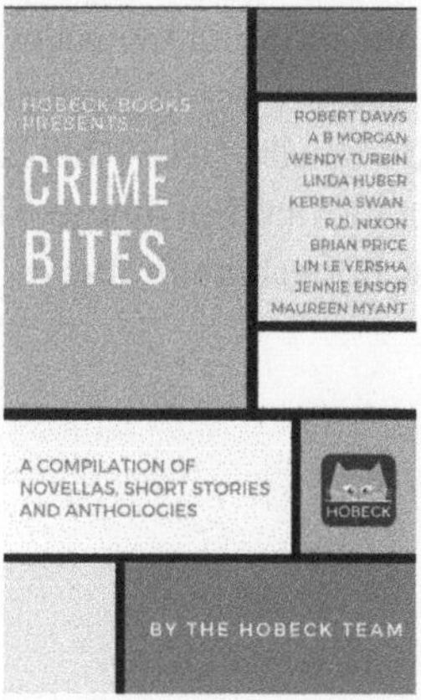

- *Echo Rock* by Robert Daws
- *Old Dogs, Old Tricks* by AB Morgan

- *The Silence of the Rabbit* by Wendy Turbin
- *Never Mind the Baubles: An Anthology of Twisted Winter Tales* by the Hobeck Team (including many of the Hobeck authors and Hobeck's two publishers)
- *The Clarice Cliff Vase* by Linda Huber
- *Here She Lies* by Kerena Swan
- *The Macnab Principle* by R.D. Nixon
- *Fatal Beginnings* by Brian Price
- *A Defining Moment* by Lin Le Versha
- *Saviour* by Jennie Ensor
- *You Can't Trust Anyone These Days* by Maureen Myant

Also please visit the Hobeck Books website for details of our other superb authors and their books, and if you would like to get in touch, we would love to hear from you.

Hobeck Books also presents a weekly podcast, the Hobcast, where founders Adrian Hobart and Rebecca Collins discuss all things book related, key issues from each week, including the ups and downs of running a creative business. Each episode includes an interview with one of the people who make Hobeck possible: the editors, the authors, the cover designers. These are the people who help Hobeck bring great stories to life. Without them, Hobeck wouldn't exist. The Hobcast can be listened to from all the usual platforms but it can also be found on the Hobeck website: **www.hobeck.net/hobcast**.

OTHER HOBECK BOOKS TO EXPLORE

Silenced

Silenced is the compelling and gritty new thriller by British author Jennie Ensor. A story of love, fear and betrayal, and having the courage to speak out when the odds are stacked against you.

A teenage girl is murdered on her way home from school, stabbed through the heart. Her North London community is shocked, but no-one has the courage to help the police, not even her mother. DI Callum Waverley, in his first job as senior investigating officer, tries to break through the code of silence that shrouds the case.

This is a world where the notorious Skull Crew rules through fear. Everyone knows you keep your mouth shut or you'll be silenced – permanently.

This is Luke's world. Reeling from the loss of his mother to cancer, his step-father distant at best, violent at worst, he slides into the Skull Crew's grip.

This is Jez's world too. Her alcoholic mother neither knows nor cares that her 16-year-old daughter is being exploited by V, all-powerful leader of the gang.

Luke and Jez form a bond. Can Callum win their trust, or will his own demons sabotage his investigation? And can anyone stop the Skull Crew ensuring all witnesses are silenced?

Pact of Silence

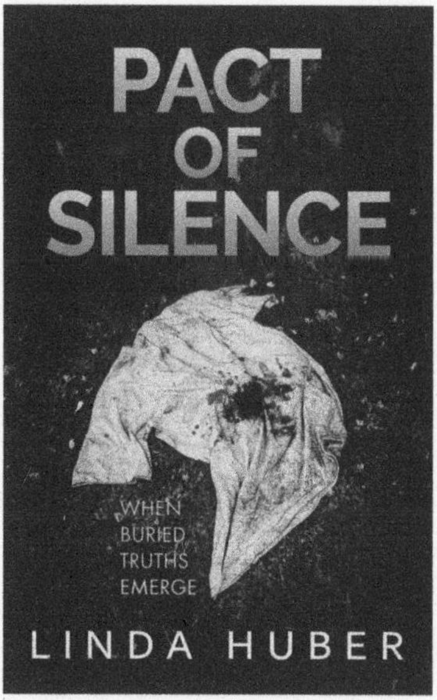

'What an emotional rollercoaster! Darkly addictive and packed to the rafters with secrets, I was flipping those pages, desperate to see how it unravelled.' Jane Isaac, psychological thriller author

A fresh start for a new life
Newly pregnant, Emma is startled when her husband Luke announces they're swapping homes with his parents, but the rural idyll where Luke grew up is a great place to start their family. Yet Luke's manner suggests something odd is afoot, something that Emma can't quite fathom.

Too many secrets, not enough truths
Emma works hard to settle into her new life in the Yorkshire

countryside, but a chance discovery increases her suspicions. She decides to dig a little deeper…

Be careful what you uncover
Will Emma find out why the locals are behaving so oddly? Can she discover the truth behind Luke's disturbing behaviour? Will the pact of silence ever be broken?

Lightning Source UK Ltd.
Milton Keynes UK
UKHW041021150922
408907UK00002B/237

9 781913 793913